# Barrowbeck

# Barrowbeck

## ANDREW MICHAEL HURLEY

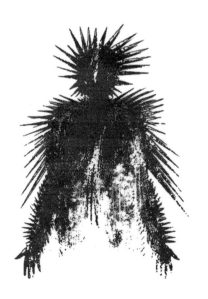

JOHN MURRAY

First published in Great Britain in 2024 by John Murray (Publishers)

1

A CIP catalogue record for this title is available from the British Library

Hardback ISBN 9781399817486
ebook ISBN 9781399817516

Typeset in Baskerville MT by Hewer Text UK Ltd, Edinburgh
Printed and bound in Great Britain by Clays Ltd, Elcograf S.p.A.

John Murray policy is to use papers that are natural, renewable and
recyclable products and made from wood grown in sustainable forests.
The logging and manufacturing processes are expected to conform
to the environmental regulations of the country of origin.

Carmelite House
50 Victoria Embankment
London EC4Y 0DZ

www.johnmurraypress.co.uk

John Murray Press, part of Hodder & Stoughton Limited
An Hachette UK company

For Jo. Twenty-five years x.

Among the hills the Echoes play
A never, never ending song

William Wordsworth,
'The Idle Shepherd Boys'

# Contents

# First Footing

It is likely that Barrowbeck's original settlers were
drawn there by the river and the seclusion of the valley.
Refugees, perhaps, from a less hospitable territory.

L. S. Hunter, *The History of the North of England*

After the raid, after the bloodshed and the burials, the marsh-
folk fled east along the riverbank, depleted in numbers.

They had been walking for a whole day now, the party
ever more fragmented by fatigue at the rear and an eager-
ness to keep moving at the front. Those leading the way had
to judge each footstep so carefully in the snow that they only
occasionally glanced up. When they did, it felt as though
they were passing through a stretch they had already navi-
gated, as in some nonsensical dream. Covered in white
drifts, everywhere looked the same.

The boy, Mabglas, could not be sure if he was truly
awake. No matter that his feet ached, or that the cold seemed

to cut straight through to his skeleton, to be thrown into exile like this was so sudden as to seem unreal.

Only two days ago, the village had been languishing in a wonderful normality. The first signs of a squall had been blowing in off the sea but that was nothing out of the ordinary for the season. They knew how to prepare. There was no panic. They had simply set to work and fastened down any thatching that was loose, re-dug the drainage channels, hammered the poles of wicker fences deeper into the mud, heaped up firewood indoors, and moved their animals off the salt-pastures to higher ground. Across the marshland, they had been getting on with the business of living as they'd always lived. But now half the men were dead – the chieftain, Prif, and his son, Gogwyn, among them. And the survivors had been forced out of their homes into the slush and snow with whatever they could carry of the little left to them by the marauders.

Mabglas had only the clothes he wore and an oak-wood staff. But he needed nothing more, Dewin, his teacher, had told him. For men like them, he said (and Mabglas liked to be called a man), for men who swam between worlds, the fewer trappings they had the better. To be attached to something, to rely upon it, was a weakness that the gods would exploit whenever he went to barter with them.

He should not have undue affection for anything. Not even his master. He had to be different. Free of love. It was good that he had no mother and father any more and did not remember them. Orphans made good shamans. Nothing he cared about could be taken away from him. He had no one to weep for in situations such as this. He should not even bewail the loss of the village. They would build another. Just as if he broke his staff he could easily cut himself a replacement. He should keep a clear head, said Dewin. His duty lay in vigilance. Let the others mourn.

At present, their grief was largely silent and seemed to have been deferred by a mutual unspoken agreement. When they were far enough away from harm, then they would cry.

Everyone kept their own counsel. The men wrestled with whatever shame and guilt they felt; widows remained impassive for the sake of their newly fatherless children – some only babies – who chewed their thumbs and clung to their mothers, subdued by the violence that had swept through the village with all the pitilessness of a winter storm. Worse than a storm, in fact. A storm, they could have weathered. They'd been more than ready for the high wet winds that lashed the coast at this time of year. But they could never have predicted the coming of these wild-bearded giants with their clubs and spears. Nor their cunning. For they had crept into the coppice wood above the village with such uncanny stealth that they had not snapped a single branch underfoot or disturbed a single bird from its roost. It was only as they'd started to charge down the hillside and let out their battle cry that the trees behind them had erupted with crows.

*

The men of the village had fought back with courage if not expertise. They were farmers and fishers and reed-cutters. What chance had they stood against these taller, stronger brutes so drunk on the thrill of slaughter? It had all been over within moments.

Once the raiders had gone with the sheep and the cattle and the salt fish, when those who had hidden themselves away emerged, the extent of the viciousness became clear. Here was Fadog, here was Cambugail, Bram and Corrath. Stuck like pigs where they had been cornered. Prif they found face down in the rushes, his back stabbed open to the white of his spine. Gogwyn decapitated. The utmost insult. Or was it a punishment?

As they buried the dead in the high barrow, they wondered aloud what they had done to anger the gods – why these barbarians had been sent to kill them. The marsh-folk were not greedy in any sense; nor were they vain or ambitious. Prif had never been bellicose. Nor had any of their previous chieftains. Each had inherited his father's benevolence. Likewise, Gogwyn, steadfast, generous Gogwyn, whose cheeks had still been ruddy when they'd laid his head beside him in the grave, as if his soul was protesting at his needless death and refused to leave.

For an explanation, they had turned to Dewin, their shrewd, white-haired brother with an understanding of things preternatural, or as much understanding as anyone *could* have. But all that he had been able to say for certain at the time was that to try and bargain with these gods of carnage – which Mabglas knew was what the villagers wanted him to do – would prove fruitless. No amount of pleading or bribery would dissuade them from recommencing their game. And it was a game. Part of the grand game of war the gods returned to now and then when they were in want of entertainment. As boys enjoyed clashing their armies of little wooden warriors, so the gods pitted one clan against another. Indeed, some gods *were* like cruel children, Dewin said. Children with sharp sticks and an insatiable fascination for watching things suffer. But unlike children, they could not be chastised or changed. Their toys could not be taken away.

They had revelled in the combat, he said. They would want an even gorier spectacle next time and send the invaders back to kill everyone they came across, with no mercy for women and children. They would take the village and all it contained for their own. The gods had decided.

For the marsh-folk, there had been no choice but to leave as soon as they could and use the course of the river as their path.

Mabglas tried to instil some comfort in those walking beside him by reminding them that it was past midwinter now, as though that mattered when the days were still so short and dim and cold. However hard they beat their arms, however strenuous it was to wade through the snow, the chill was unavoidable and made all the worse by the fact that they had been strenuous to see out the harsh weather in the shelter of their homes. The way they talked, when they talked at all, they missed the hot stones and steaming cauldrons of their hearths as much as they missed the dead. And to think of those savages, they said, sitting in their houses enjoying the warmth of a fire while they were out in the open shivering . . .

Here inland, the gods Gawl and Eira, who roused fierce blizzards whenever they met, had left wide plains of deep snow that rolled to the rise of the moorland in the distance.

To the marsh-folk, those hills were unknown and untrodden. No one had ever been so far. In ten generations, there had never been one among them adventurous enough to go off and explore the peaks and valleys. It would have been dangerous and sacrilegious. Dangerous *because* it was sacrilegious. There were plenty of stories about the fate of those who – by accident or more often reckless curiosity – had intruded into some hallowed place.

Years ago, a man from another clan, somewhere east, had set off one night and walked over the edge of the horizon so as to catch sight of Heulwen, the Sun goddess, before she dressed herself in the blinding robes of morning. For spying on her nakedness, he had been nailed to the earth and seared every day until he was nothing but bones.

North of here, a little boy had climbed a tall tree on a clear night and torn open a patch of the sky to find out what lay beyond the stars. Peeking through the hole, into the foundry of the gods, his eyes had melted like ice.

So went the tales that cautioned against foolishness. And even for men like him and Dewin, thought Mabglas (men who swam between worlds), knowledge had its limitations. Certain marvels had to remain hidden. The Sun in her nudity. The furnaces behind the curtain of the night. And the birthplace of their own dear Arfon, their river.

Somewhere in the folds of those hills on the horizon was the womb from which she continually sprang anew to wind her way to the marshlands of the estuary – the briny kingdom she ruled over jointly with Old Salo of the Sea.

He could be petulant, especially at this time of year, and distracted by the task of stirring up rainstorms and tides, but Arfon had been kind to the marsh-folk thus far, and they had venerated her with such love that it didn't seem too presumptuous to hope for her protection and sympathy now. After seeing what these rabid dogs of men had done to the village, outraged that innocent blood had polluted her waters, she might feel moved to provide them with somewhere else to live. A sheltered bend or a quiet sister-tributary secreted in a wood.

But after a day of walking, they had come across no such places. Only black swamps of dubious solidity. Or the small frosty islands of oxbow lakes. Nowhere was suitable or safe. All was exposed in these flatlands. And they were forced to spend a sleepless night squatting in the roots of thrashing trees along the banks, not even daring to light a fire for fear that the wild ones would find them.

From the muttered conversations Mabglas overheard in the dark, there was a growing feeling that they had expected too much of the frozen Arfon. She was weary at this time of year, too drowsy and inert to concern herself with human affairs or the blood-sports of the other gods. No, they were travelling without her knowledge. They were alone in this foreign countryside.

When the morning came, with a sky as downy as the snow, some wanted to turn around, thinking it better to take their chances back in the village; better to die in their homes – their precious homes – than freeze out here. Freeze or starve. They had left with so little between them, nothing but some cobs of brittle bread, half a sack of berries, and two strings of dried mushrooms that were as tough as twists of dead skin. Despite favouring the most needful, the food had all but gone. If Arfon was not going to provide them with more, then what was the use of carrying on? While they still had the privilege of choice, they should be kind to themselves and choose the swift death of the club or the spear.

But come, see, said Dewin and he led them closer to the river where he proved his eminence in occult matters by show-ing them what he had noticed and they had missed. Here the ice was thin and if they looked closely, they could see the rush of the current beneath the surface, the bubbles of Arfon's breath. She was still with them, he said. She was still their guardian. She led them to these inhospitable places of creaking bogs and roaring trees only to urge them into the hills.

The hills? The thought of going there troubled them more than anything else. It gave Mabglas pause too. He thought of the man pinned down and roasted by the Sun's heat. He remembered the boy whose eyes had turned to water. What punishments could they expect if they were to tramp into the place of Arfon's miraculous, endless birth?

Dewin seemed sure that she would give them refuge; more than just refuge, she would offer them a new place to live. They could not think of the marshland village as theirs any more. They could not go back. They were not *meant* to go back. Arfon was calling them to her.

To put so much faith in one of the gods – even one with a legacy of kind-heartedness – sat uneasily with Mabglas. But Dewin's certainty of Arfon's beneficence spread to the others and grew all the more credible when the sky cleared into a morning of bright sunlight. It was a providential sign that they could all interpret. For the first time since they had left the village, something other than fear and sorrow passed between them.

Mabglas knew that he ought to resist the seduction of hope as strongly as he ought to abjure any sadness or regret. Dewin had told him that often enough. But it was hard not to share the joy of believing that, after what had happened, there was a place of sanctuary waiting for them. He wanted to live rather than die. He could not quite bring himself to feel guilty about that, even though he had been instructed to think of his life as something entirely disposable. His life didn't belong to him anyway, Dewin had said. He was but an egg being passed among the gods. One day, one of them would close their hand and crush him.

For now, though, Arfon cradled him and the others, and the going was better the further east they went. The forests of the upland country were winter-bare but tangled and dense and had sheltered the riverbanks from the worst of the snow. It felt as though they were at last making progress even though the river was forced to take an ever more sinuous course into the heart of the moorland.

In these narrow dales, the slopes ran more or less straight down to the river-edge with no room for building or farming. It was all rockfall and scree. Useless for their needs. But towards sundown, after passing through the jaws of two limestone crags, they came to a long, open valley; a silent trough of snow and blue shadow closed off by a steep wall of fells.

Some made the comparison of an eel trap. But a dead end was to their advantage, said Dewin. This was a hidden place. A place of privacy. No one had been here before. Theirs would be the first footprints. Their voices the first to resound here. The first voices of a new village.

Didn't they see it? he said. Couldn't they see that here lay all the makings of a settlement far better than the one they had left behind? There was land they could use for pasture.

A wood of oak, ash, willow and holly that was perhaps abundant with beasts that had yet to become wary of men. A stag here might be lured out of hiding by the presence of strange new beings and stand and stare in wonder as an arrow came its way.

He was always convincing, perhaps too convincing, thought Mabglas, as the others started to assume that all would be simple from now on.

Yes, they would catch something gullible, build a fire, fashion a spit, eat well, sleep out the night in that grove of yew trees and tomorrow begin to fell what they would need for the posts, braces and beams of new houses. They still had an axe. The invaders hadn't robbed them completely.

One of anything was better than nothing.

Every village began with a single blow to a single tree.

They passed around the aphorisms with an air of triumph, until Dewin cautioned them to remember themselves. It was only by Arfon's grace that they were here in this haven at all, and they should acknowledge their debt to her before they took anything from it. And so, standing at the edge of the river, they gave thanks and assured her of a proper offering when it could be made. They hoped that she would be satisfied with a promise. They hoped that she would see that they were bound by circumstances. It was not a slight. All manner of rightful devotions had been suspended since they'd been turned out of their homes. They had even postponed the observances of their own grief.

Following the burials in the barrow, there were cere-
monies of remembrance that ought to have been performed
until the moon had been through its wane and wax and
looked again as it had done on the day of committal.
Everyone was expected to mark the various stages of bereavement in which the dead were first longed for then celebrated
and finally allowed to slip away into the past.

Until now, the marsh-folk had been too afraid to make much
noise, but here they were alone and secluded, and as they went
into the trees to find shelter and firewood and food they lifted
their voices in the songs of lamentation that were owed to the
departed. To Mabglas it sounded like relief as much as sorrow.
Relief that they had at last begun the formalities of mourning,
but a greater relief that they were still alive, saved for a special
purpose. If they were meant to be here, then they would not
be made to shiver or go hungry for much longer.

Yet, as they picked through the wet deadfall and others
went deeper to look out for the coming of any curious deer,
the wind rose until the wood sounded like the sea when Old
Salo was at his most irascible. Then snow came. Not powder
shaken down off the branches but a fresh blizzard that tore
through the trees.

Mabglas had assumed that Gawl and Eira had passed
through the valley and gone off to overwhelm some other
place but perhaps they had been here all along, sleeping off
their labours, and had been woken by the marsh-folk's intrusion. Or were they angry at the reverence shown to Arfon?

Pride and envy were just as much the failings of the divine as they were of mortals.

Whatever the reason for this sudden wrath, the snowstorm brought the night on early and shook the trees with such force that it seemed as if the wood might collapse. The gods would not think twice about burying them. What were a dozen more broken bodies?

There was a cave on the fellside, and although Mabglas privately sided with those who fretted about wolves, he agreed with Dewin that there was nowhere else to go and helped the weakest among them up the slope through the driving snow.

The air inside was sour, never breathed by humankind before, and the low ceiling hung with pellucid spikes of ice. They could not be sure if they were merely hearing the sibilance of their own voices or if they had already disturbed whatever lived there. The babies cried and were hushed, but it was impossible to be silent. Even cautious whispers echoed too freely against the rock and drifted away down fissures and passageways that they could not see. For they had no means of making a fire. The branches they had found were soaked to the heartwood and if combustible at all would have only filled the chamber with suffocating smoke.

And so in that tar-black mouth in the hill, in the bone-grip of the night, in the expectation of wolves, some took turns to watch while others tried to sleep.

The storm would pass, Dewin told them. By the morning Gawl and Eira would have blustered away to some other part of the world and forgotten about them. Fury did not last long. It *could* not last long. Fury was tiring, even for the gods.

Comforted by his words and his toothless smile, the children wilted against their mothers' chests and into an enviable oblivion where there was no hunger, and there were no ominous noises in the dark. But for Mabglas, sleep was as thin as water, and he woke repeatedly from dreams of wolves and wild men until his time for vigil came around and he was roused to replace Dewin.

He did not want to think of his master as dishonest, but he could not shake off the thought that the old man was imparting his wisdom so as to *appear* wise rather than with genuine insight. Still, it was necessary for the others to believe that he was confident and in command. Especially now. They needed someone to lead them. A new chieftain. Perhaps it would be an act he'd learn himself in time to come, thought Mabglas. This *seeming*.

Nonetheless, they would only trust Dewin for as long as his predictions proved true, and as the storm went on unabated and was no less fierce at dawn, deference to his knowledge started to ebb. They'd been tricked, some said. Perhaps even their own precious Arfon had been complicit in the plan. She was in league with the gods who'd sent the savages. It was all part of the game to pretend that she was their saviour when in fact she had brought them here only for Gawl and Eira to finish them off.

It was wild talk, and Dewin did not tolerate it for long. Arfon had not betrayed them or abandoned them, he said. She was being held captive just as they were. Gawl and Eira had thickened the ice and submerged her in so much snow here that she had no power. It was a question of weakness, not will. She wanted them to have this valley. She had promised it to them. If that was not true, then why did Gawl and Eira seek to retain it with such force?

The logic seemed sound, but it was not a solution. An explanation was not a strategy. If Arfon really was imprisoned and unable to protect them, the others said, then they would soon succumb to the cold or starve or be eaten alive, or all three. So, what were they to do? Rely on the gods' sympathy?

They would bide their time, said Dewin. Meet rage with patience. It was winter. Gawl and Eira had work to do elsewhere. They could not stay here indefinitely.


And so on his advice, they waited out the day and then another night with nothing but meltwater to put in their stomachs.

Mabglas had known hunger before. They had all known lean seasons when they'd had to ration their supplies. But their bellies had soon become used to less. They had never gone without. There had never been days of nothing. Never such a famine as this.

The agony of it was inescapable. Emptiness shrivelled their guts and tapped at their thoughts as constantly as the icicles dripped with water. With the cruellest clarity, Mabglas pictured the glorious butchery of a fat boar. As if it really dangled before him, he saw the carcass being slit from groin to thorax and the hot blood and blue innards piled and steaming in a basin to be minced and stewed. Then would come the jointing and the skewering and a thick haunch set to blacken over a fire, the skin blistering and bubbling. The smell of it. The taste of it. The mercy of it. Oh! It was too excruciating to imagine.

If he could only sleep then that would give him some respite. But gnawing hunger kept him wide awake. It was the same for everyone. It was why they talked so – as a distraction from the pain and the thought of pain, and to shut out the distant yelp and whine of wolves, who were ravenous too, but cannier with it – experienced in it, more patient. They were merely waiting until the groaning lumps of man-meat in the cave became too feeble to resist them. And then they would come with their blue unblinking eyes and their teeth and their hot breath. Everyone knew what wolves could do if they were starving. Tear out a person's throat. Carry off a screaming baby by the arm.

To try and keep such thoughts at bay, they turned their conversations to the marshland, but spoke of it as if it was a place they'd been away from for years not days. The setting for an old fable. They recounted the accomplishments of

Prif and Gogwyn and the other dead men like the feats of the ancients, like the feats of gods.

They missed the bleating of sheep and goats, the lowing of their cows, the cry of seabirds, the sound of the wind in the reeds, the tall sky, the smell of the pools and the creeks. They missed their houses and their hearths and the odour of warm bread and meat. It always came back to meat.

On went the famishment and on went the storm. If the wind died down or the snow seemed to thin out, a tremor of optimism passed among them and for a moment it took away the pangs of apprehension, but it wasn't long before Gawl and Eira resumed their assault, their indignation still not satisfied.

A consensus arose for an attempt at appeasement, but Dewin was sceptical. The gods here in the valley were as cruel as the ones who had sent those howling animals to attack the village. Would *they* have been pacified with a few trinkets and tools?

But the others were insistent that they tried *something*, and into the sack they passed around went bright beads of amber, the three sharpest arrows, a good whetstone, the axe. Then there were bone rings and knots of hair and strips of blood-ied cloth and other keepsakes of the ones they had buried.

Celyn, the wife of poor Gof, whose head had been smashed open like a jar, was getting close to her time and, finding some privacy in the gloom, she milked her breasts into the basin she had brought. Then the nursing mothers did the same, and this inestimable donation was set between the rocks outside with the other tributes. It was all rightly generous and well-meant and they reassured one another that it would be enough. No god was above flattery.

It was true that old, bad-tempered Salo had been usually satisfied with their acts of reverence. Fed with lamb's meat and beer at midwinter, he would at least give them forewarning that his deluges were imminent. He raised the wind and set the reeds whispering. He threw the clouds with increasing speed across the sky. The air grew salty. And then when the gulls came in off the sea in flocks so large and loud that they darkened the marshes, it was an indisputable sign that a storm would soon follow.

And Arfon had been ever appreciative of the gifts they had thrown into her spry, laughing waters. The garlands of blossom at May time. Apples in the summer. Sheaves of wheat after harvest. In return, she had given them water to drink, water to wash in, smooth rocks to ring their hearths, and upstream beyond the coppice wood she had scoured away the soil along the banks to the thick clay beneath, which made durable cups and bowls and provided rendering for their houses.

Yet the gods here in the valley were not so easily bought, as Dewin had predicted. Perhaps it was not Gawl and Eira at all, thought Mabglas, but some wanton spirits unknown to them, ones with even less concern for honour. They took what had been offered but seemed glad to mete out even more punishments, new punishments. They not only had control of the wind and snow but some means of making the weak even weaker and touched them with a sickness that emptied their bellies and bowels of what was left inside.

The young ones shrieked in pain. Mothers and fathers tried to comfort them. Full-wombed Celyn lay down like a sow, fearing that the gods – or the other marsh-folk – would think her baby the next necessary sacrifice.

While she held herself, men argued about whether they should stay put or go out and find food.

What food? some said. Leaves and berries? There were none. And they could not hunt for anything of flesh when the gods had taken their arrows.

Well then, they could find some firewood at least. It was not far to the trees.

But in this weather? came the reply. They would be dead before they were ten paces down the fellside. They were too weak. How were they to carry enough wood back to the cave if they found any at all?

The disagreement escalated into accusations of cowardice and emphatic declarations about a man's duty to bravery, do or die.

They were livid from hunger, unreasonable and delusional, and their voices rose and redoubled in the hard hollow of the cave. They might kill one another, thought Mabglas, before the cold or the wolves or the hunger got to them.

Dewin struck his staff against the wall and cried out until – one by one – the voices dwindled.

He would go and speak to the gods, he said. He would try and broker some deal. If they wished the marsh-folk gone, then he would demand a cessation of the storm while they left. If there was some compromise by which they might stay, he would try and discover the terms. If the gods were only interested in another massacre, then at least they would know.

To travel to the Other-world was no small undertaking. It required concentration and incantation, food of special properties. And time. Though that, like many other things, had been stolen from them too. They would have to make do with what they had.

Mabglas took off his cloak and spread it on the ground for a blanket. Dewin lay down on his back and the others came to sit around him as he started to whisper to his soul, calling it up from the depths with the same words, over and over. Words from the language of the gods that Mabglas was slowly learning.

To Dewin, they were familiar after so many years, and as he talked himself into a trance he spoke louder still, his voice rising over the buff and boom of the wind in the cave. There was an authority in his tone that Mabglas had yet to acquire. He was still too unsure of himself. He could coax his soul to the surface, he had even managed to extrude it from his body, but after so much effort he felt exhausted. Whereas

Dewin, although he now lay silent and corpse-like, was alert and primed. He fixed his eyes on Mabglas, meaning that he was ready for the boy to feed him.

Opening up the otter-skin pouch he carried, Mabglas used his finger to stir the mush inside – a mixture of certain toadstools and mashed henbane. The smell of it was putrid, like a dirty wound. And the taste was worse. Though Dewin was used to it.

After coating the thumb of his right hand – the hand of wisdom – Mabglas pushed it between the old man's lips and felt his hard bare gums sucking off the paste as a child suckled the teat.

Once he had swallowed it down, he set his eyes on the rock ceiling and the marsh-folk laid their hands on his body so as to hold it steady when his soul began its exit. Mabglas had seen Dewin thrash like a netted fish before now, and they would all need to put their weight on him. He was immensely strong. Not that anyone would think it to touch him. Under his cloak, his muscles were like twines of thin rope, his bones sticks.

Mabglas felt the old man's skinny chest start to shake, then his hips twisting, his legs straining to kick out. They held him tighter as his soul gradually slithered out of his navel and into the ether that lay between the world of passing things and the world of the deathless gods.

It was of a translucent, viscous substance, and to move through it was rather like swimming in the weedy parts of the river on a sunny day. Bright but cloudy. And just as everything changed when he leapt from dry land into water, so it was when the soul left the body.

In the course of his apprenticeship, Mabglas had only been given small amounts of the paste so as to gradually inure him to the flavour – which was a struggle in itself – but, more importantly, he had to be acquainted with the peculiar sensation of otherness too.

Even after ingesting the tiniest smear, he did not feel like 'him' any more. 'He' was not a body but the thing that floated free and *observed* a body and found it beyond strange, a joke even. It had nostrils! Hands!

It was so small and scrawny. So temporary too, as Dewin had said. A body was merely something to be worn for a while before the soul was cast out and into another. Certainly not a thing that should be thought of as precious. It would only come to rot in the barrow. And before that, it took only old age or illness (or hunger) for a body to become a burden that one would gladly throw aside.

Well, in moments of desperation, perhaps.

Even when someone grew palsied and cankerous, they hesitated to solicit death too eagerly, not because they particularly wished to linger on in agony but for fear of what the gods would choose to do with their soul afterwards.

One could long for new-birth in a body that would know more joy than the one before; one could lie there clutching an amulet in the grave – as Prif had done – and hope for good fortune; a grieving family could proclaim the upstanding deeds of their mouldering loved one aloud from new moon to full; but the gods were unpredictable, as the attack had proved. Who knew what they were thinking or planning? Who could say how they made their decisions about a person's fate? If they were so fickle, then being someone of great munificence and virtue in this life gave no assurances of a favourable progression in the one to come, and wickedness was perhaps no impediment to reward.

The soul that had been inside Prif might have already been stuffed into a worm, the long chronicle of his benevolence immaterial. Whereas one of the wild men who had rampaged through the village cracking open skulls and stamping on brains might be given the body of a mighty horse, say, as his next host. But only for as long as the gods allowed it. Only until the horse was hacked apart in battle or worked to lameness and death.

It had been the way of things since the Earth-world had been shaped by Light and Dark in a past so distant that it was beyond even Dewin's reckoning. And if his master could not comprehend such things, Mabglas could not hope to grasp the true scale of time.

He wondered how many bodies his soul had passed through before it had come to be in the one he had now. A soul had no memory of what it had previously inhabited, but the thought that he might have been a spider once or a slug or a sand-flea made him shudder. He was as grateful to have no recollection of that as he was saddened to have never known what it was like to be a hawk or a bear or even a wolf, if he had ever lived inside such animals.

Although these questions troubled him, he thought about them endlessly, and Dewin had warned him that he would have to overcome distractions if he hoped to come and go from the Other-world unscathed. He would need his wits about him.

So far, he had only swum to the borthwen, the gateway, once, and with immense effort. He had only snatched glimpses of the gods, like shadows flickering behind a water-fall. To pass through, he would need a greater dose of Dewin's paste and an even larger dose of stamina and cour-age. Deeper knowledge too. He would have to be able to decrypt the complex language of the gods and learn how to parley with them if he was to stand any chance of acquiring their assistance and their intercession and – on occasions such as this – their mercy.

Dewin had been successful in the past. He had persuaded Old Salo and Arfon to bring them fish the summer the nets had come up empty from the estuary day after day. And in that strange season when the lambs had been stuck fast inside the ewes, he had brought Groth, the goddess of springtime, to deliver them safe and well.

Yet, such victories were never certain. Pleas, promises and sacrifices were accepted on some occasions but not others. Dewin had spent his lifetime trying to discover why, and

Mabglas would too. When it came to the subject of divine will, the increments of knowledge that a teacher could pass on to a pupil were always slight. It would take many wise-folk many years to fully understand the gods. That privilege would not fall to Mabglas but to another far into the future. Or it would never be realised at all. Perhaps humankind was destined never to grow out of its long infancy and as such the gods treated them as simpletons to be strung along. They will play with you, Dewin had warned him. They will agree, then disagree. They will seem kind when they are not. They will ask to be revered, then call your adulation a ploy.

Thus, a conference in the Other-world could be drawn-out and eventually come to nothing. There was no telling.

The negotiations were still not done. Dewin was still absent. He stared up at the roof of the cave. Even his breathing was barely perceptible. His body remained rigid under their hands.

As time passed, and then more, and Dewin did not stir, Mabglas feared that the gods were holding him in the Other-world, incensed that he had trespassed there, just as his people had trespassed into the valley. Or they were torment-ing him for sport, blowing his soul around as if it were a feather. They might do so for a thousand years if they so wished, long after Dewin's body had turned to dust. It would be a mere moment's entertainment to them. They might keep his soul captive forever, come to that. Dewin had spoken of such things. Think of a rat with its foot in a snare, he'd said, a rat yanking at a tether for eternity.

Mabglas could not imagine it. He did not want to try. For a thing to have no end unsettled him greatly. To be trapped and in pain was a recurring nightmare. A waking nightmare here in this cave when he shivered and hungered so. And if Dewin were to fail and they were to perish and leave these cold withering bodies behind for good, well then it did not seem so bad any more. All this would be over.

Ah, he had come to that, just as Dewin had said he would. Craving death as a welcome deliverance. There was no question that the cessation of this suffering would be a blessing. It could not come soon enough. And yet he could not quite hasten it along either.

Behind him, Mabglas heard a cry of surprise. It was Celyn, who had been sitting quietly in the dark, keeping her distance from them, still anxious that they would want her child if Dewin was unsuccessful.

It's stopping, she said, and moved towards the entrance of the cave.

Outside, there was clear bright air for the first time. When the last flakes of snow had come down, the wind died too. After the relentless pounding of the blizzard, the quiet felt like something sanctified and the marsh-folk did not dare to speak. The wolves said nothing either. Even the tap of dripping water stopped. Echoes dissipated. And there was something close to silence, until Dewin took a deep inward breath.

Mabglas attended to him straight away, as duty (but not love, never love) required. He wiped away the foam of spittle that brimmed at the old man's lips and dribbled a little cold water over his eyes to bring him round. There was a reluctance in returning, Mabglas knew that. He had felt it himself. It was something like disappointment to be back in the prison of the body after being so free.

But the others would not let Dewin lie there struck. They shook him and called to him. They were impatient to hear the verdict. They needed to eat. That was understandable.

Was the end of the storm just another trick? they asked. If they were to go down into the wood to gather fuel for a fire would the gods entomb them in more snow? Would the gods return their arrows and their axe? Were they to be duped by false hope again and ousted from this place too?

No, said Dewin as Mabglas helped him to sit up. No, the gods had agreed to let them stay. They were no longer angry. They could see that the marsh-folk meant no harm.

They had promised to bring the Sun to the valley so that she could melt away the winter. They would release Arfon from her torpor. They would bud the trees and fill the dale with deer and boar and waterfowl.

But wasn't it like the gods to renege on such assurances? some said. Wasn't that amusement to them? How could they be trusted?

This covenant was different, said Dewin. They had done something that they had never done before and given him a vision as proof of their honest intentions. One so vivid that it was as though the things he had been shown had already come to pass. It could not be a hoax.

To assuage any further doubt of the gods' clemency (and allay any remaining uncertainties about his competence) he described what he had seen of the coming springtime.

Warmth and sunlight.

The fells streaming with bright waterfalls.

They had built strong houses next to the river, he told them, with good timber for the scaffold, and thick reeds and hardy grass for the thatch. In long pastures of goldcups and star-flowers, there were many sheep and goats. A herd of cows swollen with milk. A virile bull. Plump fish wriggling in the stew-ponds.

All this would be theirs, he said. The gods wanted nothing in return. Only that the marsh-folk – or the valley-folk now – should always remember that they were custodians here.

No.

*Servants.*

Dewin corrected his translation of the word the gods had used.

Servants.

Though in what way, he did not know.

# To Think of Sicily

## 1445

For almost an hour, the plough had been stuck in the middle of Copelands Furlong as if the earth was attempting to claim it. But now at last the men were moving away again down the field, one driving the ox onwards with a stick and a short, threatening command, the other steadying the tip of the share as it cut the furrow.

The soil in the field had only just thawed sufficiently for it to be turned over and where shade sat all day, winter ice lingered. But everywhere else there was mud of varying consistencies, clods to puddles. In the days since Candlemas, melt from the moors and heavy rain had swollen the cloughs and the river, and the pasturelands closest to the banks had flooded. One of the Copelands' ewes had died after stumbling into a water-logged ditch, and the lambs inside her had perished.

It was the fault of the Sicilian. No question. He had made the animal demented. Just as he had called down the deluge and set the very earth against them. Such facts had passed into folklore within a few days. In the village, they were already telling stories about the Dark Vagabond.

Isobel Copeland watched her husband bullying the ox. Her daughter, Jayne, watched her man, Matthias Leach, set his body at an angle as he tried to drive the plough forward.

'That field will be riven with as many curses as gutters,' said Isobel, for she knew how incensed both men would be by the obstinate clay.

'They would be as well to wait a day or two,' Jayne said, as she watched them struggling again. 'It will still be frozen in parts.'

'Two days, three days, a sennight, forever, it will make no difference if the land is bewitched,' her mother said. She spat on a piece of coarse cloth and rubbed it hard against the back of her hand.

'It is not bewitched,' Jayne answered.

'But all is wrong,' said her mother.

'Wrong how?'

'The earth steers the plough.'

'How can it be so?'

'It is full of mischief,' her mother said. 'Did you not see how long the soil held onto the blade? It even muscles the ox aside. Do you see it, Agatha?'

She lifted Jayne's daughter, a pale tot of four, and pointed at the beast wading in and out of the sucking mud and lurching away at a diagonal from the trench. The two men beat the animal back into line, but their cries were small on the air. The crows wheeling above them were far louder and far more fascinating to Agatha, who copied their grating calls until her grandmother told her to hold her noise. They were wicked birds, and she should not learn their language.

'Child, go and collect the eggs before the rats start a feast in the coop,' she said and sent her away with a basket.

Jayne watched her go, the little dog, Vinegar, leaping around her in his jollity. She could not remember her own childhood.

But in the dream she'd had the previous night of that beautiful garden with its fountains and terraces, she had *felt* what it was like to be a girl again. She had looked at the trees and the birds and the animals with true astonishment.

How she had come to be walking barefoot in that place, she did not know – only that those lawns and pathways were hers to enjoy for as long as she pleased. There was no time there. The sun was forever at its zenith. The grass was so dry and warm.

The kick Matthias had given her for oversleeping had been nothing to the agony of leaving that place.

'The fleece, Jayne,' said her mother, working the cloth hard between her knuckles now.

The dead ewe had been moved to a corner of the yard away from the pen, though this seemed only to have aroused curiosity and suspicion in the other sheep and they wedged their faces between the palings, their eyes all a-startle as they watched the women go by. They would start to lamb soon. The valley would become loud with bleating as the young were let out onto the fells. The new-borns would soon learn the limits of their heft.

Jayne thought of the pretty white goat she had seen in the dream. A kid with little grey horns standing in the shade of an olive tree. Her mother had been there too, utterly enchanted by the creature. She had picked it up and stroked its chin and imitated its cries, as Agatha had mimicked the crows. Aye, her mother. It was hard to imagine.

In the dream, she had been so happy and had remarked to Jayne how strange it was to meet in this paradise and that they would have much to say about it on the morrow.

What had seemed vivid at the time was absurd now. Silly enough to make for a brief diversion as they worked, thought Jayne. But her mother was too short-tempered for idle chatter.

'Did you not sleep well?' Jayne asked her.

'You know that I did,' her mother answered. 'Were we not both slug-a-beds this morning? You must still feel your husband's boot in your leg. I feel your father's in mine. And I shall know it again if we are lax. Put her on her back.'

Between them, they rigged the sheep, a ton-weight in death, bloated from drowning with its coat still sodden, and

Jayne put down the milking stool she had brought to sit on while she sheared.

The ewe had been hexed. That was the unanimous opinion of the village. And so the carcass would be burned soon enough, but not before they had removed the fleece, which – the priest had cautioned them – was too valuable to be turned to ash. Wool built churches. Wool allowed them to glorify God. A sheep's coat was sacred. Nothing untoward could hide there. Was that not evident? The good women of England would not be encouraged to sit at the spinning wheel or the loom if the Devil could somehow conceal himself in the warp and weft.

'*Was* it witchery?' said Jayne. 'Think you that? Truly?'

'The priest confirmed it,' her mother replied.

'Not drowning? Sheep are witless sometimes.'

'The animal was bewildered by other means,' said her mother. 'That stranger had some . . . cunning.'

'He was a good man. Did you not say as much yourself?'

'His appearance made it seem so at first, perhaps.'

'And not his manner?'

'His manner?'

'Was not Agatha taken with him? She is ever a shrewd judge. And did he not favour us with a gift?'

Her mother worked the cloth into her palm, making hard circles against the heel of her thumb as though she was trying to bring out the shine in a coin. Like Jayne's, her hands were perpetually cut and split. Scars lay across scars. The most recent punctures, from dragging away the boughs of the hawthorn tree that had blown down into the pig pen, had been healing well with the balm the Sicilian had left them, but now she had opened the wounds again and brought the rag away bloody.

'Why do you do that, mother?' said Jayne.

'Your father does not like the smell of that . . . substance,' she said.

'And you?'

'I do not care for it either. Not now.'

She knew when her mother was being untruthful. Rather than averting her gaze, as most would do, she looked at a person straight and with a stern eye, as if to fend off any accusations of falsehood before they were voiced.

'It was giving you relief from your sores,' said Jayne.

'Aye, and what else might it do? Send me wandering into the marsh like this lady?'

She shook the ewe's foreleg and its heavy head lolled from side to side.

'He must have fed her some of that ointment,' she went on. 'The foreigner.'

'Wherefore, mother?'

'To tangle its brain.'

'But to what end?'

'No end but malice itself. It is the Devil's great joy to spoil what God gives to us.'

'The Devil put him up to it?' Jayne said. It was irrefutable in the village, but she did not believe that her mother thought it true.

'The Devil could not have been unfamiliar to him,' she replied.

'So certain?'

'Anyone who has walked from the other side of the world in pilgrimage must have considerable sins to pardon.'

This too had been agreed upon.

'Is that not more a sign of true repentance?' Jayne said. 'He might have stayed in his own country and resigned himself to being damned. Yet, he left to seek absolution.'

'Jayne, your father is already much abused for letting the man stay,' her mother said. 'Do not add to his troubles. Break the bottle. Pour the oil into the river. The water will carry its poison away.'

'Poison? It is a salve, mother,' said Jayne. 'Is that not evident? Look at my hands.'

She did, and said, 'It surprises me that your Matthias has not scoured them to the bone. Does he tolerate the smell?'

'He has a cold,' said Jayne. 'He cannot detect it.'

'Well, pray it continues,' her mother replied. 'And in the meanwhile, cleanse yourself.'

'And make my skin weep blood like yours?'

'Would you rather be thought an accomplice of that black-bearded fellow?' said her mother. 'Nay, do not scoff, woman. If they cannot hang him, they may well hang you in his stead. Here.'

Jayne declined the cloth that her mother passed to her. 'There is no cause to worry now,' she said. 'The oil is all used up.'

'In truth?'

'Aye. It is gone,' said Jayne. She wished it was not so.

~

The Sicilian had passed through the valley three days before, a pilgrim heading north to York or south to Chester, perhaps. They could not tell, and he could not explain. But that was no matter. He had been caught in a snowstorm while crossing the moor and needed shelter.

The weather here, especially in February, was the common adversary of all, villager or wanderer, even a wanderer as singular as this one. And to have booted him along the lane or back up the fell would have been cruel. A sin, no less, the priest had said. For here was a servant of God, and God would remember those who had rejected such a virtuous mendicant.

But the priest had guests in his house already and could not accommodate another, and so it had fallen to a family of his choosing to give lodging to the stranger. 'Mr Copeland,' he'd said. 'Good man.' And proceeded to explain that to give succour to one so devout that they would willingly walk across the moorland in wintertime to honour a saint or relic would please the Lord well. And for that reason – or rather for that reason *alone* – had Jayne's father permitted the Sicilian to stay in the haybarn until the blizzard subsided.

In between their labours, the other villagers came to look at him. Children sat at his feet and stared for a while until they were called away by mothers who were at once nervous and exhilarated to meet the man's eyes. The blacksmith, the miller, the shepherds, woodsmen, thatchers and their prentices looked in and went away again, incurious after the first jolt of the pilgrim's darkness. He was just another vagrant with a hat for a begging bowl. A tramper with a crucifix. He would not stay for long. They could not understand him anyway. And they had work to do. It was the duty of the women to attend him.

When Jayne had knelt before him with a bowl of water and scrubbed away the muck and the grass and the thorns, she found the Sicilian's feet to be broad and flat and there were faint marks where his broken sandals had bitten into his skin. Older damage had cured into mere discolorations. For someone who had walked so far, he was remarkably untarnished. His grazes were nothing next to the injuries she had seen on others who had come in off the moor with lacerations and breakages remarkable enough to draw a crowd. Bites from wild dogs. A snapped shinbone. Ulcers to rival Job's.

There had been a lunatic woman once, whose bare feet were split to the bones at the heels and oozed a yellow pus that smelled like the innards of a hoof boil. She had been walking the hills for years, she had said, looking for Judas Iscariot. She had God's written authority (in the form of a piece of scratched-on slate) to pardon the poor devil his sins. Damned for a kiss. 'Twas nothing.

Within a few days her feet had rotted, and she had died with toes as thick and black as blood sausages. Yet the Sicilian looked as though he had suffered in no other way than to stain himself. He had been walking for so long, Jayne thought, that the north country dirt had seeped into his skin for good, as his hands and feet were hardly less brown when she had finished washing them.

He seemed to understand her puzzlement.

'Siciliano,' he said, prodding his chest. 'Siciliano.' And then motioned this way and that. Was he lost? If so, he was undeterred, always smiling.

Seeing that little Agatha was amused by the way he flapped his hand, he did it all the more and made her laugh as she had not laughed for some time. It was delight, thought Jayne. How rare it was here. Even at Agatha's age, a child of the valley was starting to understand that their life would be one of endless work. And only rarely would there be any distractions from the routines of the day and the season. It was why the Sicilian gave her so much pleasure.

Unlike many of the others in the village, the girl had shown no fear at all of the man's dark eyes and reached out to feel his beard and his short, tufted hair. He ran his breath across a small set of wooden pipes, making the noise of a cuckoo and an owl and then to please her further, he took from his skin bag a seashell shaped like an ear and a lead flask of holy water, which he gave her to hold. He seemed to enjoy her fascination and allowed her to put the sack on her knee to search for the next plaything.

She brought out a tiny square of dirty linen, which the Sicilian carefully unfolded to show them some strands of hair.

'Maria,' he said. 'Maria Mater.' And closed his eyes and beat his fist against his heart with so much passion that they feared his ribs would break.

He was very thin. Everywhere. His wrists and ankles were all bone. He had such hollow cheeks. How long had it been since he had eaten? Several days by the look of him. Other villages had not been so generous perhaps. But which ones he had passed through, it was impossible to know. What he had seen, he could not describe.

When other travellers happened into the valley, they were as glad sometimes to lay down the news they had been carrying as much as their belongings and their tired, aching bodies. Thus had Barrowbeck come to know about wars and executions, trickery and treason, and while Jayne had dutifully denounced the wrongdoers in each case, she enjoyed hearing about them as much as the descriptions of castles, cathedrals, bridges, boats and the sea.

The sea. The Sicilian would have known it. But she could not ask him what it had been like to leave one land for another, and he could not have told her. No matter how long he talked for, she failed to grasp his meaning. All that was clear was the adoration he had for the Holy Virgin, and the three strands of her hair.

Given the vigour of his exaltations, Jayne had thought that he might be fasting out of a special fealty to the Blessed Mary. For when she and her mother had brought him bread, cheese and ale, he had made a gesture of sweeping something off his palms as if in refusal.

He could see that this puzzled them and he plucked at his frayed black smock and the grimy rope around his hips.

Ah, he had no money. He could not pay. But they shook their heads at his concerns and said, 'Eat, eat' – little Agatha, too, in mimicry of her mother – and mimed with their fingers until he understood.

'Grazzi,' he said and bowed and bowed again before putting the food aside on the hay to take out a small stone bottle from his bag. Inside was dark green oil that he rubbed into his hands until they glistened like burnished wood. The smell was that of herbs unfamiliar to the two women, not bay or rosemary but something flowery and sharp in the nose. It was a token of respect, Jayne assumed, to sweeten his hands before eating the food of strangers. A custom in his homeland, she thought. Was that what he'd been trying to say as he went about his ablutions? It was all out of reach behind his soft mellifluous words, which were beautiful to listen to but lost on her. Such a waste. The most exotic of emissaries was here in the haybarn and he would leave as inscrutable as he had arrived.

The next morning, he was already gone when Jayne and her mother went in to gather feed for the ewes. He had left behind the bottle of his fragrant oil in such a place that made it clear it was in recompense for the food they had given him, and not something he had simply forgotten.

Had they not found it, they might have thought him an apparition. A Sicilian! In Barrowbeck! Beating his chest with love for the Virgin Mary and smearing his hands with that spicy ointment. He had been a thing of fable, like a chimera or a crocodile. No, nothing so menacing, thought Jayne. More a playful faun, with his set of pipes.

She would have liked to have kept him, somehow, and looked upon him whenever she felt the desire to be amazed. But then it was as well he hadn't stayed. After his departure, the thaw had come and then the flood, and then the ewe had drowned in the swamp at the edge of the pasture-field. The Sicilian would not have survived the retribution.

For a day, Jayne had worried that she and her mother had shown him *too* much hospitality and that, given the torrential weather, he might return to avail himself of it again. A dog could always be found where it was fed best, as her father said. And in the village they would have thought of him as a dog, less than a dog. They would have beaten him and noosed him from the tree by the Celts Cave. The priest would have taken the boys and girls, little Agatha too, to throw stones at the hanging body to drive out the Devil. For it was known that he could squat in the dead long after the last breath had been drawn.

As much as Jayne longed to set eyes on the Sicilian again, it was to her relief that he had not come back. Just as the magi were warned to bypass Herod's palace on their return journey, perhaps God had directed him along a safer path to his home. If indeed it was his intention to go back to his own country.

She did not have a number for the miles between here and there. And would he remember Barrowbeck? Cold England? This muddy valley? He might think of them as privations he had deserved. For his pilgrimage was one undertaken in penance. She could tell. He carried such humility with him. The heaviest of all his belongings. He had not come expecting charity, as pilgrims usually did, but had made a point of reimbursing them for his supper by leaving the oil. The wicked had no such concerns about courtesy. Just as they had no inclination for remorse. Whatever the Sicilian had done, it seemed to Jayne that he was sorry. That he had travelled so far and did not yet think of himself as forgiven was not, as her mother and everyone else assumed, evidence of a sin so heinous as to be unpardonable, but rather a dissatisfaction with his own efforts at reparation. That made him a man of principles, not the Devil in a friar's robes. Atonement was, for him, a lifetime's work, a lifetime's walk.

Jayne almost envied him, and then dismissed such a notion as iniquitous. She should not wish to be a sinful person. She did not wish it for one moment. Only that she might be tested, like him, in some manner. Sent out into the world to prove her faithfulness.

In her head she held the names of well-known missionaries – Saint Columba, Saint Brendan, Saint Ingrid of the Hills, and others too – and while she could not recall the full list of their accomplishments – though they were all surely magnificent – it gave her pleasure to simply picture them moving, even if it was in somewhat fleeting images. A man pulling on a pair of oars amid much spume and spray. A woman in a cloak being blown along a windy ridge with a lantern in her hand. There was always a tumult to these invented scenes.

She felt certain that she would be able to withstand the hardships of a pilgrim. Welcome them, even. Tempests, pain and hunger would be the very things that urged her onwards. They were trials that had purpose. After seeing them through, a person would be changed.

Whereas here in the valley, adversity led nowhere. Aye, to endure it day by day, to covet nothing more, to confess any thoughts of cupidity, however small they were, gave certain assurances of reward in the next life, and that ought to be plenty. That ought to be all. Was not heaven superlative?

But that madwoman looking for Judas on the moors, as touched in the mind as she was, she had seemed so *unbound*, so convinced that she really had been entrusted with this sacred task that her only concern was to fail in it. She did not worry about being imprisoned for her oddness or her heresy. It would have seemed to her unthinkable that anyone would want to hinder the Lord's work.

If only she were to be called in such a way, thought Jayne. If the Virgin, say, were to appear before her – as she had with others – with a message on a scroll saying go here, go there, do this in my name, then no one would have the authority to prevent her from obeying the command. Not her mother or her father. Not Matthias. Or the Under-Tenant of the valley. Or the priest. Or the Pope himself.

Only, there was Agatha. What about Agatha? The child who had lived after three before her had been born too early as clots of sinew and blood. She could not abandon her.

But then had not Saint Catarina of the Desert kept a maidservant, a travelling companion? One who played the tambourine and sang in gladness as they crossed the Sinai. Aye, Agatha could sing and play, and they might fall in with other pilgrims just as merry, like the ones who had come down into the valley on a wet afternoon the year before, cheering themselves through the final mile by chanting and carolling, as if a host of wild angels had descended from the clouds on the moor.

A day later, they had gone again – away to the next place, a cathedral town or a shrine, the distance no object since they could march all the way to the far points of the compass if they wished. How would it be, Jayne thought, to set out one morning and walk into the rest of Christendom?

A shake of her arm and there was her mother, irritable at her for falling into thought and slowing up the work.

'Be lively, Jayne,' she said. 'They will want to see that everything is in hand.'

She rolled the sheep onto its flank and held the animal fast so that they could take off the other side of its fleece.

Jayne looked at her mother's face – studied it, in fact, in a way she hadn't done for some time. Ruddy chops, broken teeth, veinous temples, hard eyes. How old she was, she did not know for certain. Forty years, give or take. One of the more elderly in the village, certainly. Though she had always been a woman of aches and solemnity. It is what I will become, thought Jayne. Then Agatha. And any other daughters that might survive. And their daughters.

She had prayed, and still prayed, for sons. At least, they might go off soldiering. They might see France. Or even Sicily. And not just in a dream.

It was where she had been taken in her sleep. She was certain of that. The garden had belonged to the Sicilian.

It had smelled of his oil. She and her mother had found the ingredients growing against an old wall – the bushes stirred by a warm wind. They had enjoyed the heat on their skin and the trill of the crickets in the grass. In the fields beyond the garden there had been shepherds singing. More faintly still they had heard a bell tolling from one of the white church towers that sat among the distant hills and vineyards.

Here, there were only cries of anger and distress. The plough had tipped over and Jayne watched Matthias and her father both pushing at the handle trying to right it again. Thin, surprising sunlight came and went, casting the men's busy shadows and the more inert shadow of the ox over the rippled earth.

It was, for a moment, like an allegory the priest might use as an illustration of some eternal struggle.

'I dreamt last night,' said Jayne, as she considered the thought.

But her mother was not interested.

'You need not be so delicate with the shears,' she said, keen to set Jayne back onto the task in hand. 'She will not feel anything now.'

'I did not want to wake,' Jayne said. 'Though it did not seem as though I was asleep.'

'You should not let your father hear you speaking so mistily. He will think you addled as well as idle.'

'I was in that stranger's country,' Jayne continued.

Her mother was perturbed that she had mentioned him again.

'What does it matter, woman?' she said. 'The fleece.'

'You were there too, mother,' Jayne said.

'Enough now.'

'Do you not wish to hear what you said to me?'

'I will have much to say to you now if you chatter on.'

'You were so very content.'

'And I would be so again to see you plying the shears.'

'It was pleasant to hear you laughing.'

'Then you are pleased by very little.'

'You thought it extremely fine,' Jayne said.

'To laugh?'

'No, mother, the garden.'

The word made her mother turn away and watch the men in the field.

'What is it?' asked Jayne.

'Hand me the blades,' her mother said.

'Something gives you dread?'

'Aye, your father's birch.'

'Only that?'

'Is that not enough?'

No, it was not a whipping that troubled her. Not after being a wife for so long.

'You dreamt of it too,' Jayne realised. 'The garden.'

Her mother fixed her eyes on her. 'No.'

'But I see that you did.'

47

'Look again.'

With her mother still defiant, Jayne said, 'There was a goat kid. Do you remember it?'

'How could I?'

'You held it in your arms as if it was a child.'

'Strange things happen in dreams.'

'You picked from the fruit trees,' Jayne went on. 'You ate an orange.'

She put her palm close to her mother's nose.

'This was the smell of the place, was it not?' she said.

Her mother pushed her hand away.

'It cannot be true that two should have the same dream on the same night,' she said. 'It cannot be proper, either.'

'I do not think it *was* a dream,' said Jayne. 'We were there as we are here now. Flesh and blood.'

'And yet you were asleep with your husband and daughter. And I with your father.'

'Then by some marvel we were here *and* there.'

'Or by some witchcraft.'

'Witchcraft would not have spirited us away to a garden so beautiful.'

'Eden had its serpent.'

'Is it not marvellous that we were in that place together?' said Jayne.

'Truly, woman,' her mother said. 'But what of that?'

She took hold of the clippers to finish the task herself.

'You have work,' she said. 'We all have work. Even Agatha toils harder than you to-day.'

The girl was carrying over a basket of eggs, counting them as she walked. The dog, Vinegar, skipped around her ankles. His muzzle-fur was wet and bloody. Ratcatcher. He had his employment too.

In the field, the men had turned the plough and were heading back towards the farm. The ox nodded as it trudged to the thwack of the switch on its shoulder. Its belly was coated in muck. The crows rose and fell behind them, gleaning what they could from the broken earth.

Elsewhere in the valley, other men were ploughing other lots. Tussling with the land. Women were sweeping away puddles and clearing the debris that the floodwaters had dumped in barns and storehouses.

To say that the Sicilian had brought about this ruinous change in the weather, that he'd turned the fields to a gripping sludge and had – for reasons unknown – killed a ewe and her lambs was merely to ensure that when the Under-Tenant came to inspect the damage he did not blame the villagers for failing to contain the inundation or drain their fields. If they could have shown him a swinging body, bruised by stones, then that would have been a better proof of the Dark Vagabond's guilt – but a story would have to suffice.

Whether the Under-Tenant would believe it was another matter. He was not a credulous man. He took only what he could see with his eyes as the truth. And he would see that this February in his valley was the same as any other. It was the month of thaw and rain and torrents. The clay did not clutch at the plough. Animals were not put into a trance. There was only mud and bad luck and inadequate preparation. None of that was the Devil's doing.

The Sicilian was a good man, God's man. How selfless of him to give away what little of his fragrant oil was left when he would need it more. Not only to soothe his feet and cleanse his hands but to remind him of his home. That was why he had left it behind. So that others could enjoy his garden too.

But to Jayne, the smell of it was already fading. It would soon be gone. She would stink of soil and yeast and animals, this ewe's greasy coat.

'Be about it now and help me,' said her mother. 'They will be full of fury if they see it is not done. This is not our only labour of the day.'

Taking up the edge of the cut fleece, Jayne pulled it tight so that her mother could slice the rest away with more ease. She worked the shears quickly with force and severity. A woman with a grip that could leave finger-marks on granite. Stony herself in all respects. But in the dream – or whatever it should be called – she had been much amused by a bird in the garden, a bird with a little crown and green skirts. She had pursued it with as much glee as Agatha would have had in seeing it strutting off in front of her, yowling.

Across the warm grass she had gone, clapping and whistling the bird through the olive groves and the cool dry cypress wood until, back out in the brilliance of the noonday sunlight, it had thrown up its tail into a fan of eyes that were as wide as hers.

And she had said to Jayne – and said it most sincerely – that they were truly blessed to be there. She had never seen feathers so colourful. Nor a thing so transformed. How wonderful it was to think that Sicily had such creatures.

# The Strangest Case

## 1792

*February 28th, 1792*
*Midnight*

Sleep eludes me for a second night, dear Brother, while this, the strangest of cases, remains warm to my mind. I have not hitherto imparted to you all that has happened here in Barrowbeck these several days, but now that the trial, or at least my connection to it, is complete, I shall endeavour to commit the entire affair to paper so that you might better appreciate my insomniac condition – and perhaps, in your wisdom, offer some strategy by which I might begin to comprehend these incidents.

You know already, from my letter a fortnight past, that May Calvert (a mere babe when you quit the village some seventeen years ago) was found dead by the river in Fitch Wood and I have named her father, Peter, as one of the two men accused of her murder, alongside this George Haydock of

Halifax. But you know not of the details. Indeed, I have been in dispute with my conscience as to whether I ought to impose them upon you as directly as I must. For the circumstances of the crime are no less disturbing than the grisly homicide itself. Never have I known the courtroom here at the Hall to be so awash with tales as outlandish and grotesque as those told by the two men at the stand. By the third and final sitting, when all evidence had been submitted, I was only too glad to retire to the antechamber with Squire Underwood and Reverend Austwick to consider the verdict.

'Well, gentlemen, what make you of it?' the Squire enquired of us, and the Reverend made certain that he was heard first.

'They are murderers, my lord,' came his adjudication. 'Nothing could be plainer,' he said. 'I say we condemn them as such, put an end to this absurdity and go to lunch.'

I flatter myself, dear Brother, that I have in my letters communicated *his* character to you well enough since his arrival at Saint Gabriel's some years ago, and that you know him, as I do, to be a man who prides himself on his common sense. This is not an unadmirable trait, especially in a clergy-man, but it leads him to conclusions which beg for proof beyond his own assumptions. He is not a man to change his mind. Nor is he a man of much Christian compassion. Granted the power to do so, he would have sent Peter Calvert and George Haydock to the gallows there and then and kicked away the stool himself.

I said to him, 'There is nothing plain in any of this at all.' For that was most evidently true.

'Then you are prepared to give the defendants' account some credence, Mr Kennet?' the Squire asked me.

'They seemed to tell it genuine,' I answered.

'Seemed?' Reverend Austwick said, and you can conceive his sneer. 'For parish constable, Mr Kennet, you have much to learn about the guile of malefactors. You would acquit them on the strength of how they seemed? Peter Calvert *seemed* a fond father and yet his plan was to give a man a horse in return for killing his daughter. Read your Bible, sir. It has much to say about sheep and wolves.'

I said, 'He is a good man at heart.'

Which, Brother, you surely believe to be true as well.

'Then if Mr Calvert acted against his character,' said the Squire, 'he was perhaps preyed upon by this man, Haydock, for money?'

I explained that Haydock would have chosen in Peter Calvert the most unsuitable victim for extortion. 'The Calverts are as poor as dirt, as you know, my lord,' I said. 'That grey mare is the sum of their wealth.'

'Then does Peter Calvert suffer from some mental imbalance, think you?' the Squire suggested. 'He had not the scattered speech of a lunatic in court.'

'No, I do not think that he is ill, sir,' I said. I believed that wholeheartedly. I still do.

Reverend Austwick then smiled in the hollow way I have described to you on several occasions, as though all was beneath him.

'Then you consider what he says to be truthful?' he said. 'You believe that his daughter became the possession of some *thing* from the river?'

'Peter Calvert could not have invented such a story,' I said. 'And why would he?'

'To conceal the true motivation for the child's murder,' Reverend Austwick replied.

'Which is what?' asked the Squire.

'The answer is obvious,' the Reverend said. 'The girl was with child, as Haydock testified. Calvert knew that he could not feed another mouth and thus he sought to resolve the matter.'

The Reverend knew, as did I, that Haydock had testified to no such thing. 'He only *suspected* that May was bearing,' said I. 'By his own admission, he did not know *why* he had been employed. He did not consider that his business.'

Reverend Austwick directed his response to the Squire.

'I am merely making an inference, sir. The girl was, shall we say, *well known* to young men in the valley. So I have heard.'

'But if she *were* with child,' I said. 'And if Peter Calvert were determined to cut short the development, the woods and fields are filled with poisons that can flush out the womb right quick. Hellebore, Feverfew, Tansy. Even I am familiar

56

with the names. Any farmer could have made an infusion without recourse to a recipe. There would have been no need for him to have had May killed. She need only have drunk some brew of herbs to rid her of the inconvenience.'

'Inconvenience?' Reverend Austwick sniffed. 'How polite.'

'Mr Kennet has a point, though, Reverend,' the Squire said, much to my satisfaction. 'If those indeed were the circumstances, such a deadly solution seems too excessive.'

'Then there was some additional shame in the pregnancy,' replied Reverend Austwick.

'You mean the child was Peter Calvert's?' said the Squire. 'If child there was?'

'You pile one slander upon another, Reverend,' I told him. 'You must offer evidence.'

'The evidence lies in logic, sir,' he said. And then petitioned the Squire. 'Think on it, my lord. If Calvert really did believe his daughter to have been seized by something unholy, why did he not call upon me to pray for her release? Why pay a brute like this man Haydock to dispatch her?'

'Perhaps he feared you would not believe him, sir,' I said.

'More likely he feared the penalty for his sin,' said Reverend Austwick.

'Why do you persist with these assumptions?' I returned, not a little acerbically, I have to say. 'They bring us no closer to understanding the cause of any of this.'

'We are but mortal men,' the Reverend said, speaking to the Squire rather than to me. 'I fear that discovering what compelled Calvert and Haydock to embark on their deplorable course of action must fall within God's purview now. Indeed, I consider it our duty to bring these two miscreants before His heavenly court as soon as we may. They have confessed to the conspiracy, and we must be satisfied with that. The motive for their brutality is no longer our concern.'

'It is the concern of those who live here,' said the Squire. 'They will look to the three of us for an explanation. There is great discontent.'

'Then, sir, we must use the opportunity to enlighten them,' Reverend Austwick said. 'Wean them off this drivel about sorcery. Such things belong to the centuries of the past, not ours. They work among the marvels of science every day at the mill, and yet they talk of goblins?'

The Squire said nothing, which Reverend Austwick took to mean that he could not see the discrepancy.

'It surprises me, my lord,' he said, 'that a man of your education would give a story such as the one you have heard a moment's consideration.'

'I am here to consider all that comes before me,' returned the Squire. 'And I have to agree with Mr Kennet', he said, 'that Mr Calvert and the man, Haydock, did not appear insincere in their description of the events.'

'Well, if not insincere,' Reverend Austwick said, 'they were most certainly delusional. Was not this Haydock reeking of brandy when he was apprehended, Mr Kennet?'

'My understanding', I said, 'was that the drink was intended to restore his nerves, after what he'd seen.'

Reverend Austwick dismissed my words with a turn of his hand.

'He saw nothing. It is a design upon your clemency, sir,' he said to the Squire. 'These felons must be denounced for what they are. Let those in the village mutter about demons if that is their wont. But the court must be seen to be unswayed by superstition.'

Before Reverend Austwick had finished, the Squire was gesturing for him to cease.

'Yes, yes, quite,' he said.

His authority notwithstanding, I felt it incumbent on me to remind the Squire of May's condition in death.

'But my lord,' I said. 'You saw the body. From head to toe it was as soft as the clothes she was wearing. How could Haydock have rendered her so with his bare hands?'

'Mr Kennet,' said the Squire. 'Do not doubt that I have pity for the girl and for Peter Calvert. He has clearly lost his wits, even if he appears lucid. But the Reverend is right, we cannot endorse rumour. We can only proceed on facts. And the facts before us are that a murder has occurred, and two men have admitted to the plot which led to it. Anything else will have to remain unproven here. Our duty to the matter is done now. Let the Lent Assizes bring the case to its end. They will see that the girl is given justice.'

'A wise conclusion, sir,' Reverend Austwick said. 'We have wasted enough time on the misfortunes of this whore.'

Thus, our deliberations came to an end. My entreaties to unravel the enigmas of the affair went unheeded. The two men, Haydock and Peter Calvert, were taken back to the Squire's cellar until they could be transported to Lancaster gaol. And they sit there now.

It surprises me that neither have made any appeal. Not even in court did they protest against the Squire's judgment. Peter Calvert seemed numb, and Haydock did not reproach him for sending him off to do his odious job so unprepared. Indeed, Haydock did not seem to know where he was. He gave his testimony as if recalling a nightmare.

I have endured many liars in my time and, contrary to the Reverend's slighting of my ability, they are rarely so skilled at it that I cannot penetrate their deviousness. But Haydock was not one of them. Nor has Peter Calvert any craft in him. Would you say that he was an artful man? No, nor I.

Then what is there to do but take the accounts of these two men as the truth?

As the Squire justly said, and as I have reported, Peter Calvert did not seem mad as he spoke in court. He was, by degrees, distraught and tearful, I grant you, but he did not go gibbering from one topic to another as a man insane might have done. His story was well-given and methodical. It is why I can so clearly relay it to you now.

It began, he said, about a month before. His daughter had been spending more time than usual at the river, taking the horse there to drink so that she could have the excuse to go and meet a boy from the village, Calvert suspected. He knew when she had been with a boy. There was a change in her disposition that made her languid and absent-minded and she smelled, too, like a tom cat, he said. And had she returned to the farm so, he would have shaken confession and repentance out of her, as he always did, as any good father had the duty to do. But she did not seem like that at all. Indeed, the first few times that she had come and gone from the wood, he was satisfied that she had visited the riverbend only to sate the horse's thirst and not her own.

Yet he began to notice her looking at him strangely. She studied him, he said, with an intent that he found most disquieting. It was as though she was reckoning something, devising a strategy. Though for what purpose eluded him in the moment.

He enquired of his wife if she had noticed the same in the girl, but she could see no change. Nor could May's brothers and sisters. To them, she was as she always had been. But that was the cunning of the thing, Calvert said. It only gave itself away to him. A detail that Reverend Austwick pounced upon in court.

'A most convenient aspect of the plot, no?' he said, prompting some uneasy laughter from those watching the proceedings. 'Do you deem queer looks to be a reasonable basis for murder?'

Peter Calvert answered in the negative and explained that the peculiar way in which May had begun to regard him had only been a foretaste of far more troubling alterations to her behaviour.

He began to follow her to the river, he said, and watched her licking the sweat off the horse's neck. He watched her eating things that turned his stomach. And she appeared to lack any feeling in her body. The river was still much too cold for anything other than washing, but she did not seem affected by it and would swim out into the deep of the bend and dive under the water for longer than the otters. Concerned that she would drown, Calvert had on one occasion come to the brink of wading in to rescue her, only to see her surface and allow the current to take her some way downstream, her body undulating as though it was liquid itself.

These and other phenomena he reported to his wife and yet she would not believe him. Indeed, she considered *him* to be the one affected in judgement. He told the court that she imagined he had eaten some bad pork and that a parasite must have worked its way from his gut to his brain. Or that he had been addled by the dried mushrooms he liked to steep in milk for his supper. He had made an error, she suggested, and picked not Honey Waxcaps in the autumn gone but Brown Sickeners.

Had Peter Calvert eaten such things, then his mistrust of his daughter might well have been explained. But he had not. And his belief that May had been somehow *replaced* continued to cause much disagreement between him and his wife. When neighbours called, he probed them for their opinion of May's character – a query they thought most odd, for in their company the girl was quite ordinary. Yet, if Calvert attempted to have some dialogue with her, she would only scrutinise him and say nothing and he would become so provoked that he tried to beat her into answering.

His wife, not unreasonably, took exception to what she saw as persecution, and by and by Calvert found his meals left on the outside step and he was exiled to sleep in the hayloft. Yet he feared for his family, especially little Edwin, Franny, Joe and Arabella, and once his wife was a-bed at night, he took up a vigil in the children's room.

May would come to the door and look in but seeing him there she went back to her chamber, and he was glad that he had decided to watch over the small ones. Yet one night, fatigue engulfed him and he dozed in the chair until the candles were almost down. When he woke, May was standing at the bedside with a billhook in her hand and studying her brothers and sisters while they slept as a dog might look with delight at a pack of cornered rats. He had no doubt that had he not raised an alarm, then May – or rather this *thing* inside her – would have done them great injury.

\*

I trust that I have explained well enough the reasons as to why Peter Calvert did not seek help from anyone in the village. His difficulty was one of substantiation. Or the absence of it. If he had called me to the house, I would have gone right enough, but I would have found a dearth of evidence and so, bereft, I would have been justly dubious of his claims. How *should* I have proceeded without proof? Yet I long now to have had an influence on him. At least I might have instilled in him *some* rationality and perhaps turned him away from seeking the remedy for his troubles in those primitive philosophies of the past.

He had in his possession, he told the court, a small book from before Cromwell's time, one that had been acquired by his grandfather and which contained some accounts and illustrations of witchery. I suspected that it had been handed down as an object of value rather than a set of treatises to be studied, but he could read to a limit, said Calvert, well enough to recognise his own predicament within the pages.

It was, he explained, with the book in his hand, a demon's highest pleasure to occupy a human body and dissolve the person inside the skin. Thus was he obliged to concede that May had been dead for weeks, and that he had a duty to both end the violation of the girl's corpse and turn the fiend out before it did harm to the rest of his family.

A picture in the book showed him what had to be done – not simply a birching, such as he'd given her before for her lustfulness, but an execution. And while at times he felt bold enough for that endeavour, it was boldness in fantasy only and he knew that he could never undertake to do it himself. For, outwardly, May was still too much like his daughter. Hence did he travel to see this George Haydock in Halifax on a market day.

You will remember, Brother, even from our brief and infrequent visits there those less than salubrious men who come to trade in things other than sheep and cattle. The hawkers in the alleys. Those fences who would touch us on the shoulder and bid us look into their sacks of contraband. For you and I, they were faces that came and went in the crowds, but Peter Calvert knew them all by name. He knew which men to approach for certain services. And thus he sought out Haydock in the smoke room of the Crossed Hands in order to commence this terrible business.

The agreement made in principle, they strolled together thereafter through the market square, and Haydock itemised the conditions of his employment. Above all, he had no wish to be sensible of any motive, he said. Calvert was to think of him merely as a tool. He would not explain to an axe why it was to cut down a tree, would he?

On this point, Calvert said that he was much relieved. Had he been forced to provide the reason for his engaging Haydock, then he feared that the man would have thought him a fugitive from Bedlam. And he suspected that men such as he would consider it too hazardous to enter into a contract with anyone they presumed mad. The discretion of a maniac could not be trusted. Nor their promises of payment. But Haydock had been satisfied that Calvert was sound on both counts, and after inspecting the horse that was to be his fee they made the necessary arrangements and drank a glass of strong spirit to bind them in the conspiracy.

It was to be done well away from the farm, Haydock had attested: in Fitch Wood, when the girl took the horse down to the riverbend. And so he followed her there late one afternoon and hid in the trees to wait.

Both the girl and the horse went into the shallows of the river, she to wash herself, the mare to drink its fill. When the girl was done, she led the horse out of the water and tied it to a willow bough while she knelt on the bank to wring out her tresses, examining her hair as though it was something alien to her.

Though he had desired not to know why her father wanted her dead, Haydock said that he had pondered it since market day nonetheless. He had never been appointed to kill anyone so young, and his guess was that the only crime the girl could have committed to warrant such an exacting punishment was to have caught some young man's eye and got herself seeded. Though that in itself was hardly calamitous enough to merit ending two lives and so he had to conclude that her sin was more particular. One that had condemned her and the child alike. He would not be drawn on what he considered the nature of the wrongdoing to be (and so Reverend Austwick came to his own conclusions) but only said how aggrieved he had felt that Calvert might have duped him into snuffing out an innocent.

He was not so hardened to his work, he said, as to be unmoved by his deeds sometimes. He profited from violence, that was true. He had to eat. He had rent to pay on his rooms. But he took no pleasure in it, even if it was a skill at which he had become proficient. And he was much relieved, he said, if he was able to convince himself that whomever he had been hired to dispose of had not suffered unduly at his hand. For this reason, he was pleased to see that May Calvert was not visibly expectant and was in fact thin for a farm girl. Her skull – in his words – would give like dry cake.

As he moved closer, he saw that she was now starting to dig between the tree roots with her hands as if searching for something. Perhaps a favour stashed by her paramour, he thought. He had seen it before, illicit lovers leaving one another gifts in the hollow of a tree or in a buried box. He had stolen them now and then. Pretty things sometimes. Rings and lockets. Here in this grasping village, he did not think he would discover anything of worth, but if the girl had a token of affection upon her person when she was found then the blame for her death might be fixed on this boy of hers, whoever he was.

Haydock left his place of concealment in the willows, took out his cudgel, and advanced with the stealth he had perfected through the years of his abominable work. The girl had her back to him, he said, and he was able to stand close enough behind her to see the freckles on her arms.

She had finished scraping at the earth and seemed to have found what she was looking for, but when she opened her hand it was filled with worms. As they writhed in her palm, she studied them for some moments, in the manner of a blackbird, said Haydock, and then selected one, the most bloated and ribbed, and lowered it into her mouth.

To watch her chewing the thing had sickened him to his stomach, he said, but it had sickened him more that she had a life so pitiably poor that she was obliged to eat what crawled in the dirt. And in the moment – oh such a merciful man – he thought that the blow from his club might be her salvation.

He had learned through practice, he said, to act with swift-ness and precision, and without hesitation he struck the girl hard across the back of the head. The force sent her onto her belly, where, to his liking, she lay immobile and unbreath-ing for the several minutes he waited to ensure that she was dead.

Yet, when he went to untether the horse, she stirred and woke and got to her knees. She had only been concussed, stunned into a kind of idiocy – for she smiled at him as though she had not felt the clout he'd given her at all and continued to gnaw on the worm, her teeth covered in brown flakes of skin. It was a detail, he said, that he could not forget.

He went at her again, thinking to break her neck, and beat her twice at the top of her spine. Yet she did not scream out. Nor did she resist him. She gave up her body as if it meant nothing to her. When he grasped her hair and pulled back her head to expose her throat for his knife, she looked at him as if it were all but play.

He did not often favour this method, he said, for he was then burdened with the disposal of his bloody clothes. The blade was a last resort. More a weapon of defence. And so unnerved was he by her demeanour that he slashed her gullet to end things quickly.

But the girl did not bleed as he expected her to. There was no hot spray. What came forth was more akin to pitch, he said. A black, viscous discharge that oozed rather than gushed from the cut he had made. And then the same emerged from her mouth, her nose, her eyes and ears, from every opening in her body, staining her skin and her dress, and thickening into a puddle in the grass.

Behind him, he could hear the horse straining at its tether to get loose, but he stood transfixed, he said, as the girl began to sink in on herself and fold to the ground, until she lay flattened and shrivelled, her head like an empty wineskin.

In the moment, his single thought was to retreat. He had no interest in his payment any longer and left the mare tied up to save his own life. He could not recall his flight through the trees or the fields. Such was his terror that when I found him lying soused with drink on the lane out of the village, he begged me for more grog, anything to make him sleep. He could still hear it, he said, the sound of that poor horse shrieking in the wood.

~

That was his testament as given, Brother, and I beg pardon for imparting the facts without reserve. But as a physician, I trust that you would wish to be acquainted with every detail in order to make the best possible assessment of the case.

I am confident that Haydock reported truthfully what he believed he had seen. He must have been greatly affrighted by *something* or he would not have confessed so frankly – not only to his purpose in coming to Barrowbeck but to the whole of his vile career.

Perhaps he thought he had witnessed the manifestation of something infernal in Fitch Wood, perhaps the corporal form of the Great Evil itself, and that made real the hellfire he had always imagined awaiting him.

This is speculation, I admit, but is it not said in countless chapters of the Bible that sin might be wiped away if a man would only turn to God and repent? Then does Haydock, by this candidness, hope to give himself up to the noose in this life in order to be redeemed in the one to come? Does such an intention seem credible to you, Brother? I know not the conclusions I should draw, and I would fain hear your advice. A voice of reason would be most welcome and comforting to me. There is such unrest here. I have never seen everyone so frightened. And by its subtle alchemy has fear turned to anger.

Since Haydock gave his account in court, and its repugnant particulars have circulated in the village, a party of men that you know as peaceable fellows has been out in the valley hunting the Calverts' mare. And in preparation for it being found, others are building a pyre on the green.

They are to burn a horse, Brother, unless I can find the words to appease them. Or do I say nothing and let them bring these horrors to an end in the way that will give them satisfaction? Is this how peace is to be restored? For I am moved to think that until a devil is found, they will go on searching for one here, fathers passing on the mantle and the musket to their sons forever.

Oh, that you were here to explain it to them better than I.

Your servant,
Martyn Kennet.

# After the Fair

## 1899

This year, there'd been more animals than ever before. Miniature apes swinging through tiny Japanese trees. Polar bears the size of mice. Elephants small enough to be held in the hand. Alligators like newts. And a hawk with the wingspan of a moth high up in the rafters of the tent.

Eleanor would have happily taken any one of them home, but no one had any choice about the animal they were given if they won the competition. It was Pascal who decided.

Tall and chalk-white in his Pierrot costume, he'd moved about the tent surrounded by a skirt of children all pleading to hold one of the tiny snakes that curled about his fingers. Their excitement had been contagious, and Eleanor had allowed herself to be caught up in it too, stretching out her hand, trying to catch Pascal's eye.

Her mother thought that she was getting far too old for it now. To be so enthralled by that silly zoo, playing games with a clown, it hardly befitted someone of her age. 'You're sixteen,' she'd said. 'Working.'

But there was nothing silly about Pascal. And he didn't play games. He came to Barrowbeck every springtime to see whom he could trust with his animals, who was the most observant. That was the test.

When he bowed, they had to bow. When he grinned, they grinned. He stood on one leg, and they had to do the same and stay as balanced as they could.

Once the contest had begun, Alison Thwaites and Fred Guiseley didn't last long and soon collapsed into a heap. Then as Pascal jumped from side to side, clicking the heels of his pink Arabian slippers together, a few more went. Emma North and Oswald Heaton, Arthur Croasdale and his brother Norman. Now Pascal made butterflies with his hands, causing Florence Lythgow and two little boys, the Mewith twins, to tie their fingers in knots. They went off to sit on the hay bales sniffing back tears to try and hide their disappointment.

But Pascal saw that they were upset – he saw everything – and screwed his fist next to the black teardrop on his cheek. Some, like Eleanor, had the wherewithal to copy him. That was the mark of experience. And being older than most, she had more stamina too. Whereas the younger ones quickly dropped out one by one, she was able to match Pascal's increasingly intricate jigs and poses until only she and June Harrison were left. After blowing them both a kiss – which they sent back to him – Pascal lay down on the ground, laced his hands over his belly and pretended to be a corpse, not moving an inch, his eyes wide open, his teeth clamped together.

Eleanor and June did the same and lasted a good length of time. But the other children were quick to shout when they saw June blink and so Eleanor was named the winner.

No one was allowed to sulk in defeat. No one was allowed to be envious. No one could even *think* jealous thoughts or Pascal would know and disallow them from competing next time. And so everyone clapped, as happy for Eleanor as if they'd won themselves, and gathered around as Pascal gave her a box made of yellow card.

Inside was a tiger no bigger than a new-born kitten. When she went to stroke its head, it bared its sharp, pin teeth and circled the box, flicking its tail. And then, as the winner had to do every year, Eleanor mimicked the creature she'd been given so that she left the tent reminded that her life and the life of the animal were now one.

That the day of the fair was always so eagerly anticipated, and the way it permitted certain treats and excesses, made it akin to a second Christmas for most people in Barrowbeck. Not least in its transience. For as spontaneously as the tents appeared on the green at dawn, like gifts waiting to be opened, they vanished again just as suddenly overnight. The saying was that the fair went where the wind took it, and

Eleanor had always imagined that the marquees and the animals, the buglers and drummers and the various troupes of acrobats, jugglers, jesters, freaks and fire-eaters were all gathered up in a single gust during the night and swept away to the next village.

And although everyone acknowledged that the brevity of the visitation was the very thing that made the fair special, they couldn't help but feel despondent when it was over. Any means of prolonging the fun or, rather, suspending the return to dreary ordinariness was welcomed, which was why the Doctor had always drawn a good-sized crowd.

He was a man who held himself in such high regard that he made sure to arrive at the precise moment the church bells were ringing noon so that it seemed as if his coming had been ordained by the greatest of authorities.

If he was Vanity, then his pony was Suffering. A docile, jaded nag that only ever looked at the floor and was laden down with bottles of the tonic folk bought for gout and constipation, udder cysts and sheep scab; a panacea that, according to those who used it, served people and animals equally well.

Although he *looked* like a doctor with his beard and his black suit and his homburg hat, no one could say for certain what he was. He might well have been an engineer, for along with his sweet, tar-like medicine, he peddled certain hand-made devices for lancing and prising and scraping that were of great use to farmers. But once the transactions were over and his money pocketed, he took off his coat and rolled up his sleeves to sermonise about the dangers of the fair with the passion of an evangelist.

'Do not be fooled', he liked to say, 'by the antics of the tumblers or the smiles of the pretty girls who swallow swords. And take care not to indulge that capering clown. He above all is not to be trusted. Think of the way he lures children into his tent with the promise of living toys.'

The Doctor couldn't anticipate when the fair was going to arrive, he was always chasing it, always a day late, and so he could only lecture about its evils after the fact. He gave the same address about Pascal every year, and Eleanor always went to listen for the tradition of it, for the entertainment of it. Most people did the same. Apart from the Sour Faces, who came to nod and applaud with their glum, browbeaten children in tow. One or two joined their ranks every now and then, but for the most part the Doctor came and went as a spectacle on the green, and nothing changed.

Yet his arrival that day, a bright dewy Sunday in March, was attracting more people than usual. Word had spread about the large wooden chest the pony had carried in on its back and the two acolytes that the Doctor had acquired since his last visit: a mother and daughter from another village, who stood beside him, conscious that everyone was wondering who they were.

As the crowd grew around her, Eleanor felt something inside her hand. She hadn't noticed, but John Hatcher had worked his way to her side. He pressed his thumb harder into her palm, urging her to grip it so that he could pretend she was holding something else. She knew what he was thinking. The week before, she'd seen him wading naked from the river after his bath and as he'd gathered his clothes, he'd started up with 'Hark, Shy Maiden', hoping that, like the girl in the song, Eleanor might be persuaded that death was just as quick to take the young and that the dark earth rotted pretty green eyes and rosebud lips just as it did old, shrivelled dugs. She should make herself a woman, went the chorus, before her final day, or give herself, a virgin, to the cold and lonely clay.

He had laid a claim on her, whether she liked it or not, and he seemed to think that by this proclamation alone he possessed her in perpetuity. It was now his duty and his right to fight other boys who looked at her or talked to her, and he showed her the bruises on his face and the scabs on his knuckles as proofs of his devotion.

'Come with me to Fitch Wood,' he said in her ear, and she twisted her hand free.

He grinned in a self-satisfied way, as though he thought she was playing a game of hard-to-come-by, and he whistled that song again, thinking that the threat of dying chaste would prise her open. As if being jabbed with his thing (which was no bigger than his thumb) would make her fulfilled.

Once she'd tamed the tiger, she thought, she'd send it out at night and have it tear up John Hatcher's throat while he slept. He wouldn't even hear Death coming.

'Time flies fast away, away . . .' he sang and put his hand around her waist and held it there for longer than he usually did in public, taking advantage of the fact that everyone was distracted by what the Doctor was going to say as he quietened the crowd.

Normally, he began his sermon about Pascal with a burst of righteous anger – 'Corruptor! Charlatan! Parasite!' – but there was something different about him this year. He had a look of serenity, a look of triumph even.

'At last, at last,' he said, clasping his hands and shaking them heavenwards in thanks. 'At last, this deviant, Pascal, has been found out. His methods have been exposed.

'It has been discovered of late by scientists in London', he went on, 'that a special compound of powders is cast into the air inside his tent, which, when inhaled, induces vivid hallucinations, particularly in the juvenile mind.'

Undeterred by the cynical laughter from his audience, he said, 'Now think for a moment. Think rationally. How *can* those animals be so small? There must be some trick. The oldest trick of them all, in fact. For there is nothing in the cages whatsoever. It is merely a flea circus.'

The Sour Faces clapped enthusiastically and looked down on their children as if to say, *there, didn't we tell you so?*

John removed his hand from Eleanor's hip to join in with the applause and gave her a scornful smile, the insinuation being that she'd been conned all these years too, that she was still a child. On the day of the fair, he'd ribbed her mercilessly about her obsession with the little animals and had tried to drag her over to watch what he called the *real thing* – the two brown bears called Gog and Magog that were dressed in crowns and gowns and made to wrestle in a boxing ring.

But she'd not been fooled. The tiger was real enough. The Doctor was getting desperate. Powders?

Capitalising on the encouragement he'd been given by his devotees, he squatted down and opened a drawer in the wooden chest at his feet. He took out a small jar, held it up, shook it twice and green dust clouded inside.

'This was extracted from a boy over the way in Cragg Morton,' he said, sending it around. 'It is a dried blend of the various moulds and funguses that grow so plentifully in your wood here. Even a small quantity such as this is capable of tricking the brain into a permanent state of delusion.'

'Hear that, Eleanor?' said John and pinched her cheek and grinned. He looked like a ram with his brown teeth and his thick forehead, though if she were to tell him so he'd think it a compliment. On a day the previous autumn, she'd walked up to Prospect Farm to get away from her mother and he'd followed her along the lane, calling, hooting, whistling. At the gate to the sheep field, he'd caught up with her and gripping her wrist he'd made her stop to watch the ewes being tupped, as though that might have persuaded her that being tailed was natural and necessary.

'Harken to the shepherd boy,' he'd sung, 'come maiden, lie with me. No flock grows from being coy. No lambs are born from chastity . . .'

Any child of his, she'd told him, wanted strangling at birth, and, thinking that her hostility masked some latent desire for him and his little dangling spike, he'd laughed at her as he laughed at her now.

But how would he laugh when the tiger raked open his neck and crunched his Adam's apple?

She shook herself loose from his hands and went to stand a couple of rows further forward with the children who'd participated in Pascal's competition. Because she had won and because she was the eldest, they looked up to her, and when the jar came around, she reassured them that such a tiny amount of this green stuff couldn't ever do *anything*. It was a scepticism that everyone apart from the Sour Faces seemed to share, and the murmur of incredulity grew into loud exchange with the Doctor.

'How did you get it out of the boy?' someone called.

Holding up the jar, old Jacob Mewith, the twins' grandfather, said, 'What did you do? Make him sneeze?'

'I have some apparatus, a machine,' the Doctor said, which increased the volume of laughter all the more.

It was the same every year. A Punch and Judy show. It was the reason Eleanor's mother didn't come to watch. She had no interest in the Doctor or the fair and was glad when both had passed through the village and life could return to how it had been, how it *ought* to be – which, for her, meant work and woe and church on Sundays. She'd been there that morning, on her knees, thanking God for all that she didn't have.

'It's tea,' someone said.

The jar had been opened now and a few were taking it in turns to sniff the contents.

'Or dead grass,' another suggested.

But the Doctor had anticipated their distrust and called forward the girl he'd brought with him.

'You have doubts, of course,' he said. 'You should not be expected to take my word alone. But Mary here is the proof. Until she received the treatment, she believed herself to be the owner of a wolf no bigger than a shrew. She believed *herself* to be part-wolf too. Howling, biting. Now she is quite cured, as you see.'

The girl, who was the same age as her, thought Eleanor, looked down at her feet. Her mother put an arm around her shoulder and implored the parents watching to take the remedy on offer.

'Nothing else will work,' she said. 'Nothing you can say will stop your children from going to the fair.'

The Doctor nodded sagely.

'It is true, too true,' he said. 'Pascal's skill is in making these hallucinations seem so pleasurable. Thus, do your children slip out of your hands and into his. Your words of warning cannot compete with his . . . chemistry.'

The Sour Faces agreed. Eleanor heard John call out, 'Hear hear' behind her.

'Before poor Mary had the narcotic drained out of her,' the Doctor went on, 'she was as in thrall to Pascal's Fair as the opium fiend is to the druggist's den. Whenever it returned, she could not resist its draw, could you?'

Mary wouldn't answer, and the Doctor lifted her chin and touched her pale cheek compassionately.

'The fault lies not with you, my dear,' he said. 'There is no shame in being deceived by the Devil when his tricks are so artfully contrived to charm the young. You are not his only victim. There will be others here in Barrowbeck, I have no doubt of that.'

It was as much an invitation for agreement as it was a supposition and he scanned the crowd for a few moments until Georgie Mitton's mother cried, 'Yes! My boy.'

She was one of the Sour Faces, long since persuaded by the Doctor to keep her son indoors on the day of the fair. But her Georgie managed to sneak out anyway. The previous year he'd won a tortoise that he kept in a matchbox.

'Bring him up,' said the Doctor. 'Hurry now.'

As Mrs Mitton dragged Georgie to the front she wept and smiled with relief. Since her husband's cloddy, fattened heart had carried him off, and there'd been no Mr Mitton at home to rule the boy with a rod of iron, Georgie's misbehaviour around the village had been a source of constant worry. But now there was a reason for it. He wasn't to blame. And nor was she. The boy had been contaminated.

'See how he struggles,' said the Doctor, as he opened the lid of the box. 'That is Pascal's poison at work. Only the clown's mischief would make him fight so.'

Some of the other mothers called out for Georgie to be let go. And when the Doctor began to take out the hoses and clamps of some medical paraphernalia, even the other Sour Faces looked dubious about what this antidote would entail.

'What I say is true, is it not, young man?' the Doctor said to Georgie. 'You do feel lured to the fair, don't you? Even though you try to listen to your mother's advice?'

Georgie said nothing and the Doctor clicked his fingers to stop him gawping at the crowd.

'You do not *wish* to be disobedient, do you?' he said, laying a priest-like hand against the boy's temple. 'You would have me take away the temptation, if I could?'

Georgie nodded, or the Doctor moved his head for him.

'Good, good,' he said, and gave a signal to Mrs Mitton to hold him steady.

She did her best, but the lad was strong for his size and she called on the help of the mother of the girl who'd thought she was a wolf. Between them, they took an arm each, giving little Georgie reassurances that everything would be fine, that he'd be better soon.

'A few moments is all it takes,' the Doctor said and began to fit a leather hood over the boy's head, making him cry out in panic.

The sudden noise startled the Doctor's pony, and the girl, Mary, stroked its neck to keep it calm, seemingly glad that she had something to occupy her. She couldn't bring herself to watch Georgie struggling as the Doctor yanked down the hood and tied the laces at the back.

There were no eye holes, no perforations which might have allowed him to breathe, but only a brass cylinder on the front, like an elongated pig's snout, with two rubber tubes attached. One led down to a set of foot-bellows, the other into a glass jar like the one still being passed through the crowd.

'Watch now, see,' said the Doctor and he began to pump the contraption with his heel.

Georgie squirmed and gave a muffled scream. He booted out blindly, crouched down and twisted but then suddenly stiffened and began to shake as if in a seizure, his hands as hard as crabs, his feet kicking divots in the mud as his mother held him from behind.

'Yes, the sensation is strange, most strange, but it will cause him no damage,' said the Doctor, trying to placate the tension that was rapidly growing in the crowd. 'Quite the opposite, I assure you.'

Some shouted at him to stop. Fathers made threats. There was never any malice in Pascal, they said. They'd been to the fair when *they* were young. Nothing bad had happened to them.

But they were not to be listened to, said the Doctor. They were more infected than their sons and daughters.

'In you', he said, 'the venom has fulfilled its assignment and made the fair seem nothing more than innocuous fun. You are, without realising it, making fresh victims of your children every year.'

Before they could protest any louder, the Doctor waved his hand.

'Look now, look,' he said and beckoned everyone forward to inspect the jar. Those at the front swore that they could see green powder puffing up inside and their amazement was passed back through the crowd. John Hatcher sidled past Eleanor and the children to see for himself.

'There it is,' said the Doctor, still working the bellows as Georgie convulsed in his mother's arms. 'You have the evidence.'

Now there were murmurs of admiration. The defiance in the boy was being removed right before their eyes with vacuums. Eleanor saw a palpable relief in those around her.

Mr Rye wouldn't have his door knocked on after dark. Mrs Grant smiled to think that her apples would be safe from theft. The Deacon gave thanks that the name 'Georgie' wouldn't be gouged into the pews ever again. And the boy would no longer be able to disrupt the class with stories about his tiny tortoise, Miss Slater was thinking. When he next opened his matchbox, he'd find it empty.

The Doctor declared Georgie's treatment over and removed the device from his head. The boy looked bewildered, weak in the legs. He'd wet himself too, and his mother gathered him to her chest, pecking him with kisses.

'You're a good boy,' she said, 'such a good boy now. It's all done with. It's all over. Good Georgie.'

But these theories about toxic powders couldn't be true, thought Eleanor. She'd held the tiger not an hour ago. She'd felt its weight. She'd brought it to her nose and smelled its skin. She'd seen its teeth and fed it scraps of pork rind. She'd heard its quiet snarl. It had looked right at her with its luminous gooseberry-coloured eyes. If she were to go home now, it would still be there. It couldn't have disappeared.

She began to try and thread her way out of the pack of bodies but there was a surge around her as the parents of Fred Guiseley and Alison Thwaites and Emma North came to find their children and haul them forward, jostling to have their little ones cured next. And not wishing to seem negligent of *their* children's health, others followed on behind. Those who'd scoffed at the treatment only a few minutes before were now arguing about which of them deserved it more.

Those among the Sour Faces whose children had defied them and snuck out to the fair felt that they had the best claim of anyone: after all, *they'd* been right all along . . . and no one had ever listened . . . and now it had all come out . . .

A knot formed of bickering grown-ups and boys and girls pleading to be taken home. And the green was filling with more and more people. Even those who did not usually turn out to listen to the Doctor's lecture had heard the commotion and come to watch him demonstrating his cure. Impressed and convinced, they were trying to catch their children before they could escape.

Eleanor saw June Harrison's father seize her by the hand and then felt someone grasping her elbow with the same roughness. It was John Hatcher, laughing with his brown teeth as he pulled her towards the Doctor. 'Make this one next,' he called. 'She's wild. Be quick.'

And seeing her trying to wrench free of his grip, watching her biting his hand, hearing her roaring, the others stood aside and made way.

# Hymns for Easter

## 1922

It was by sheer chance that the young men who stood before Corin Hale had survived. They were not stronger or braver than the dead. Nor had they been allowed to pull through as some kind of reward. It wasn't as though God, if a God there was, had saved them because of their saintliness. They were no more virtuous – and some far less – than those from the village who had succumbed to Maxim guns and howitzers over in France. In fact, it was arguable that the ones who had fallen at the Somme and Neuve Chapelle, and everywhere else, had been the true recipients of any divine approbation. They might be strolling white-robed in the perfumed meadows of Paradise, whereas these rather dishevelled basses and tenors over-egging the crescendo of *and trust in his redeeming blood* had to try and live with all manner of scars and severances.

Their injuries were of great interest to the younger ones in the choir, and the gang of little trebles Corin taught during the week peered over the tops of their *Hymns Ancient and Modern* stealing glances at the men opposite:

Herbert Gough, a stonemason, gassed at Ypres, struggling on with only a single working lung.

Philip Wardley, once a weaver at Swinside Mill, once an esteemed athlete, his name etched six times onto the Barrowbeck Fell Race cup, confined to a wheelchair now with his trouser legs pinned up.

Robert Heysham, old Wesley's eldest lad from Moorfoot Farm, tall and bull-brawny with a glass eye of a different colour to the other.

And next to him was Gilbert Lampland, who spent his days thumping away with a meat cleaver in the backroom of his family butcher's shop. A young man as pale as milk, with a torn bottom lip that even when he had stopped singing made him look as if he had an invisible hook in his mouth.

'We'll try the last verse once more, gentlemen, if you don't mind,' said Corin, when the hymn came to an end.

'A moment, a moment.' Herbert Gough gestured for him to wait and retched up mucus into a handkerchief embroidered with the words 'Come Back Safe'.

Rather cruelly, but predictably, the boys in the choir called him Mr Cough rather than Mr Gough; to his face sometimes, knowing that his hearing wasn't sharp enough for him to tell that they were being impertinent.

If Corin ever caught them at it, he gave them short shrift, and now and again he'd had to punish one or two with a caning the following day at school. Surprisingly, the worst offender was Tommy Croasdale, who might have been expected to show more respect to the war wounded, given that both his father and his uncle had been killed. But he was always mimicking Herbert Gough, going about hunched and wheezing as he acted out the poor man's fits of breathlessness to the great amusement of his pals.

He was only twenty-five, Herbert, but seemed elderly already, as did the others who'd served.

In all, the war had reduced the men's section of the choir from a score to a baker's dozen. Of the thirteen who remained, eight had been too old for the call-up, like Corin, and the rest, born at precisely the wrong time, had been maimed to dreadful disfigurement, with poor Roland Archer coming off the worst.

Shrapnel and surgery had given him an appalling pocket of a face and he'd become a virtual recluse. The only time he ever emerged from his house was to accompany the choir at the Wednesday practice or the Sunday services, where he would arrive excessively early so as to hide himself away in the organ loft.

He had always been a very fine musician. A little wasted on Barrowbeck in all honesty. He could have held his own in a minster or a cathedral. Saint Gabriel's was lucky to have him. He kept the choristers in tune while Corin kept them in time, and between the two of them they had – by degrees – revived something of the proficiency and repertoire that the choir had enjoyed before the war. But it would take a long while before it was the same. In fact, with all the time in the world, these men might never quite return to how they'd been.

Herbert folded away the black sputum and indicated that he was ready to resume.

'If you would, Mr Archer,' said Corin, looking up to the half-closed curtains of the organist's cubby hole.

Roland played a bar of introduction to 'There Is a Green Hill Far Away', and Corin brought the choir back in to re-sing the final lines.

'A little gentler this time, please,' he said.

O dearly, dearly has He loved,
And we must love Him too,
And trust in his redeeming blood,
And try His works to do.

It ought to have come across as a quiet contemplation of Christ's suffering and sacrifice, but they went at it fortissimo as before – with the one-lunged Herbert Gough somehow outdoing them all – and Corin thought it best to move onto 'Jesus Christ Is Risen Today', where they could bellow alleluias to their heart's content and get it over with.

It seemed to go this way at every practice. It took a few hymns for them to find the correct intonation and control, and then a couple more to tease out the subtleties that certain songs required. And Father Wadlow always seemed to walk in and listen at the wrong moment.

Not wishing to give the impression that he had come to interfere or to judge, he would make it seem as though he had been happily engaged in some other task outside, when – lo! – the sound of Christian voices raised in exaltation had enticed him into the church. Thus, he would appear with a pair of shears or a bicycle pump.

In he came now wearing gardening gloves and carrying a trug of weeds in the crook of his arm. He sat in one of the pews halfway down the nave, trying to enjoy what he was hearing but wincing every so often as though he was being afflicted by spasms of indigestion.

A delegation from diocese headquarters was coming to Mass on Easter Sunday for the dedication of the war memorial, and being chairman of the Remembrance Committee – by his own appointment – he wanted everything just so. He was a priest of that ilk. Finnicky. Petulant.

As the hymn drew to a close, Corin had no doubt that he would have some criticisms to make, all of them veiled in his specious self-effacement and the usual backhanded compliments.

'Yes, it was . . . there were some . . . I must commend the *earnestness* . . .' said Father Wadlow, amid the choir's coughing and paper shuffling.

Taking off his gloves and leaving his little basket on the pew, he came forward, a bald, rabbity man. At the pulpit, he was considered a good orator, but only because he was reading from a script. In everyday conversation, he fumbled and stuttered.

'My only concern, Mr Hale,' he said, 'is that it might be construed as . . . boisterous . . . I don't know . . . I'm no singer myself . . .'

The men and boys regarded him with a contempt that he either missed or chose to ignore.

'I'd say it was rousing, certainly,' Corin offered.

'Rousing, yes,' replied Father Wadlow. 'No question . . . stirring.'

'Which seems fitting for the Resurrection.'

'Naturally, naturally . . . a time for joy,' the priest half-smiled. 'But for the consecrating of the memorial . . . something less . . . exuberant, I feel? I think our watchwords ought to be decorum . . . solemnity . . . you've made your final decision on the piece, I take it?'

'Well, we've been making a pretty good fist of "When I Survey the Wondrous Cross",' said Corin.

Father Wadlow clearly didn't like the crudeness of the expression or, rather, its suggestion of optimism as opposed to confidence, but found something outwardly encouraging to say nonetheless.

'Ah, yes good . . . very apt . . . very . . . ceremonial . . . ' he replied and put his hands behind his back, and Corin realised that he wished to hear the rendition now so that it might be vetted.

'Page fifty-six, gentlemen,' he said and nodded up to Roland, who he knew would be watching through the gap in the curtains and waiting for his cue.

Pensive, understated notes flowed from the organ pipes and with a languid turn of his hand – which Corin hoped would translate into a softer sound than the one he'd got from the choir earlier – he set them off singing.

It took a few bars for the men to stop overpowering the boys, but after some more pointed gesticulations, Corin managed to settle them all into a balanced and quite beautiful harmony.

And then he heard it again.

The same as at the rehearsal before and the one before that.

It was just the acoustics of the church, with its gritstone pillars and its high ceilings, but it seemed as if there were more voices than choristers.

The others had remarked upon it too as they'd practised these hymns for Easter over the last fortnight or so, and some had said, without hesitation, that it had to be the seven dead men returning to swell the ranks. For weren't spirits said to be drawn to music?

Whether they truly believed that or not, Corin didn't know, and perhaps it didn't matter. It was just a pleasant thought, and if he listened carefully enough he fancied that he could pick out Daniel's particular timbre too. He'd been such a sweet tenor, his boy.

\*

Tender in tone and tender in character. That was Daniel through and through. People had always warmed to him so instinctively. People had always turned to him for advice or praise.

At the outbreak of the war, he'd been training for the teaching profession in Manchester, and in that respect, the apple hadn't fallen very far from the tree. Indeed, Corin couldn't recall a time when Daniel had ever wanted to do anything else. He would have made a splendid grammar-school master. Admired. Beloved. Destined to be long remembered by his pupils. A very eligible bachelor in time to come as well. He could have had his pick. Along with Suzanna's high cheekbones, he'd inherited her chestnut hair and her piercing seamstress's eyes – all of which had given him a natural handsomeness.

He'd been nineteen – and only just – at the start of it all, but in the photograph of him in his cap and uniform he'd sent them from Catterick he seemed much older. A smudge of a moustache too. His baby boy with a moustache!

Every so often, Corin would take the small portrait out of the drawer of the wardrobe to remind himself of Daniel's face, but Suzanna couldn't bring herself to look at it any more. Nor at any of Daniel's letters home. She still hadn't seen the official missive from the Army Record Office first-hand.

Corin had read it out to her the day it had arrived – *It is my painful duty to inform you* and so forth – and she'd said nothing. Not one word as he'd wept and shaken in the hall-way and felt the world keeling over.

He'd wondered then if MISSING, BELIEVED KILLED (stamped at an angle on the form, as though in haste or indifference) had put the thought into her head that there was still some hope the boy would turn up alive. But there was no equivocation about what it really meant. She wasn't naive enough to think otherwise, not Suzanna. If she had genuinely believed that one day Daniel would arrive on the doorstep with his kit bag over his shoulder hungry for bread and jam as though he'd only been walking over the moors, then she would have anticipated his homecoming with great excitement; she would have made plans. But she wouldn't even talk about him, and she wouldn't entertain Corin doing so either. How deftly she changed the subject or found an excuse to leave the room if he tried. And so he had stopped bringing the lad up in conversation.

Her grief was too private to share, perhaps even unpronounceable. It could only produce a numbness in her. She had the vacuity of someone dazed.

In their own way, everyone in the village was still reeling from the sheer strangeness of what had happened. A decade ago, who could have ever imagined that their boys would end up in a foreign field five hundred miles from home facing men who wanted to kill them?

Who would want to kill his Daniel? His gentle, thoughtful Daniel who had his mother's pretty smile and could barely grow a moustache. And yet, hadn't the lad taken up arms to slaughter the young men of Germany? Hadn't Philip Wardley and Gilbert Lampland, Herbert Gough and Robert Heysham and Roland Archer and the rest done the same?

A great many had joined up within the first month of the war, roused and rallied by the military band that had come to Barrowbeck with a squad of recruiters from the West Yorkshire Regiment.

Corin had taught nearly all of those who'd taken the king's shilling and he knew that since the horizons of their lives stretched no further than the fells that encircled the village, it hadn't been the intricacies of central European politics that had ignited their passions. That wasn't condescension, but a fact. And one they would have agreed with.

No, they'd gone off to fight because everyone else was doing the same and they didn't want to be thought of as cowardly, or because they had been stirred by the marching music, or they feared the Germans might invade, or they had heard that the Bosch army was atrocious and sadistic, or simply because they liked the idea of soldiering and the licence it gave a man to be ruthless.

Most Saturday nights Robert Heysham would end up in a fight outside the Jester (for which he atoned on Sunday mornings with a rigorous contribution of bass during the psalm) and had probably enjoyed the thought of giving some German fellow a bloody nose to put him in his place too.

Not everyone had been so ardent. Corin knew that there were some in the village who had found the whole thing as unnerving as him. They'd never have disclosed their opinions in public, of course, and he could only speculate about who'd shared his anxieties. He suspected that June Harrison would have confessed to a feeling of revulsion, so too Eleanor Hatcher, the Kennets, David Wray and Clarissa Jones if they'd had the chance, if they could have been confident that no one would pillory them for being conchies. Yet that was exactly how they would have been seen when everyone else was so besotted with the war. And Corin, as a teacher, would have been hounded out of the classroom if he'd spoken his mind.

He wasn't a pacifist or a socialist, nothing so committed as that, and indeed those things required the very kind of zeal that he had found so disturbing in his militant neighbours. There had been plenty of them too. The fervour for flag-waving had arisen quite naturally, even among the most mild-mannered folk.

It had been the rheumy, white-haired ladies and gentlemen of the parish council who – with the same enthusiasm and diligence that they applied to the organisation of the harvest festival – had arranged for the regiment to visit the village. They'd been the ones who'd decked out the church hall with bunting and had rallied a small battalion of their own to serve up sandwiches and tea on the day.

And from Sunday to Sunday, Father Wadlow had reeled off thrilling sermons about Christ's special love for soldiers and how He would lend His might to any army that fought on the side of righteousness.

The fever had been inescapable. Even as he'd walked home from the school at the end of the day, Corin had run the risk of being collared by Austin Thwaites or Reuben North, men in their fifties like him. It'd been, *we'd show them, wouldn't we, Mr Hale? We'd put the Hun on the back foot, eh?* The assumption being that Corin would have signed up without question if he'd been the right age.

It didn't matter how old men were, there were some who still liked to think that they'd be able to best an opponent in a fair and honourable fight. That if they were called upon, they would have the toughness and the skill to prevail. They were thinking of knights in storybooks, perhaps. Contests of chivalry. For more than once, he'd heard such men disclose how envious they were of their sons being given the chance to prove their mettle and win their spurs.

But at the start of the conflict it had seemed as if the entire world had become a playground, with everyone from politicians to pit-diggers acting like children enthralled in some grand game, and children themselves, especially boys, full of patriotism and exhilaration. Corin had never seen the lads of the junior class so animated, and it had taken all his energy to keep them focused on arithmetic and spelling when they were far more interested in what had happened at Mons and Tannenberg and the Marne and if the Germans really were devils and if his own son would become a soldier.

'Yes,' he'd told them. He had no doubt of that.

The letters Daniel had sent from Manchester in the Michaelmas term of 1914 had been full of commendation for the war – a war of urgent necessity in his opinion – and Corin suspected that the lad would have been confused, even suspicious, if anyone close to him had tried to change his mind about enlisting – something which Daniel had pledged to do should the conflict continue.

Suzanna had been swept up in it all from the start too. She'd done her stint behind the trestle tables on recruitment day, pouring tea, and she had been captivated by Father Wadlow's sermons. Corin had watched her from his seat in the choir stalls and thought how elated she was to have her instincts validated by scripture.

There had never been any doubt in her mind that the fight in France was a fight for goodness *by* the good. And so when Daniel had joined up in the first few weeks of 1915, whatever apprehensions she might have had about her boy becoming a military man were outweighed by pride. She set the photograph of him on the mantelpiece, and made much of it whenever anyone visited, gushing over his alacrity, his bravery. Corin could always give a convincing performance of how enamoured he was of Daniel's courageousness too, but he'd felt as though he was watching it all unfold from afar. His son and his wife completely unreachable.

It pained him that he hadn't spoken more candidly to Suzanna, but she was a single-minded woman, more certain in her understanding of the world and its people than anyone he had ever known. It was what had made her so attractive to him when he'd first met her. And trying to talk her out of her convictions would have only made them more steadfast. She would have worried about his standing at the school, the reputation of the name Hale in the village. And had he somehow managed to coax Daniel out of picking up a rifle, she would have considered it selfish of him to foist his own views upon the lad and so make him a pariah too.

She might have thought that then, but not now. Who now but the most foolish or blinkered would not wish that they'd kept their sons or husbands or fathers hidden away here for the duration? Yes, for a time, to have done your bit was a badge of honour as prized as the medals the men had brought home, and even when conscription had begun there had been no loss of appetite among the next lot of recruits. They'd wanted the same adulation as the ones who'd gone before them.

But now almost four years on from the Armistice all that was starting to matter less and less. No one talked about the war any more. What was there to say? The price of the great folly was evident enough in those who'd made it back and was to be set in stone on the green for all time.

The choir began the closing verse, the descants from the boys pure and bright and yet subtle enough to pass as reverential.

> Were the whole realm of nature mine,
> That were a present far too small;
> Love so amazing, so divine,
> Demands my soul, my life, my all.

On the last line, Corin motioned for the ritardando – although they slowed down intuitively enough anyway – and then made them hold the final note until he closed them off.

The echoes of their voices, and the voices of the absentees they'd wished into being, lingered above the choirstalls as indistinct rumbles and whispers and then faded.

Father Wadlow nodded with something that resembled approval, even admiration, though it was obvious he was formulating a more exacting verdict.

'Excellent, yes . . . moving . . . though I wonder . . . might it have been a little too . . . what's the term? . . . *allegro*, is it?' he said, turning and glancing up to where Roland sat, as though to lay the blame at his fingertips.

'Too lively?' said Corin. 'You think?'

'A touch.'

'Yet it shouldn't be a dirge.'

'No no, quite . . . but certainly contemplative, no?' said Father Wadlow. 'An elegy . . .' he went on. 'Though you'll know best, Mr Hale . . . I am but a layman when it comes to the finer points of music, as you know.'

After another smile, briefer this time, he looked at his watch and went back down the aisle to collect the sheaf of cat grass and nettles he'd ripped up in the graveyard.

'Well, I must go,' he said. 'Errands . . . do carry on . . . don't let me stop you . . .'

The men and boys watched him open and close the east door, and when he'd gone and the latch was down, Corin said, 'Once more?'

'Aye, but for us,' said Philip Wardley. 'Not for him.'

They began again and the dead men sang too. There was Georgie Mitton's wavering alto and Jack Mewith's deep-chested bass. Just about audible were the delicate trills that Peter Hollinhead would give the r's in 'Prince of Glory' and 'Christ my God'. And perhaps the wayward Tommy Croasdale in the trebles could hear his father's creamy baritone, as Alfred Tasker could hear his son, Benjamin; as Corin could hear Daniel again, even more distinctly this time. It was the same, it seemed, for some of the others too, and they looked away from their hymn books to the empty misericords as though their former occupants might at any moment materialise. It felt almost imminent, almost real, their voices being so crisp.

He would try his utmost to convince Suzanna to attend Mass in the morning, thought Corin. Even if she were to sit in for one hymn it might begin to offer her some contentment. If she closed her eyes and listened hard, she too might be persuaded that Daniel was still here, his voice revived by other voices. But the chances of her coming were slim. She had not set foot in the church since the lad had been killed. She had removed her Bible from the mantelpiece long ago and hidden it in the back of a cupboard, angry and ashamed at being fooled. Where she thought Daniel was now, Corin didn't know. He couldn't rightly say himself when God had so obviously turned his back on the world and devolved the fate of human lives to sheer luck. Daniel had been unfortunate, that was all. In Corin's view it was far better to believe that. Endlessly pondering why *his* little boy had been turned to dust at Passchendaele and not someone else's, well, that was the road to madness, one that Suzanna was further down than he'd thought.

Mostly she *got on*, as people here did, as they had always done, and subscribed to the somewhat hackneyed mottos of resilience that had been passed down generation after generation in the village. She didn't dwell on things. There was no point crying over spilled milk. What was done was done.

It was bad form to make an exhibition of grief when everyone had been affected, and Suzanna was of the mind that she and Corin had not even suffered the most. There

105

were children who were now fatherless. The Croasdales had lost two boys. So had the Mewiths. And for the parents of Philip Wardley and Gilbert Lampland – and especially Roland Archer – it had to be harder in some ways to see their sons mutilated than to know that they were dead.

But her stoicism and graciousness were fragile, a self-administered palliative and not a cure, and during the build-up to the memorial ceremony, she had retreated to her bed with a fever that was not really a fever so much as a plausible excuse to absent herself from joining in. And yet, the stone would remain where they planted it on the green. She would have to pass it sooner or later. Perhaps in time, it would become easier for her. Or never.

The hymn ended, Corin thanked the men for their efforts and the chancel was filled with talk of who they'd heard singing and if the congregation might hear them the following day.

With their books shelved, the boys were like greyhounds in the traps, and after Corin let them go, they charged down the nave and out through the porch to go and play football. He hadn't the strength to shout at them to slow down. None of the men were interested in doling out discipline either and mooted the idea of a pint in the Lion before they headed back home for their teas.

'You'll come, Corin?' said Robert Heysham.

'I won't, thank you,' he replied. 'Not today.'

Herbert Gough wiped his nose. 'There's nowt int book about staying dry on Easter Saturday as far as I know.'

'Another time,' said Corin.

'The missus, is it?' Philip Wardley asked.

Corin said, 'I promised I'd be back as soon as I could.'

They seemed to understand.

The door at the bottom of the stairs to the organ loft opened and Roland Archer joined them, with a thick woollen scarf wrapped around the lower half of his face. The other men offered to buy him a drink, knowing that he would refuse, which he did with a silent shake of the head; nevertheless he appreciated their fraternity as they clapped him on the shoulder and asked him if he'd heard the extra voices too. He had, he said. Or, like the others, it was more that he wanted to think it true.

But what of that, thought Corin? They ought to be allowed to hope that when these ailments carried them off as fairly young men, they would have the chance to return home to Barrowbeck now and then. It only seemed right that the next life would afford them that choice.

They made their way out as the clock struck four and Corin closed the door behind him. Putting on their cloth caps one by one, the men made their way along the path through the churchyard, talking about the weather, the price of timber, a horse that had been lamed, boots and beer. Once through the lychgate, Roland scuttled away to the sanctuary of his mother and father's house on Back Lane, and the others sauntered across the green at the slow pace of Philip Wardley in his wheelchair.

Corin watched them pass the war memorial, which was still wrapped up in tarpaulin and rope, ready to be unveiled by the bishop's representative in the morning. Although it wouldn't be much of a revelation. In the last couple of weeks at least half the village had stopped by at Hardwell's to watch the masons at work. Corin had been too. He'd not told Suzanna, but he'd gone in on the day they were chiselling the last of the deceased into the plinth.

How they had got through the task, he couldn't imagine. According to Herbert Gough they'd tried to think of the work in terms of so many serifs, stems, strokes, ascenders and apertures – the letters just shapes and nothing to do with the names of people they'd once known. But it couldn't have been as easy as that.

Daniel was there between *Frederick Guiseley* and *Oswald K. Heaton*. THESE WHO DIED THAT WE MIGHT LIVE IN PEACE ran the inscription beneath, a sentiment which seemed already old-fashioned. It belonged to that febrile summer years before of hoopla and high romance, drums and trumpets.

Whatever a dozen deaths had brought to Barrowbeck, it wasn't peace. Yet, it was abhorrent to think that the sacrifice might have been wasted and so the village had agreed to pretend that it had been an offering to a higher purpose.

On the day of the Resurrection tomorrow, hopefully a dry morning, after the Grace and the closing hymn, the faithful were to process from the church and gather at the new cenotaph. And there Father Wadlow would read John 3:16 and the choir would sing of martyrdom, and the mothers and fathers, the brothers and sisters, the sons and daughters, would lay their wreaths against the limestone column with its sculpted dove and rifle.

And then there'd be dinners to be made and eaten. Work to think about. The next term to face. Time would go on.

A gust of wind crossed the green and knocked off Gilbert Lampland's hat. It rolled and skittered over the grass, stopping and starting, making him give chase as if in pursuit of a disobedient terrier. Corin could hear the others laughing and he smiled himself. To feel heartier today than the day before, that was all anyone could ask for.

And maybe it was because it was springtime too. A brisk, sweeping springtime that drove the shadows of clouds swiftly over the steep flanks of Pilgrim's Fell and Lord's Pike. Chattering birds were lofted up into the sky over the church tower. Cherry blossom blew across the road like snow. The trees that had been soaked by the rain that morning shook themselves onto railings and pavements and gravestones. And then the sun emerged again and suddenly everything wet was blinding. Daffodils jigged. The weathercock turned.

In it came, bold April. Winter forgotten for another year.

# Natural Remedies

## 1938

The early summer that year had been so warm and wet that it had turned Prospect Farm into a brimming Eden. Whenever it rained, the hedgerows seemed to swell all the more with foxgloves and poppies, bindweed and brambles. And among the thickets of hawthorn, honeysuckle grew in such heavy yellow swags that the smell of it in the evening time was almost too much to bear. It was a perfume from perilous antiquity, when gods still meddled in human affairs. It was the breath of Venus. The scent that hazed the whispering Arcadian cedar woods and induced the virginal young to sleep and dream of love. And more than love. Of bodies entangled in furious pleasure.

Rose had never known June to be so full of fragrance, colour, clamour and profusion. What had struggled to grow in previous years – White Lady, Archangel's Promise – now bloomed and sprawled from cracks in the yard. Surprise followed surprise. Two days before, the dogs had discovered a drowsy adder tangled in the woodpile. Strange iridescent hoverflies and tiger-striped bees came to burrow in the clematis and sweet peas that thronged the walls and fences. In the cool of the evening, droves of dark, plum-sized snails invaded the allotment, drawing down thrushes and blackbirds that hammered through the shells for the succulent meat in an almost orgiastic frenzy.

But it wouldn't have mattered if the snails had been left to gorge themselves to bursting, thought Rose. These last few months, the garden had given her and the Mister far more than they could possibly eat themselves, more than could be sold down in the village even. She'd given away the surplus to the needy of the parish and, in her estimation, must have left at least a hundredweight of potatoes, onions, carrots, leeks, radishes and turnips at the church door. Some pears and apples too, which had ripened early, too early for the Mister's liking. They'd become too fat too soon, just like his spring lambs up on the moor.

He was a man who fretted nightly over his account books and liked to know the price of things he had acquired. A man at his most uncomfortable when he felt himself in debt or doubt. It troubled him greatly that he'd had no choice in being favoured like this (no other farm in the valley had gone as wild as theirs) and what he might have to give in return for all this astonishing, unearned abundance. It was too generous an endowment. He couldn't accept that they'd simply been blessed. To him, it was the opposite of that, in fact, and after weeks of biting his tongue, he'd finally laid the blame on Rose.

'You brought this on. You shouldn't have planted another of those seeds. It's not natural.'

But if it was wrong, then why had nature come to the farm with such force? Nature *wanted* the seed to grow. And it had.

'Those poor people you've made promises to,' he'd said. 'They're barely older than children. It's not right, Rose.'

And off he'd gone to the Lion so that he'd be out of the way when the Hutchinsons came.


He thought that she was being heartless towards Judith and Henry, but when a couple as deserving as them was so desperate for a child she found it hard to see good people going unrewarded.

She'd known them all their lives and it broke her heart that they'd been married for almost three years now and not had any luck. It was Judith rather than Henry. The problem lay in her womb. She'd come out of her mother twisted at the belly like a dishcloth, and so there'd been every chance that she'd struggle to conceive when she got older.

Yet she'd been patient. She'd tried all the remedies: Happy Aphrodite and Mother's Flower, Bethlehem's Glory and Fill-the-Cradle. The things that worked for most girls most of the time. Still, she'd remained as empty as Celts Cave.

And so, today, it had come to this. But not without due deliberation on her part, Rose assured herself. The Mister scolded her for being reckless, but this wasn't a gift that she gave away to just anyone.

'Time was they'd have hanged you,' he'd said. 'There are some down in the village who'd hang you now, if they knew.'

That was why she chose carefully. No flighty girls or loud-mouth husbands, no one who was likely to go running off outraged to the church or chapel. Only when she was convinced of a couple's discretion did she make the offer.

Sympathy played its part in who she approached, of course it did. She couldn't help but feel sorry for some people, like the Hutchinsons. And before them, the Wardleys and the Collinwoods.

Philip Wardley had come back from France in a wheel-chair, half a man. And Caroline Collinwood, who'd spent her best years nursing her diseased, cantankerous mother, had been midway through her fifties by the time the old crow had passed. She'd married soon after the funeral, but too late in life to have children. And so Rose had invited her and her husband, Edward, to the farm – as she'd done with Philip and Bernadette Wardley – to see how willing they might be to listen to what she had to say, whether they might believe that she could give them what they wanted.

'But after what happened to our Hazel,' the Mister had said. 'You'd put other folk through that? It's pure cruelty, Rose.'

It was nothing of the kind. All she wanted was for people to know the happiness that she'd had. It *would* have been cruel if she hadn't been truthful with the Wardleys and the Collinwoods, but she'd been honest from the start. She'd told them about Hazel. They'd known what to expect. She hadn't coerced them. They'd made the choice in the full knowledge of what it meant. Just as young Henry and Judith had done.

They'd both been very quiet since they'd arrived, and sitting drinking tea as they waited for the rain to stop had only made them more anxious. It was being here and realising that the *idea* of all this was one thing and the actuality was something else. No doubt Judith would be asking herself – and not for the first time – if it mattered that the child wouldn't really be hers, whether the ache of wanting a child was really the ache of wanting to *grow* a child inside her, and if she'd be able to feel the same affection for something she hadn't carried.

It was likely to be a private quandary. She wouldn't have asked Henry his opinion. It was too difficult for husbands to fully understand. When they imagined having sons and daughters, they saw them not as beings that had come from their bodies, but as fully formed, bright-eyed pixies who skipped around a maypole or went charging through a corn-field with a kite on a string. It wouldn't be quite so important to him where the child had come from. But it would be different for Judith. Rose knew that well enough. When Hazel had been born, she'd felt such extraordinary joy and yet a sense of unfulfilment too. An incompleteness.

Still, that uneasiness had been quickly suppressed, and Judith would soon put it to the back of her mind as well once she realised that the child idolised her. When their eyes met for the first time, she'd see it, instantly.

The rain stopped, and even though it looked as though there'd be another shower soon, she said to the Hutchinsons, 'Come on, then. While it's fine,' and opened the back door.

She'd delayed taking them across the allotment for the sake of their clothes as much as anything. Rather endearingly, they'd come in their finest for the occasion. Henry in his church suit, Judith in a plain but pretty floral dress she'd made herself. It would have been a shame to make them go out in a downpour when they'd made such an effort to look smart.

Hooking the basket she'd brought over her arm, Judith took Henry's hand and Rose led them through the garden. The pair of them were awestruck by the sprouting, bloated greenery, intoxicated by the incense of the mint, marjoram, thyme, sage and rosemary.

'And the honeysuckle, my god,' Judith said, stopping to smell a patch of the stuff growing among the ivy. 'It's so strong. It's as if you're drinking it. Come and smell it, Henry.'

But he was looking over the gate into the pig pen.

'Your Tamworths . . .' he said with a grin, marvelling at how much they'd grown, speculating about what they'd fetch at the cattle market.

'And are these gooseberries?' asked Judith, lifting the fronds of the bush by the path and getting the answer with a spike in her finger.

It was talk for talk's sake. A means of putting off going to the greenhouse, even though they both desperately wanted what was waiting for them inside.

'Are you ready?' said Rose. The Hutchinsons nodded, tentative and yet full of longing, as the young often were. She squeezed Judith's little hand and cupped Henry's boyish cheek. 'Well then.'

She took them past the patches of raspberries and peas, the canes laden and bending, past the bed of elephantine marrows, between the sagging boughs of the fruit trees and out to the very end of the garden where the white-framed greenhouse sat with its windows lightly sheened in condensation. Thin grey smoke idled from the chimney.

The door was always locked – to keep out the Mister as well as any other inquisitive pests – and Rose took the key from her pocket, giving Judith and Henry a smile.

'It's a happy day,' she said.

'I know, I know,' Judith replied, steeling herself. Henry too.

But once inside the greenhouse, with the door closed behind them, they were apprehensive once more and stood irresolutely by the pots of tomato vines, staring at the raised bed and the plant that sat there in the dark soil. A green-leaved thing, like a cabbage but the size of a prize-winning pumpkin.

It had grown well, thought Rose, since she'd brought it inside. It was always necessary to do so. The sun and rain got things off to a good start, especially in a summer like this, and in an ideal world it might be left to grow outdoors until it was ready, but it was too prone to being eaten. She could keep off the birds with wire netting and the birds in turn more or less decimated the crawling pests, but in the latter stages of ripening, the plant began to give off a smell that was attractive to rats and foxes and nothing would prevent them from tearing the thing apart if they were determined. Years ago, before she'd really known what she was doing, they'd got into the garden a few times and left a scene of carnage.

'Come,' said Rose, beckoning Judith and Henry over. 'It's all right.'

She took their hands and placed them on the globe of leaves.

'There. Press your fingers in. Can you feel how it won't give?' she said. There was a particular firmness to these plants when they were ready to be unpeeled.

'Can I help?' asked Henry, already taking off his jacket.

'No, love,' said Rose. He couldn't. Not in the way he meant. It was best that she was the midwife here just as she was down in the village.

'Go and see how warm the water is,' she said, looking at the pail she'd left by the woodstove.

Glad to have something to do he went over.

'Still cold,' he said.

'Well, stoke the fire,' Rose told him and then turned to Judith. 'You stand back, petal,' she said. 'You don't want that dress of yours stained.'

Judith did as she was told and took a step away, holding the basket in both her hands.

Unwrapping the plant was an intricate and messy business. The outer husk was thick and dry and required not a little brute force to tear it off. Underneath, the overlapping layers were more delicate, more like wet skin, and, from experience, Rose had found that a wooden butter knife was best for getting under the edges and turning back the leaves.

Between each one and the next was an oily yellow sebum that smelled of a butcher's counter – the odour that attracted vermin. But the Hutchinsons made no mind of it. They stood side by side, holding hands, and looking on as Rose teased up each wide leaf and then carefully cut it away. It couldn't be rushed. It had to be as gentle a process as possible.

Gradually, she stripped off the bulk of the green skins and got down to an even more delicate-looking part of the plant, at which point Judith let out a short breath and smiled at Henry.

'Did you see?' she said.

The flap Rose was picking at bulged, and when she folded it aside there was a small pink hand beneath, clenching and unclenching. Thankfully, there were five fingers this time. The Wardleys' boy had suffered more than his share of mockery at school. Children could be so brutal.

'Can I?' Judith asked, unsure if she was allowed to touch the baby yet.

'Of course,' Rose said. 'You're the mother, aren't you?'

Judith pressed her fingertip into the little palm and the child gripped it hard enough to make her gasp and laugh. It was strong. They always were.

'Not long now, little love,' Judith said, bending to kiss the tiny knuckles. 'You'll soon be out.'

She twisted her finger free and let Rose continue taking off the coverings. After a few more cuts with the knife, the rest of the arm emerged and then a meaty-looking foot that was wedged between the elbow and the hip. They grew very curled up, these children, with their knees next to their ears, their spines bent like caterpillars, and sprang open with some vigour when the leaves that had been holding them in place were taken off.

As Rose went on, the other arm fought its way out, then the other leg broke free, quivering. Another layer or two down she came to the head, where an almost transparent green film covered the baby's face like a caul. The sudden flood of light caused it to stir, and as it moved from side to side, its nose made a tiny tent, its mouth a hollow.

Rose scrubbed off the membrane in a way that probably seemed heavy-handed when the rest of the procedure had been so calm and careful, but the baby needed to breathe for itself. It needed to begin its life with a wail, just like any other child. And soon enough, when its mouth was clear, it started to bleat in the lamb-like quiver of a new-born.

It had all its teeth already. Its tongue was small and sharp like a pink thorn, but it would thicken and soften.

Like the others Rose had grown, the child was sexless, though the Hutchinsons had already decided to bring it up as a girl and call it Lily.

'Keep her still now,' said Rose, and Henry held down the jigging legs. 'Judith, take her arms.'

With the baby pinioned, Rose snapped off the stalk grow-ing into the navel, a little green fluid dribbled out, and the birth was over.

Henry looked on, mesmerised, and Rose had to ask him twice to go and fetch the water. With a nudge from Judith, he brought over the metal pail that had been warming in front of the woodstove, unable to take his eyes off the baby, his daughter, kicking among the leaves.

'Is she all right?' he asked.

'She'll clean up, don't worry,' said Rose.

They did look a mess at first, these children, with strings of resin stretched like gum between their legs and under their arms but it came away easily enough.

The heat of the fire had taken the chill off the water, yet Lily still cried bloody murder as Rose washed her skin and sluiced out the sludge from her nose and ears. She was still screeching when Rose handed her to Judith, who had been waiting joyfully and anxiously, crying herself.

The weight of the child seemed to surprise her, or alarm her even, but she wrapped Lily tight in the blanket, as though bandaging a wound, and held her to her shoulder.

Petted and comforted, Lily quietened down and looked at Judith with brilliant green eyes. They were always green at birth and then faded into brown as the child got older. In fact, the change in colour was one of the signs that a child was getting close to its time.

There was no telling when that would be for Lily. The Wardleys' boy had been seven, the Collinwoods' just five. She'd been a little luckier, thought Rose. Hazel had been nine. Though once her eyes had lost their brightness, it hadn't taken long for her to deteriorate. She'd started to sleep for longer. Her appetite had withered. She'd stopped talking. And then her skin had dried out. So quickly too. In a fortnight, it had gone from paper to lace. Then the flesh underneath had turned to something like flaking bark, the bones to brittle twigs.

But she'd not been in any pain, even if the Mister thought otherwise. These children never suffered at the end any more than a leaf suffered when it yellowed. Nor did the decay come as a surprise to them, in the way that a tree was never shocked by autumn.

'But it's as if they're just toys to play with,' the Mister had said.

No, it was more like enjoying a garden, thought Rose. It was what these children *gave* that mattered. And what they gave was love, in forms as various as wildflowers.

Love, the promise of.

Love, the finding of.

Love, the gaining of.

Love, the memory of.

Love that endured, unlike everything else in nature.

# An Afternoon of Cake and Lemonade

## 1970

The boys and girls his father brought home that afternoon were the same as all the rest: poor children from poor towns deemed to be in need of some fresh country air and God's enduring love.

As soon as they got off the minibus, they were like caged things freed. Some clambered up the trees, others threw gravel at the cross on the roof of the chapel, two boys fought over which of them was going to ride the bicycle they'd found leaning against the wall of the manse. Jason's bicycle. A present. He'd turned eighteen that day.

The youth worker who'd come with the children did her best to rein them all in, clapping her hands and telling them to remember what they'd learnt about being respectful and polite and so on, while the last person stepped down awkwardly off the bus: a small boy with bowed legs and cumbersome corrective boots.

'This is Nicholas,' Jason's father said, bringing him over with his hands on the child's narrow shoulders. 'You'll take care of him, won't you?'

The other children jostled past him in a game of tig, ruffling his thatch of dirty blond hair, patting his face. Nicky Rickets, they called him. He grinned as though he was trying to assure himself that it was all just good-natured rough-and-tumble, and Jason saw that he had no front teeth. Those that remained were brown pegs that needed to be pulled out or would fall out soon by themselves.

He was so short and thin that he might have been even younger than Jason had first thought, and he half expected him to start sucking his thumb – for the meat on the bone as much as for the comfort.

His mother would remind him that these boys and girls were often *malnourished*. She mouthed the word rather than saying it out loud, as though it was impolite to draw too much attention to such things.

Calling, 'Children, children,' in the voice she used to fetch in the cats at night, she emerged from the manse with the Outreach Committee: Mrs Lythgow, Mrs Pike, Mr and Mrs Middlegill, strange Keith Smeer, and the wholesome, ever-growing clan of busty, strapping Fairwoods – each of them carrying a tray of lemonade and cakes.

Seeing the treats, the children stopped what they were doing and charged towards the house as the youth worker, whose name was Sunita, begged for restraint. Before a riot ensued, Jason's father went over to help, but Nicholas stayed put, chewing the skin around his thumbnail.

'Don't you want a drink?' Jason asked him and he shook his head.

He was going to be one of those who never spoke the whole time they were here. There'd been a few like that. Or they were loud and wild. One or the other. Mutes or maniacs. Nothing in between. All through the summer holiday they'd been ferried in from Salford and Huddersfield, Barnsley and Oldham and every run-down place in between. And Jason had been expected to welcome them and play with them and share what he had; *all* that he had. Even his new bicycle now.

But it was good for him, his father said. He needed to understand how fortunate he was to be loved. And that love wasn't given to be hoarded, but to be disseminated. A thousand people might be nourished from a single store of grain. And what did any man profit from holding to his heart the things that others needed ... etcetera, etcetera.

It was as if privilege was something he'd actually demanded, thought Jason. But he'd never asked for anything he'd ever been given. Not love. Not these unsparing parents. Nor any of the things he'd received that morning for his birthday. A chess set. That bicycle. If such things were so corrupting, then why had his mother and father bestowed them upon him in the first place? They'd been made to seem not like gifts at all but as objects by which he might contemplate the repercussions of his inborn covetousness. For wasn't it true that an abundance of possessions made a person insensible to those who required the most sympathy? That was Luke. And Matthew said much the same thing too. Likewise, Timothy and Proverbs. Poor in spirit was the man of wealth who could not see through a poor man's eyes.

'Empathy, Jason,' his father had said to him as they'd washed up after breakfast that morning. 'It's all about empathy.'

It was all there in 1 Corinthians 13. And standing at the pulpit, he'd often open the Bible at that passage and wag it at the congregation saying, 'This is your heart' or 'Here is your life', or something similarly dramatic. 'Your mission in a nutshell,' that was another phrase he liked to use, meaning that in that single chapter lay the whole of one's Christian duty. Nothing was as important as love. Words meant nothing unless they were backed up by *actual* acts of charity. That they were tucked away here in Barrowbeck was all the more reason for them to go out and *look* for the destitute or the sinful and bring them into the fold. To that end, he'd allowed a tramp to stay in the box room one Christmas Eve and invited an ex-thief to give the lesson at Pentecost.

When he'd first come to the village from Bradford, his new parishioners had been intimidated by such radical notions. Venturing into the most squalid places to share

Christ's love, casting oneself down among the lowly, was all very well in Tong and Manningham, very likely *necessary*, but that was a mission for inner-city God-folk, not them.

Yet, they'd been won over, they'd been convinced of their importance, they knew that God was watching and waiting, and now they couldn't get enough of Keith Mallowdale. Or 'Pastor Keith', as he insisted they call him. He wanted them to think of him as their shepherd.

He'd found his most stalwart disciples in the Outreach Committee who toured the slums of the towns and cities beyond the moors, seeking out the lost and needy and making arrangements to bring them to Barrowbeck for a day of respite. Drug addicts. Battered wives. The homeless. These troubled children off council estates. The more deprived the better. Because that way they could feel as though they were shining a light into the darkest places.

Still, in Jason's estimation, it wasn't empathy they felt for the wretched souls they paraded about the village but pity, which was just another word for relief. It was really, *Thanks be to God that we are not like them*: hopeless, toothless, malnourished.

They came and went, the tramp, the thief, and all the rest, and Jason had never seen them again. Just as the children he was forced to befriend for a few hours never returned. It was as though a glimpse of compassion was all that was needed to set their grisly lives on a better course. And so long as they left the valley feeling that kindness was at least present *somewhere* in the world, then the Pastor and his wife and the saintly, satisfied congregation could be content that they'd done their duty.

Jason had been made to believe that his kindness towards these children was essential, but what difference did it honestly make? At six o'clock they'd be herded onto the minibus and driven back to wherever they'd come from, and their lives would go on as they had before. If they were sad about leaving Barrowbeck, then more fool them. The grey, stone chapel was cold all year round. The manse was tiny and smelled of damp. The wood behind it boggy and largely impenetrable away from the path. When the wind was high enough, he could sometimes hear faint voices coming from the loony bin at the old hall down the lane and felt as though he might as well be one of them for all the freedom he had.

Once, when he'd been cycling past the grounds, some mad old duffer had spoken to him from the other side of the hedge he was pruning. Whether he was *supposed* to have been out on his own with sharp tools in his hands was unclear, but he'd seemed harmless enough. Just weird. He'd talked as if he'd stepped out of the previous century. On and on he'd gone about the apple trees in the garden. And what a sanctuary the valley was. And how lucky they were to live there.

But there was nothing worth coveting about the place at all. The children would soon see that if they stayed. It wasn't a playground but a dungeon. The fells were as good as walls.

And they'd realise that the reception they'd been given here at the church was a show of virtue put on for their sake, a matinee. Did Nicholas think that it was cake and lemonade here every afternoon?

He didn't seem to want any, mind, and kept his distance from the other children as they sat on the lawn sucking through straws and licking buttercream off their fingers.

'There's plenty for everyone,' said Jason.

Nicholas sort of shrugged, gnawed at his thumb again and moved closer to Jason's side, a shadow in his shadow.

Christ. Why did he have to be so afraid? He could choose not to be.

The children were asking for more food, but Jason's father wanted them to show some appreciation for what they'd already received. And so as politely and patiently as they could, the members of the Outreach Committee shushed all the conversations and then sat down, holding hands with the children, encouraging them to close their eyes.

Jason nodded at Nicholas to do likewise, though he wasn't sure if he'd be able to just fold into the grass with legs like his, or if he'd need some assistance. But he managed by himself, which Jason was grateful for. He didn't want to have to touch Nicholas if he could help it.

'Dear Lord,' the Pastor began, turning his face to the sun, his eyes closed, enraptured. 'We give thee thanks for the food we have enjoyed and the daily nourishment you give our souls. As we go now to enjoy the cool water of the river, let us be reminded of thy baptism . . .'

Hearing 'thy' and 'thee', some of the other children yawned or tried to suppress their laughter, and even before the Amen they were chattering again, some already on their feet and scaling the garden wall.

But Jason had been taught not to judge them. They hadn't had an upbringing like his. They didn't know any better. They were caught in a cycle. Their parents didn't know any better either. Allowances had to be made. Their behaviour was best met with understanding.

Before the children had a chance to run too wild, Jason's father directed everyone through the gate into the wood. Nicholas hobbled after them, hanging back with Jason, still with nothing to say.

The path to the river led through the trees for half a mile or so to May Calvert's Corner, where the Outreach Committee arranged picnic blankets and set down more bottles of lemonade and more boxes of cake. Here, the banks were shaded by willows and alders, but the bend of water lay in bright sunlight and the other children wasted no time in tearing off their plimsolls and socks and wading in, splashing one another, screaming, gasping at the cold, the boys grappling. But Nicholas sat with Jason and the adults, picking the daisies from the grass between his bruised, crooked shins.

Sunita regarded him as she fanned herself with the lid of a cake tin.

'Poor lad,' she said to Jason's father. 'He has it worse than any of them,' and, not quite sotto voce, she relayed the facts of Nicholas's life. No dad around, mum working the streets, an older brother who knocked seven bells out of him when he'd been drinking.

The Pastor shook his head. How awful for the boy. How cruel the circumstances of his life.

'Well, I'm glad he's here,' he said.

At least in the valley Nicholas was away from all that ugliness for a time, and through the eyes of the kind-hearted souls who'd brought him to Barrowbeck, God would see his suffering too.

But didn't God see everything at all times anyway? thought Jason. Surely he knew Nicholas already. He must have watched him being pummelled by his brother. He must have intended it, in fact. If everything was God's will, then he had *chosen* for Nicholas to have a violent life; he'd given him rickets and rotted his teeth. In which case God was a fucking sadist.

'Don't you want to go and paddle, sweetheart?' Sunita said, reaching over Jason's lap and squeezing Nicholas's arm.

'It's not deep,' Jason's father assured him.

The weeks of dry hot weather had made the beck shallow, and it rushed so loudly over the pebbles on the bed that the children had to shout at one another to be heard.

133

'Jason will take you,' the Pastor said. 'If you're worried about falling in.'

'Undo his boots for him,' said Jason's mother, glad, it seemed, that she wasn't the one sitting next to him. The thought of touching his feet clearly repelled her too.

'Can't he do it himself?' Jason replied.

'That's not the point,' said Jason's father. 'It would be considerate to help him, that's all. Isn't that what today's all about? Isn't that what we're here *for*?' he added. 'We should be glad of any opportunity to be kind, Jason. You know that.'

He had been reminded often enough how lucky he was to have been born into God's presence. His father hadn't. Nor had his mother. They'd struggled to God's side along a winding, thorny path, and now that they had found Him and were embraced by Him, they were tasked with helping others find the way as well. That was how they, and Jason too, were expected to repay the love that God had conferred upon them. That was why God had decided that certain people needed to be maltreated – so that the saved, the blessed ones, had the opportunity to express their gratitude to the Almighty by taking these broken and unloved souls in their arms.

So went the sermons on the disadvantaged. The upshot being that the poor were essential to spiritual advancement. Their suffering always delivered the greatest lessons. Wasn't it in the stories of Jesus's dealings with lepers and cripples and fallen women, the sick, the dying, the deaf, dumb and blind, the unclean, the possessed, that Christians found their aspiration to goodness? God *lived* in the poor. To revere them was to worship Him.

Jason slackened the laces on Nicholas's boots until they were loose enough to take off. He had no socks on. His toes were filthy and twisted. His soles had a patina of grime, the skin cracked here and there. They were like the feet of a pilgrim.

'Do you actually want to go in?' said Jason. Nicholas hadn't said one way or the other. Walking into the beck over the stones might be agony for him. But he nodded.

'There, you see,' Jason's father said. 'Of course he does.'

'It'll be so lovely and refreshing on a day like this,' chipped in Jason's mother, glancing at Nicholas's stubby feet, hoping that the water might start to scour away the first layer of muck.

'Do you need a hand, Nicholas, pet?' Sunita said and made a move to help him stand up. But being so long accustomed to his affliction, he had perfected his own process, one that was efficient to him but looked horribly awkward to everyone else, and Jason's mother fretted that he was going to stumble.

'Quick, get his hand.'

Jason did as she asked and felt Nicholas hold tight, not because he was about to fall, but with what seemed like longing. He looked up and grinned with his mess of a mouth.

'Here, watch your step,' said Jason and led him down to the edge of the beck.

As predicted, he faltered on the loose stones, but then wading out a little further he found a long flat rock on which he could stand and enjoy the flow of the water around his bony ankles.

The other children were too preoccupied to take much notice of him, and for the first time Nicholas seemed able to let down his guard. He gave a small laugh, his only utterance so far, and rubbed the underside of first one foot and then the other against the soft fleece of weed, using Jason's arm for support. A shoal of minnows gathered close by, and he squatted down to look at them, poking his fingers into the water, delighted by the way the fish moved. Then, pulling Jason on some way, he rooted about in the pebbles under the surface, picking out ones that he liked the look of and holding them close to his eye, enjoying the colours.

Jason glanced back to his father and mother. They waved and then exchanged some words with one another. His father settled back on his elbows and crossed his legs. His mother shaded her eyes so that she could see. They'd both be so glad that he and this Nicholas had bonded. Every time a horde of children had come to the manse, he'd been paired with a child like him, a victim.

It was all good practice for the future. It was a foregone conclusion that Jason would join the clergy. Training. Ordination. A parish of his own. All that was waiting for him. It would happen. It *had* to happen. His father was taking every necessary step to ensure it. In his mind, if he of all people couldn't persuade his son to offer his life to God then that was nothing short of a catastrophe.

If Jason had any doubts about his aptitude, then he could rest assured that he would be more than capable, his father had told him; he would excel. He'd already proved himself a deep thinker in their Bible study groups. And as for any misgivings he might have regarding the strength of his faith, well, it was a perfectly normal thing to question, a thing that *should* be questioned, quite rightly, but these worries were entirely within his power to dispel. He had to just keep on listening to what God was asking him to do.

All summer, as these children had come and gone, he had been hearing a voice. But not that of God. That ancient devil had nothing more to say. No, the voice Jason had listened to was his own, or something like his own, a voice as loud and resonant as a bell which declared God's time to be at an end. He'd given up. He was dying. He had no interest in those striving to laud him with their acts of altruism. He had no self-regard. All those pitiful people he'd brought into being just so that they could be saved in his name were redundant now. They were the waste-products of an exercise in vanity that God didn't care about any longer. They were stuck in lives that would never improve. They deserved to be freed.

\*

137

Nicholas had found a white pebble that had been ground to an almost perfect sphere and showed it to Jason.

He said something that was lost in the noise of the beck, and Jason leant down to listen.

'Can I take it home?' Nicholas said and looked up with such hope that Jason couldn't bear it.

He squinted through the sunlight at his mother and father again, then turned back.

'Shall we do something else, Nicky?' he said, and the boy smiled at hearing his name. Those teeth of his. Jesus.

'Like what?' he replied, moving his hair out of his eyes.

'Well, let's go to the house,' Jason said. 'It'll be quieter there. You'd prefer that, wouldn't you?'

Nicholas looked past him at the others who were now on the grass and quarrelling over the food.

'Come on,' said Jason. 'I'll show you something better than all this.'

'Yeah?'

'Much better.'

'OK,' Nicholas said, and moved off through the water first, his hand in Jason's, pleased with the tiniest amount of affection, as if it was enough, as if it was going to sustain him when he left the valley.

Jason helped him to the bank and then up the slope to where the rest of the children were tucking into a second sitting of cake and lemonade.

'I'm going to take him back,' Jason said.

His mother beamed, happy that he'd warmed to the boy.

'Look after him,' she said. 'Hold his hand on the path. Don't rush him.'

He wouldn't, he said. There was no need to hurry. Everyone would be down here by the river for at least another hour. There was plenty of time.

Full of food, the bottles and boxes almost empty, the other children turned their attention to Nicholas again, calling him names, making threats. But Jason smiled. What they said or did now didn't matter. Nicholas didn't know, but it was all going to stop very soon. He couldn't wait to see the relief on the boy's face when he realised.

Carrying his heavy boots, taking his hand, he led Nicholas through the wood and up the path. The clamour of voices and the sound of the river grew fainter, and by the time they'd come to the gate they could only hear the wind in the trees. The lawn was brittle and yellow, the soil baked into cracks, and the boy's feet were dry by the time they'd crossed the grass.

Jason piggy-backed him through the gravel to the manse and set him down on the steps while he opened the door to the kitchen. Inside, the boy sniffed at the lingering smell of baking, and gazed around at the racks of hanging pans and spoons, the dresser with its delft plates, the gingham curtains, the jars of flour, sugar and spices, everything in its place.

With a nudge, Jason told him to sit at the table. Did he want a drink, he asked. A surprise? A special lemonade? Nicholas nodded.

'Close your eyes, then,' Jason said, and the boy did so immediately. His unquestioning trust was frightening at first. It was going to be so easy. But that was the way it ought to be. Quick and simple.

He took a tumbler from the draining board, one with a picture of Mickey Mouse on the side. He thought Nicholas would like it. Mickey Mouse in his wizard's costume waving a wand.

Half his left ear had been rubbed away. The colours were faded. It wasn't quite clean either. Jason held it up to the light of the window and wiped off the finger-marks around the rim. A chalice ought to be spotless, he thought.

He could recall that observation so distinctly. Those had been the exact words. The whole scene was still vivid even now, years later.

There'd been dust in the sunlight, he remembered. Wasps coming and going from the cake crumbs on the sideboard. On the window ledge, there were shrubby herbs in three terracotta pots. Cookery books leaning against a black leather Bible.

He could see Nicholas's grimy feet swinging under the chair. His little hands joined together under his chin as though in prayer. His eyes screwed shut in expectation. He could hear himself saying, 'Hold on, Nicky, won't be long.'

But clearer still was the feeling of complete certainty in what he was about to do. The exhilaration of knowing that he was at last dispensing true charity as he stirred up what he'd poured into the glass.

August the twenty-first, 1970. His eighteenth birthday.

That was the date he always gave whenever he was asked how it had begun, this calling of his.

# The Haven

## 1984

No, you are most welcome, sir. You are not intruding at all. We are always happy to receive visitors at the Haven. How fortunate it is that your walk has brought you to us on this particular day. Now you will be able to watch the last of the apple harvest being gathered.

Nature has its own clock, as they say, and we must work to its chimes. As sure as the river runs, time marches on. Day by day, the summer green is slowly turning into autumn bronze. The evenings in the valley have been misty of late. The swallows are departing. The mercury has dropped. Son Robert has predicted a storm in the coming days. He has heard it building in the air, he says, like voices in a court-room. And Daughter Ellen has given me a handful of sour blackberries every morning this week as proof that the year is on the wane. If the Master comes, she says, he will want to see not an apple left on the trees, not a thing left to rot in the grass. All must be saved. And she is quite right. The

Master has given us so much to love and care for that we must succeed in that endeavour.

Yes, sir. They are all called Son or Daughter here, no matter their age, and the Master is their father. An odious governor you might think, given the way his charges look so thin and wear such coarse, plain clothes. But this is no Bedlam. No one is put in chains. There are no loathsome supervisors to enforce good behaviour with truncheons and straitjackets. The Haven is the apotheosis of modern psychiatric care. The Sons and Daughters set the standards of their own moral conduct. Away from the malignant influences of the world that led them astray, they can choose to live in the way that they have always known in their hearts to be right and exercise restraint in all aspects.

Even though the food-stores are full, they prefer to eat in moderation. Even though they may wear whatever they wish, they opt for simple attire.

Before they were sent here, they languished in Holloway and the Scrubs and a dozen other holes, and no doubt dreamt of scaling the high brick walls like spiders. At the Haven, however, there are no fences. Containment is not necessary. All elect quite voluntarily to stay within the boundaries of the Master's land. They feel safe in these fields and pastures, and besides, none would wish to be absent when the Master returns.

144

No one knows, sir. No one here has ever seen him. Not even those who have been here for many years. But the Sons and Daughters at the Haven understand that the Master's family is vast and scattered. And so even though he is constantly on the road – we have heard lately about his acts of benevolence in places as far apart as Suffolk and Sutherland – it will take time for him to visit everyone.

But come to the Haven one day he will, and so everything is kept as the Master would wish to find it. All strive for the common goal of seeing him pleased when he appears. All are accountable and equal in the task. The only division to be found here is the natural division of labour, as each Son and Daughter gravitates to the work that best draws out their talent. Some are gardeners, some have a way with animals, both in husbandry and butchery. There are ploughmen and cheesemakers, bricklayers and cooks. Every skill is prized, yet not over-prized. No one person is above any other. Son Timothy over there, the master carpenter – his scrollwork demanded for the pulpits of modern cathedrals before his *indiscretions* – happily serves soup to the stableboy.

But come this way, sir, into the orchard. Can you see how it was planted where the light lingers longest?

Oh, many years ago, sir. In Squire Underwood's time. This was his hall. These were his grounds. He must have employed very fine gardeners for the apple trees are well-rooted and give as generously every year as doting grandfathers. There is great affection for them here. See how the Sons and Daughters swarm around them as tenderly as bees. The scene is of an antique peasantry, is it not? As though a painting by Brueghel has been brought to life.

If distinctions are not generally noted as a rule, then they are forgotten entirely on a harvest day. Today, everyone is an apple picker. All do what they can. The more agile mount the ladders and the others glean the grass for windfalls. Nothing is wasted. Even the apples that are bruised, black or wasp-eaten are kept to feed to the pigs.

I think, sir, that these men and women see *themselves* embodied in these inferior specimens, and through the Master's compassion they come to know that even things spoiled have value. Every apple, whatever its condition, is handled with great care, with love even. For the Sons and Daughters, every small touch of tenderness on their part begins to resolve the cruelties that they have inflicted on others in the past, just as one might say that another lighted candle staves off the darkness a fraction more.

Yes, you are right to think that, for some, remorse might never be dispelled completely, but what joy even the smallest step towards making amends can bring. Indeed, visitors such as yourself often express great surprise at finding this place to be one of so much hope and gladness.

146

Take Daughter Rosalind. She strangled her child. And Son Philip there, only twenty-two with side-whiskers as soft as lamb's wool, he bludgeoned a man for sport. You would not think it, the way they laugh with one another as they work. Some might argue, you may think it yourself, sir, that given the severity of their misdeeds they have no right to know happiness ever again, that it would be a fitting punishment to withhold it from them forever. And they themselves might agree in certain desolate moments alone. But the Master does not expect them to show perpetual regret for their crimes, only fidelity to him and to the success of the Haven.

And success is abundant here. The Haven is renowned for its bounty. Its milk is as thick as paint, and you will hear its meat praised far beyond Barrowbeck. Its vegetables and fruits are said to rival even Kentish produce. Look now, here comes Daughter Emily to show you the best of the apple crop. It is in rude health as you see. The Foxwhelps and the Ribston Pippins are as red as radishes. The Bloody Ploughmans as purple as beetroot. All are plump and heavy in the hand. Take one, sir. If you wish.

The temptation for the Sons and Daughters to eat as they work must be high, is it not, you ask? It must happen, you say. And there is no harm in it surely? With an acre of orchard, and twenty trees producing – what? – thirty bushels a year, an apple or two per person would not compromise the annual yield.

Perhaps not.

But this would be the worst of all offences at the Haven, sir. To take from the trees in order to pacify a gripe of hunger is to steal directly from the Master's own hand.

Ask the Sons and Daughters and they will tell you stories of other places like the Haven where some of their kin have been roundly punished for theft. A Son in the south was birched by his siblings for tempting them into stealing potatoes. A Daughter in the east made to sleep three nights in the rain for encouraging others to eat the cheese out of mouse traps. Harsh though it may seem for these men and women to be so castigated for what might be considered mild misdemeanours – we are all human, not divine – examples must be made from time to time to reassert the Master's expectations.

It is a very effective strategy. You will detect in their voices here a deep reverence for honesty and virtue.

And yet at the same time there is a degree of envy that the Sons and Daughters at these other places have actually *seen* the Master. For whenever his children are led into sin, he comes in person to pass sentence on the tempter. He appears on a white horse, they say.

Thus, secretly, they all long for someone to transgress here at the Haven too, so that they will finally have the privilege of watching the Master ride in and know his grace for themselves.

\*

It is a yearning that is never spoken of but which all share. To desire what one has been taught to abhor is an age-old paradox. A man of education such as yourself, sir, will know that in many primitive societies what is considered taboo is often acted out as a drama, a dumbshow, some piece of puppetry or mummery, lest it should become even more of a temptation by being suppressed. And so it is at the Haven. On this day each year, when the trees are bare and every piece of fruit has been stored in its proper place, the Sons and Daughters are permitted to give expression to their innermost desires.

See, as we speak, they are coming back out to the orchard with their sacks and baskets to silently recreate their afternoon's labour. They'll pretend to pick from the boughs or they'll simulate the jubilation of finding a ripe beauty in the grass.

We may join them, sir, if you'll come and play too. You'll note that every movement is more exaggerated now. Such is the nature of the performance. Make your smile wider, your mimed laughter heartier. There. That's it. You fit in well here.

But now, what's this? Can you see? Watch Son Terence there, the one as bearded as a hermit, looking about him furtively as he takes a bite of his invisible apple. How fierce is Daughter Irene's outrage. Yet how swiftly she changes. Seeing the sweet juices dripping from his chin she sneaks a mouthful of her own apple too. Did you see her?

Now look this way. Look now. Daughter Marion has noticed them from the corner of her eye. Now Son Kenneth. Now Solomon. Now Ginette, Linda, Gavin. One by one, they'll gorge on the imaginary harvest. Watch them now. Don't they do it well? Kneeling with their faces in the grass and gobbling away like swine. Aren't they fine mimics, the way they clutch their stomachs as if bloated? They can squat, they can double over, but nothing takes away the agony of their shame.

Those men? The ones still nosing about in the grass? They represent the hopeless cases, sir. Drunk on the ferment of iniquity. Snuffling for more fruit even though it will make them sick, even though they are crying.

Oh, I agree, sir. Even if it is only theatre, it is a pitiable thing to see so many faces racked with guilt and fear. Like the damned of the Last Judgement, they are infants again, wailing over their own weakness, desperate to avoid punishment. And as children do, they will try to find someone else to blame for their temptation. Someone else to offer up instead.

Yes, sir. Yes, they are looking at you. You are the only one holding a real apple after all. The one you chose to take earlier. And it was a choice, sir. Sin is always a choice. You know that well enough. That is the age we live in.

Here, let us prepare you now. We must bind your hands and fill your pockets with stones. For the river is running fast and wild and the Master will not want you swept away when he leads you into the water.

No, be at peace, sir. All this we do with love, with gratitude. It is you who will speed the Master here to the Haven. It is you who will finally reunite a father with his children. Think of that.

Now, come with us to the gates. And listen out for the sound of hooves on the road.

# Autumn Pastoral

## 1995

At Bolt & Baizeman's, at least fifty per cent of my work came about in connection with the dead. Calculating the financial worth of the art pieces left behind by the dear departed was sometimes an integral part of tying up an estate and often of great interest to those relatives who stood to inherit something, even if they pretended otherwise at the time.

Their solicitor would inform me that retaining these heirlooms for the next generation was far more important to the family than money, but then a month or two later, when that still life or that portrait, so lovingly hung above the fireplace in remembrance of so-and-so, was starting to seem less attractive than the five figures I'd suggested as a reserve, I might get a phone call or a letter saying, 'Now, if we *were* to put it in for auction, Mr Thomas, hypothetically, of course . . .'

At least Lorraine Oswald had stated her intentions directly. She wanted all the paintings that Roderick Elm had amassed in his lifetime valued and then sold as soon as possible. Indeed, everything that her former partner (or as we used to say, *old lover*) had bequeathed to her was to be disposed of. The house as well as its contents.

From what I understood, it had come as a shock to her that she'd received anything from him at all, given their long estrangement. She'd gone off to live in the West Midlands a great many years before and lived there still, while Mr Elm had stayed here in Barrowbeck.

As I pulled up at his house (or rather *her* house now) on the far side of the village, I thought that the name, Doonrigg, suited it somehow. It was a sombre place and supremely unlovely, all of it clad in black stone, and the chimneys oddly tall, as though they had some industrial function.

Still, that kind of architectural drabness held a certain charm for some people – *character* they called it – and anywhere else it would have been snapped up. But a month had passed since Mr Elm's death and as far as I knew there'd been no interest in it at all.

It was – as ever – a question of location. Other villages nearby had been invaded and more or less conquered by the middle classes of Yorkshire and Lancashire, who'd spent vast sums on barn conversions or renovated 'The Old Rectory' or 'The Old Schoolhouse' so spectacularly as to have had their handiwork featured in Sunday supplements. Whereas the buildings here tended to go to rack and ruin when they became unoccupied. New people didn't often move in, or it was my understanding that if they *did*, then they didn't stop long.

There were no jobs to speak of. That was to say there was only work for those who already lived here. And barely much of that. Those industries I'd passed on my way through the village, the type that often lingered on in these out-of-the-way places, really were in their death throes now. The stonemason's, the ironworks, the textile mill, the ramshackle abattoir – all silent that afternoon – surely made less and less profit by the day and would soon succumb to the pitiless reality of market forces and fold.

And it wasn't as though anyone would want to rush to Barrowbeck for its handsomeness either. It didn't have the enchanting, cobbled streets of Midderby-on-the-Hill, nor was it like Cragg Morton with its flower displays and its white painted pubs and its geese on the greensward.

From those places, there were, on clear days, long, scenic views down the dales. One could look out over miles of grazing-land to distant fields and coppice woods, and the sun might sometimes catch the church tower of some quiet, gradely parish. But here, the only thing to look at was the surrounding fells which felt very steep and close and at this time of year would soon blot out the sun. Even now, it was cold, with a wintry edge to the air that I hadn't noticed back in Leeds. It had rained here recently too. The cloughs choked on water from the moors. The river flowing by beside the lane was more like liquid mud. And the village itself, a quarter of a mile or so back from the house, was all wet stone and wet slate, the mist and chimney smoke mingling into a brown smog. Dogs barking somewhere.

From here, the lane continued a short way and then wound up the hillside at the very end of the valley until it came to a stop at the further of two farmhouses.

It felt such a despondent place. So stagnant. Trapped in a state of shabbiness that was as pronounced now as it had always been. Over the centuries, people must have felt, as I did, that after the long journey down the valley on that filthy rutted lane, Barrowbeck wasn't worth coming to. And yet there were those who'd spent their entire lives here. It didn't bear thinking about.

The solicitor who had been engaged to oversee the sale of the house and its effects – a Mr Crossharbour – had agreed to meet me and opened the front door as I approached.

'Mr Thomas?' he said.

'Christopher,' I replied as we shook hands, though I knew at once that he was the kind of man who would want to keep things formal.

He reminded me of a Van Eyck merchant, in the face, at least, with heavy half-closed lids and a long nose that was rather bulbous at the end. Yet, there was a military attitude to the way he held himself, as though soldiering had been his former – and preferred – occupation. He was a foot taller than me with a ramrod back and an immaculate charcoal grey suit. A crease of uniform length and straightness ran down each shin, and under the jacket was a spotless white shirt with a collar so sharp that it could have drawn blood. He wore a sensible woollen tie with – ah, there it was – a fancy regimental crest and his black leather shoes had been polished with a squaddie's diligence.

Next to him, I looked like a vagrant. I'd still not managed to get rid of the mud off my coat sleeves after changing the tyre.

'I'm sorry I'm late,' I said.

'You had some difficulty finding the place?' said Mr Crossharbour, looking at his watch. We'd settled on two o'clock, but it was gone half past.

'A puncture,' I said.

It was clearly a poor excuse in his opinion, and he ushered me into the hallway with an impatience that had me gabbling like a schoolboy up before the headmaster.

'It was a nail, perhaps,' I said. 'Or a thorn. I'm not sure. It might even have been one of the potholes in the road.'

But he wasn't interested in the particulars, only the knock-on effect of my tardiness.

'Yes, it's just that there are quite a number of items to catalogue,' he said as he closed the door. 'And you'll want to be away from here before dark.'

'Oh?'

'The electricity supply has been disconnected,' he said. 'I shouldn't imagine you'll want to work by torchlight.'

Even at this time in the afternoon, it was gloomy in the hallway with its parquet floor and its dark green wallpaper.

'I don't know,' I said; 'it might lend my job a touch more excitement than it usually has.'

He wasn't in the mood for jokes, he only wanted to get started, and he indicated the half-dozen paintings hanging between the front door and the foot of the stairs.

By the look of it, he'd used the time he'd spent waiting to fix numbered stickers to the frames. One, two, three and four were by a W. B. Garth or Garrick. The signature was indistinct. Either way, they were names I didn't know, and the work was nothing particularly special. Rather poor imitations of Farquharson compositions. Sheep on snowy lanes, downy fields blushed by rosy twilight, that type of thing. But more impressionistic, like Pissarro's winter landscapes, though far short of anything so good, naturally.

'Value?' said Mr Crossharbour, poised with a pad and pen.

I reckoned he'd been in supplies and logistics rather than on the front line. Someone with a clipboard. Anyway, his abruptness wrong-footed me and I quickly fished out my own notebook so as to seem at least mildly professional. After putting on my glasses, I thumbed to a clean page. *Elm*, I wrote, and then scrutinised the paintings again.

'I'm not sure that I'll be able to put a *specific* figure on these pieces straight away,' I said.

'No?'

'I'm not familiar with the artist, I'm afraid. I'd have to undertake some research. Is it Garth or is it Garrick? I can't quite make it out.'

This appeared to confuse Mr Crossharbour no end. Wasn't I supposed to be the expert?

'Well, this one then,' he said, moving along and nodding at number five, a large-scale canvas opposite a grimy mirror.

Thankfully, I recognised it as a William Callaghan. Probably 1780 or '90. Late career anyway. A waterfall in the sublime style. The crags reared up like something out of a Salvator Rosa and the cataract plunged as a fierce white torrent. The tiny figure standing among the rocks at the bottom to give the scene its scale was almost invisible in the vapour. *Savick Clough: Barrowbeck* read the title.

'Ah, it was painted here,' I said.

'They all were,' Mr Crossharbour replied.

'Sorry?'

'Mr Elm only ever collected studies of the valley.'

'I see,' I said.

It was a quality piece but cracking in places, a common problem with oils in damp old houses such as this. And as I said to Mr Crossharbour, it would unfortunately reduce the value.

'To what?' he said and awaited my verdict.

'I don't know, five thousand? Less, maybe? It's hard to say,' I replied, watching his face twitch with stifled exasperation as he noted down my estimate.

'Miss Oswald was hoping for a more precise assessment,' he said.

Then he'd promised her something I couldn't deliver. Not on the spot.

'You'll appreciate that there has to be a degree of speculation,' I said. 'The value of a painting is only ever approximate until the hammer goes down. And it often depends on who's bidding, of course. Get two connoisseurs with deep pockets in the room and who knows how much they'll be willing to pay. But if they don't turn up, it might be a different story altogether.'

Mr Crossharbour regarded me as if I'd been deliberately trying to patronise him and moved on – with a pointed clearance of his throat – to number six, a small charcoal sketch of the cave up on the fellside nearby.

After this, seven, eight, nine, ten and so on ascended with the wide, ornate stairs, and I thought how tedious it was going to be to listen to Mr Crossharbour grump and huff at every picture when I couldn't give him the information he wanted immediately.

'Do feel free to leave me to it,' I said, as chummily as I could. 'I'm sure I'll find my way around. I tend to work at my own pace anyway.'

He looked at his watch to imply that if I'd wanted that privilege, I should have been more punctual.

'We are up against the clock, Mr Thomas,' he said.

'I could always make a couple of return visits,' I offered, although I didn't want to and nor did he.

'I shouldn't think I'll be able to spare a whole afternoon like this again for quite a while,' he said. 'And I'm sure the same goes for you.'

It did. My diary was full for the next few months. I'd been busy all year. Up and down the country. This had been the earliest appointment I'd been able to offer Mr Crossharbour and one I couldn't repeat until well after Christmas.

'It was just a thought,' I said.

He acknowledged the gesture out of politeness but in a curt sort of way. 'Well, as I mentioned in my letter, Miss Oswald is keen to move things forward,' he said, 'so . . .'

He motioned to the drawing of the cave again. He meant to shadow me and hurry me along. I put my glasses back on and considered the work, and then the other versions of the same scene which were amateurish and poorly composed and didn't really improve by the time we'd come to the top of the stairs.

'Perhaps a hundred,' I said, 'for the lot.' Though I knew they'd struggle to make even that.


The landing was brighter than the hallway as all the bedroom doors were open and in each room the curtains had been taken down. All the furniture had been removed. The carpets too. Miss Oswald had wasted no time in stripping the house. Only the paintings remained, some on the walls, numbered by Mr Crossharbour, and some piled up under old blankets. As I expected, they were in a terrible state. Chewed at by mice and moths or encrusted with grey mould.

The ones still hanging had been slightly better cared for and were the work of local artists from the fifties and sixties: Cecil Lowden, Isaiah Berry, Patricia Stroud and the like. Landscapes and pastoral scenes. All of them of Barrowbeck. Some of it a bit twee for modern tastes but there were one or two remarkable vistas of the valley as seen from the edge of the moor by Aubrey Kilmarsh and Gwen Galloway that would be fought over if and when they came to be sold. But these were solitary gems among a great deal of dross.

'So?' said Mr Crossharbour.

'Some will do very well, I'm sure,' I said. 'But I have to say that most of what's here is practically worthless, in monetary terms at least.'

'But it all has to go,' Mr Crossharbour said. 'Miss Oswald wants nothing left. Those are my instructions.'

'Listen, between you and me, it looks as if Mr Elm was a prolific rather than discerning collector,' I said, thinking that I could be honest with him, what did he care?

'Meaning?'

'Meaning that it's ninety per cent tat, for want of a better word.'

'That's your evaluation, Mr Thomas?' he said. 'Tat?'

162

'Bolt & Baizeman's isn't a flea market,' I said, inwardly wincing at how snobbish that made me sound. But it was true. We didn't just sell any old thing. Bidders came to us because they could be assured of a certain quality. We had a long-established reputation that we weren't going to put in jeopardy just to please one person.

'If your client really doesn't want to keep anything, perhaps once we've filtered out the best items, a house-clearance firm might be better placed to dispose of the rest,' I suggested.

'If you think,' Mr Crossharbour said, though he obviously didn't relish putting the idea to Miss Oswald. She wasn't going to like it.

I'd come across that type before, those who assumed that pieces of original artwork were inherently valuable and were stunned, even suspicious, when I told them differently.

'Even if we *were* to take all this to market,' I said, 'then most of it would remain unsold anyway the state it's in. You must see that.'

If Mr Crossharbour still needed proof, then it was there when he moved me into the next room, which contained much the same sort of fare as the others: one or two minor treasures but mostly junk.

I'd said 'collector', but 'hoarder' might have been nearer the mark with Mr Elm. He'd accumulated far more than he had space to display or properly store, and all around the perimeter there were paintings stacked four or five deep.

'How did he come by so much?' I said. He'd had to have made frequent trips out of the valley to acquire all this, and that didn't seem like him somehow. My impression of him, right or wrong, was of a recluse.

'He had dealers come to him,' said Mr Crossharbour. 'And I think he had a tendency to accept pictures in lieu of rent when he let out his rooms.'

'He let them out to painters, you mean?'

'Yes.'

'What, Gwen Galloway and Cecil Lowden actually stayed here? And Isiah Berry? How fascinating.'

'They say that John Nash came too. And Hockney,' Mr Crossharbour said casually. He was, at heart, a quartermaster still, and unimpressed by artistic types.

'You're not serious?' I said, by which I meant that he might have told me beforehand. If, by chance, there was an original by either of them here, then that changed things considerably.

I think he caught some of my horrified astonishment.

'It's only hearsay,' he said.

And if true it was exhilarating, but it broke my heart to think that I might find any work of theirs mouldering away in one of these rooms.

I almost didn't want to carry on looking but I did, of course, and knelt down to pick my way more carefully through the various paintings of the valley leaning against the walls.

'He never kept an inventory, I suppose?' I said.

Mr Crossharbour shook his head. 'Not that I know of.'

'But there must be some record of who stayed.'

'I've not come across it.'

'You have all Mr Elm's paperwork, don't you?'

'Some. Not all. Very little, actually. And what I have is an unholy mess.'

'And there's nothing about his guests?'

'I think it was his guarantee of privacy that enticed them to come,' he said.

Having been through one sheaf of paintings, I started on the next, occasionally pulling out something that looked half-decent and noting the details, but if there really was an unknown Hockney or Nash in the house then it was somewhere else.

'I really ought to come back,' I said.

'I thought you were strapped for time,' Mr Crossharbour replied.

'I'll make time. Believe me.'

'No no,' he said. 'Miss Oswald won't want that.'

'She might, if there's the prospect of finding something of great value.'

'You're thinking of your commission, are you?' he said.

'Not at all.'

From his expression, I took it that he thought me disingenuous.

'Well, as I mentioned, Mr Thomas, it's just a rumour,' he said. 'Miss Oswald has heard it. She's not interested.'

'Rumours always start from somewhere,' I said. 'If we can find anything, anything at all, that tells us who boarded here then it might at least give us grounds to begin a proper appraisal of what's been left to her.'

'Isn't that what you came here to provide, a proper appraisal?'

'I had no idea there'd be so much.'

'Which is why I suggested two o'clock,' said Mr Crossharbour.

Down in the village, the bells were ringing for three. He checked his watch against the claims of the church tower.

'We should press on,' he said. 'The light. It'll go before we know it.'

'All right, fine,' I said. There was no point in arguing any further about it here and now. When I got back to the office, I'd send him the hammer price of what a newly discovered Hockney had gone for the previous year and see if that might persuade him and Miss Oswald to let me return.

'This way, Mr Thomas,' he said, and led me up a set of narrow wooden stairs to an attic studio that smelled pleasantly of linseed oil and old tobacco.

The bare floorboards were covered in little whorls of

166

dried paint, like seashells washed up on a beach. Brushes and palettes sat on a worktable as if they'd been used only that morning to execute the dozens of landscapes hanging on the walls. And by the window at the gable end stood an easel covered in a sheet and a three-legged oak stool with a seat worn smooth and pale.

It was odd that so many painters (and potentially two of great distinction) had come to stay here. I couldn't work out the appeal. Barrowbeck wasn't anything to look at. I wondered if Mr Elm had been an enthusiastic amateur and had invited all these artists to stay so that they could teach him.

'Did he dabble himself?' I said, as I started to work my way around the paintings, which varied in style and size, all of the valley, none of them up to much, nothing exceptional.

'No,' said Mr Crossharbour. 'He couldn't. He had a terrible shake in his hands. A palsy of some kind.'

'He was just a philanthropist of the arts, was he?'

'I'd hardly call him that.'

'Then what was his obsession with people coming to paint the valley?'

Mr Crossharbour mulled over a reply. 'I don't like to use the word *eccentric*,' he said. 'But I can't think of another.'

'Oh?'

'He had quite odd beliefs.'

'About what?'

'Death. His own death, I mean. What was going to happen to him afterwards. That sort of thing.'

'And what was his theory?'

'That he wouldn't really die. That this place would preserve him.'

'The valley?'

'That's right.'

'Preserve him how?'

'I'm afraid it's the peculiarities rather than the particulars that have stayed with me, Mr Thomas,' he said. 'I didn't really understand what he was saying.'

'You knew him, though.'

'I met him a couple of times when I came here to make his will back in March,' said Mr Crossharbour. 'He was dying then, I think.'

'And he was from Barrowbeck, was he?'

'Born and bred. Miss Oswald was from elsewhere, though.'

'She did well to go back there,' I said.

For a moment, I wondered if he might be so loyal to his client as to find my sarcasm offensive, but, no, there was the hint of a dry smile on his lips, good lord.

'That's true enough,' he said. 'I can't imagine that this place does anyone any good.'

For the first time there was something we agreed on.

'Still, she stayed here with him for twenty years,' he went on. 'It wasn't as if it was a flash in the pan.'

'Live-in lovers. It must have been scandalous. What sent her packing in the end?' I said, moving along to another view of the valley, late summer this time, the heather on the fells a gaudy amethyst. Horrible.

'That's not a conversation I've had with Miss Oswald, as I'm sure you can appreciate,' said Mr Crossharbour.

'Of course, but in your opinion, though.'

It clearly didn't sit well with him to talk about her, and he looked around the room before he replied, as though she might be listening.

'From what I can surmise, the relationship was quite . . . turbulent,' he said, taking his time to find the most tactful way of putting it.

'Violent, you mean?'

'Perhaps not physically, but in other ways. He kept her down, I think.'

'Down how?'

'He ridiculed her. Treated her like a child. Reading between the lines of what she's told me, at least. And she owned nothing, of course. Not then, anyway. The house was his.'

'I'm astonished she stayed with him for as long as she did,' I said.

'You and me both.'

'And she just upped and left and that was that?'

'I don't think it was so easy. He had a hold on her. It seems as if there were several aborted attempts before she finally went. He followed her, or tried to, but never found her and there was no contact from then on.'

'How long were they apart?'

'Almost as long as they were together.'

'Then I can see why she'd be surprised about her inheritance.'

'Quite.'

'Thank god they had no children,' I said, moving along to the next painting. 'That's always a complication.'

'How do you know that they didn't?'

'Well, the only reason he must have left all this to her is that there's no one else.'

'No, that isn't the reason,' Mr Crossharbour said.

'What is it then?'

He shifted and coughed, and I got the sense that he was annoyed with himself for having got into a conversation he couldn't bring to an end. I have to admit that I pressed him, all the same.

'Tell me,' I said. I couldn't help but laugh. Why was he being so cagey?

'It's a punishment, Mr Thomas,' he replied, irritated by the fact that I found his reluctance amusing.

'For what?' I said. 'Her leaving him? He knew how to hold a grudge, didn't he? Good god.'

'Indeed.'

Mr Crossharbour closed his eyes in the manner of some-one who was still genuinely baffled by other people.

'He's hung this place around her neck like a millstone,' he continued. 'She doesn't want it. She'd give it all away in a heartbeat if she could.'

'But to call it a *punishment* sounds a bit much,' I said. 'He's *inconvenienced* her, maybe, with all this bureaucracy, but is it so bad for her to have inherited a house?'

'In this case, yes.'

'You've lost me.'

He prevaricated and then with a hand on my elbow, he drew me to the window that looked out over the grounds to the rear of the house and the land that Miss Oswald now owned.

'You see the little copse at the end?' he said.

'Yes?'

'You see the boulder?'

'Yes.'

'That's him.'

'Him?'

'Mr Elm. That's where he's buried.'

I looked again at the lump of limestone sitting between two beech trees, their dropped leaves mounded around the grave.

'Can you do that?' was all I could think of to say.

'There are regulations to follow,' said Mr Crossharbour. 'But it's certainly possible, yes. As you see.'

'And is this what he meant by the place preserving him?'

'I don't know. I suppose it must have been.'

Noticing that I was disturbed, he became defensive.

171

'I was simply acting on the man's wishes,' he said. 'It was a stipulation of his will. As was the request that I dealt with his estate personally – when the time came.'

'Ah,' I said. 'I did wonder how you'd ended up lumbered with all this.'

Mr Crossharbour scratched at some splatter of paint on the window with his thumbnail. He didn't like mess. 'Miss Oswald wanted to use her own solicitor, of course,' he said. 'But there it was in black and white.'

'It had to be you.'

'Precisely. And it galls her to have to pay me, I can tell you, when she thinks that I was in on the plot.'

It sounded like the premise for a bad joke – did you hear the one about the man who buried himself in his own back garden? – and I might have laughed if I'd not been there. As it was, it seemed sick to me. Flogging a pile like this in Barrowbeck was going to be hard enough, but Roderick Elm had known that no one would ever buy a place that had a corpse under the lawn. And so Miss Oswald was stuck with it. Even though she'd left him and hidden herself on the other side of the country, he'd managed to bind her to this cheerless house in the end in the most spiteful way. It might have been her property in name, but he still possessed it in spirit, and would always possess it.

And all of this had been facilitated by Mr Crossharbour.

'I can't imagine that you didn't try and counsel Mr Elm out of it,' I said.

'I did try,' he said. 'But there were no legal impediments. And he was very determined. My hands were tied.'

He took a seat at the worktable, a defeated air about him now.

'I should have just declined his business,' he said.

'He'd only have gone to someone else.'

'Then they'd be feeling just as wretched as I do.'

'At least it wouldn't have been you.'

'But it *was* me,' he said. 'I can't ignore the fact that I helped Roderick Elm do a cruel thing. I'm complicit. Miss Oswald is quite right.'

'Can't he be moved?' I said. 'Reburied, I mean, somewhere more appropriate?'

'A person's posthumous wishes carry a lot of weight, especially when they're set down in a will,' said Mr Crossharbour. 'And I don't think Miss Oswald will have much luck in making a case for an exhumation. Wanting to sell the house won't be enough. I have told her that, but she takes no notice of anything I say. She can be quite belligerent. But justifiably so. I don't blame her.'

Despite playing his part in this ghoulish farce, I did feel sorry for him. He'd been burdened almost as much as Miss Oswald, who, quite understandably, wanted to dispose of Roderick Elm's gifts as quickly as possible. All this was costing her and would continue to cost her. Solicitors weren't exactly cheap. It was no wonder she'd been so keen to try and sell off what she could. She needed the money. And no wonder that Mr Crossharbour had demanded a valuation off me quick sharp.

He felt guilty and he didn't want to see her sliding into debt with him.

'I'd do the work for free if I could,' he said. 'But then that would be too easy a penance, I suppose.'

He rubbed his forehead and let out a deep breath from those flared nostrils of his.

'Why don't you go out and get some fresh air?' I said. 'Let me go through the rest of what's here. At least you can tell her I was thorough.'

He got to his feet. 'I will, thank you.'

'I'll be down in a while.'

'Make it a short while,' he said, consulting his watch again.

He left and when I looked out of the window there was still a little daylight on the ridge of the eastern fells, but down here it was heading towards dusk. Grey and still. Those dogs were still barking somewhere in the village.

Even if I had been able to switch on the wall lamps in the room, I wouldn't have wanted to be there after dark anyway. It sounds childish, but I'd never had such a strong urge to be away from a place before. After only an hour or so I was being made to feel claustrophobic – by the house, certainly, but by the valley itself, and I couldn't help but think of what it might do to a person over time.

I watched Mr Crossharbour go out into the rear garden buttoning up his raincoat. After tying a scarf around his neck, he put his hands behind his back in a parade-ground stance and looked over at Mr Elm's stone.

It was difficult to picture the funeral ceremony. It must have necessitated a JCB. And who had been in attendance? All the artists Mr Elm had befriended? Surely it must have seemed to them, as it did to me, that this was an outlandishly vindictive way of retaliating to Miss Oswald's abandonment of him.

People did store up anger, there was no doubt about that, and perhaps Mr Elm's bitterness had eaten away at him to the extent that this bizarre act felt justified. The man might well have been touched, as Mr Crossharbour had said. Living here would do it. But he'd not lived here alone. Judging by the number of paintings, the house had been continually occupied. If he'd gone mad, he'd done so in company.

To say that he'd been eccentric – as manifestly true as that was – still didn't explain his obsession. It didn't seem to me as though he'd acquired this mass of paintings to simply appreciate them, it was more systematic than that. The only reason anyone would stockpile so much was if they wanted something from them. Or he was trying to find something *in* them, something here in the valley that only an artist might bring out. And perhaps the sheer amount he'd accumulated suggested that he'd never quite seen what he wanted to see and had been forced to keep on looking – snapping up as many old works as he could, bringing in a steady stream of painters in the hope that one might have the vision to show him . . . what? I had no idea.

The last lot of work I needed to assess ran along one side of the room and looked to be by the same artist. There was no name to any of the pieces, but the dates were from earlier that year, from March, in fact, when Mr Crossharbour had come here to make Mr Elm's will.

They were very different to what I'd seen so far. Not realist or impressionist or even abstract, but more like illustrations from a book.

Each one showed the hills of the valley in a two-dimensional cross-section, and inside, under the skin of grass, as it were, there lived amorphous shapes that, painting by painting, mutated into large, mud-coloured creatures – like worms, I suppose – that burrowed out winding tunnels in the earth. And there was a man, naked and bearded and old, being squeezed in a motion of peristalsis along these intestinal passageways.

It was Mr Elm in the afterlife; it had to be, as his journey had evidently begun from the white stone that capped his grave. There it was in the paintings. And the garden too and the house I was standing in.

In the next picture, he was being stretched through a serpentine bend, his legs and arms as thin as rope, his face liquid and mournful. And in the next, with his body now even more elongated and twisted, he continued to be drawn towards the middle of the labyrinth where the creatures – what *were* they? – awaited his arrival.

This wasn't quite the last painting. There was one more under the sheet on the easel. A much larger piece than the others, I found, when I took off the covering.

Here, Mr Elm appeared to have reached a hollow chamber in the centre of the maze, where whatever lived there beneath the earth writhed about him like phantoms. He was stronger and younger now. Clean shaven and athletic looking. Naked, still, but with the buttocks of a Greek Olympian, and his member alarmingly engorged. Here he was virile and rejuvenated. And in a surreal touch, he had been given two pairs of arms and two pairs of legs.

Well, it was a diversion, wasn't it? The painter had just been appeasing and amusing a man in his final days. Perhaps they'd given the old bastard a laugh, these cartoons. Who wouldn't like to see themselves reborn like this? So dynamic. Who wouldn't want to be able to look into the future and see themselves cheating death?

But I noticed that there was another figure in the picture. A woman – that I took to be Miss Oswald – was crossing the lawn with a pickaxe in her hands, ready to prise up the boulder and do what? Drag out the corpse? Well, she would find it gone. She would find only a pile of graveclothes, and a tunnel leading into the hillside.

In the painting, Mr Elm watched her coming and seemed

to be waiting with great excitement for her to discover the empty tomb. His expression was one of glee, I'd say. That feels like the right word, with its connotations of satisfaction and victory.

Yes, he had a gleeful smile. And very red lips. And too many teeth. But it was the way he was so *poised* that unsettled me most. Half crouched and tense with all eight limbs primed, he was about to move at speed, like a spider alerted to the first tremors on its web.

# Sisters

## 2002

They were fascinating old things, the pair of them, thought Joyce. Emaciated Alice in the yellow-tinted glasses looked as though she struggled to see as much as she struggled to talk. Her eyes were wet and cloudy, and she communicated in a sort of rasp that Beatrice, puffy with oedema, had a habit of translating before she'd finished speaking.

'My sister says that she'll tot up the bill after you've eaten,' she explained, as she laid out Joyce's lunch.

They were dressed, as they had been every day since she'd arrived, in matching twinsets and tan leather shoes and dark, matronly tights with identical chiffon scarves around their necks. But Joyce wasn't sure that they actually *were* sisters. Alice was small and scrawny and Beatrice built from more substantial cuts of meat. Siblings could be different but not *so* different.

It was possible that they were stepsisters. Or before they'd run this guest house, they'd been nuns. 'Sisters' in that sense.

179

They both wore dainty crucifixes. But in her mind, they were really long-term lovers and called themselves 'sisters' out of propriety, as women their age might do, especially in a place like Barrowbeck.

'You have remembered that we'll be closing for the winter this afternoon?' said Beatrice, and Joyce nodded.

How could she have forgotten? Beatrice had reminded her at least twice a day that she'd need to vacate her room on Friday.

'There'll be a bus at five,' she said. 'I'd make sure that you're there waiting. It doesn't stop long, does it, Alice?'

Her sister finished off pouring a tall glass of water and ground something out of her throat that sounded like agreement.

'She says it's best to leave early,' explained Beatrice as Alice coughed into her fist.

She was a devoted, unrepentant smoker. Joyce had seen her sitting in the backyard with a cigarette at all hours of the day and night. Behind that flouncy purple neckerchief lay the scar of an operation for throat cancer, she reckoned, hence that voice of hers, like someone scraping a knife over dry toast.

'Five, yes, I'll make sure I'm there,' Joyce said, thanking them both with a smile, although the thought of moving on made her edgy again.

She'd have to go back to Manchester, all her things were there, but she wouldn't stay for long. She couldn't stay.

Somehow, the other residents of the block had found out what she'd done and now it was 'freak' and 'weirdo' all the time.

Beatrice could see that she was disappointed about having to leave and implied that it was out of her hands.

'It's this place, love,' she said, looking around the room with those small blue eyes of hers. 'It's a handful for us nowadays. It always takes us longer than we think to get everything ready.'

They weren't in the best of health, they looked after the house all by themselves, and no doubt the provision of hospitality, on whatever scale, came with a great many duties and nuisances that a guest could never imagine, but she was the only one here, thought Joyce. And hadn't they told her that it had been months since they'd last had visitors? The other seven bedrooms were surely clean and tidy already. If the sisters weren't going to open again until the spring, they'd have months to prepare for the tourist season, such as it was here, so what was the rush to sweep her out?

It wasn't as though they hadn't made her welcome when she'd turned up the week before; they had, but they must have told her half a dozen times that they'd never had anyone wanting to stay in November. People came in the summer, they'd said – fell-walkers, potholers – but no one so late in the year.

It had been a roundabout way of trying to find out why she'd come to Barrowbeck, of course, and feeling obliged to explain herself she'd said that she just wanted to get away from things, which was true. But her vagueness had perhaps only elevated the curiosity or suspicion that people here naturally had for anything or anyone out of the ordinary.

While Joyce ate what they'd served her – an over-generous wedge of meat pie, minted peas, potatoes, bread, a boiled egg, sliced and heavily salted – the sisters hovered about in the small dining room, dusting the Staffordshire knick-knacks on the dresser and keeping a surreptitious eye on her progress.

The two cast-iron radiators made it stiflingly hot and exacerbated Beatrice's rosacea until her cheeks looked like corned beef. The poor woman's clothes were uncomfortably tight, and she sweated enough for her make-up to stain the collar of her blouse. Whereas Alice seemed permanently cold, as if she could have done with another couple of layers on underneath her jacket. It was a mauve number that day, with a matching woollen skirt. A petite version of the ensemble Beatrice wore.

How did they decide what to put on each morning? Who compromised if there was a difference of opinion? Or had they drawn up a rota? Probably so. They had a procedure for everything else. And that was the only reason they were so intent on her departing, thought Joyce. It wasn't anything personal. They *always* closed on this day. It was just the way they did things. The way things had to be.

And so once she'd finished and the sisters swooped in to take away the crockery and cutlery, she smiled to herself. It was quite endearing really, this fastidiousness. And when Beatrice said to her, as if in explanation for the promptness, 'Sorry, love, but we're already behind,' she didn't think of it as a dig at her for wanting lunch and putting them out but as an apology that routine had to take precedence. She hadn't done anything wrong. She wasn't in the way. No, as the sisters went back into the kitchen, bickering in murmurs and croaks, it was clear that whatever had disrupted their schedule was a bone of contention between the two of them and nothing to do with her.

They argued a lot as they went about their daily chores, she'd noticed, but more so in the evening time when they were off duty, as it were, and their discourse switched from professional disputes to personal quarrels. Of course, Joyce had only heard one side of it but the fact that Beatrice's voice so often rose in reproach meant that Alice must have been doing something to upset her. She had the television on too loud (it usually was) or, more likely, she'd drunk too much.

It had been there on her breath now and then. Even in the morning sometimes it had been fresh and strong as if she'd had a quick nip in the kitchen before bringing out Joyce's breakfast. Maybe that was why they were running late. Alice had been at the bottle.

Joyce had a sneaking admiration for the old rascal's sedition, but then the formidable, officious Beatrice was a marvel to behold as well. She was the sensible one, the practical one. While Alice sat in front of the television with a scotch, Beatrice probably made jam and chutney and pickled things in pint jars. She did all the cooking and ironing and put their clothes through the wash, though perhaps not quite often enough.

Joyce had noticed the smell when she'd first met them. Not the flowery, pharmaceutical perfume they applied as liberally as their rouge, but rather the odour it was evidently trying to mask, one that made her think of a zoo.

It was from handling their pets, she assumed. They had three large, loud dogs chained up in the backyard, and a host of pampered, watchful cats that lolled about like Georgian royalty on the stairs. They kept rabbits too, in the scullery, Joyce thought. They bred them, maybe, to supplement their income. Lots of them, from what she could tell. The tall, pig-tailed girl from the village shop who delivered the groceries had brought several large bundles of straw every day, something which seemed to cause considerable friction between the sisters. She'd heard them squabbling about the mess it made, and now and then she'd noticed dust and strands of hay on their clothes, as if they'd been lugging the bales about.

*

As she left the dining room to go and pack, Joyce overheard Beatrice hectoring her sister again. And when she was up in her room, she saw Alice shuffle out dejectedly into the yard below, setting the dogs off, and easing herself onto the bench for a smoke. She crossed her spindly legs, took out her cigarettes and her lighter, and turned her back on a strengthening breeze that tugged at the grey shawl she'd wrapped around her shoulders – the wings of an extraordinary, yellow-eyed moth that had ventured out in the daytime.

Perhaps not a species indigenous to Barrowbeck either. Beatrice was the native here (the house was *her* fiefdom, no question) but it felt as though Alice was an outsider. Carried in on the wind years ago.

That smacked of chance, but was there really such a thing? thought Joyce. Chance was only what the surface of reality looked like from afar. Close up, it was infinitely more complex. She had read somewhere that time was not unfolding moment by moment but existed as a whole and as such every event had already occurred. Therefore, what seemed surprising, unfair or coincidental in life was merely life following the course it was supposed to follow.

From Manchester, she'd taken the first bus that was about to leave Shudehill and found herself in Rochdale. From there, she'd ended up in Huddersfield, then Halifax, then here. But none of that was accidental. Alice would understand what she meant.

She was going to miss her, thought Joyce, looking down at her again. Recalcitrant Alice, smoking herself to death. She had managed to light her cigarette at last and after taking a long drag, she crossed her arms and legs to huddle against the cold. The wind hadn't stopped skirling and blustering all week.

It surged again now in a sudden gust that yanked dry leaves to and fro and dug into the fur of the cat that stalked along the top of the yard wall. A long-legged leopard-like thing that dropped down out of sight onto the footpath that ran between the backs of the houses and the bottom of the fells.

They rose up steeply and immediately in swathes of impenetrable brown bracken. So much so that Joyce had to sit on the window ledge and look up with her cheek pressed against the glass to see any daylight. Otherwise, her view was entirely of decaying ferns and streams of plunging water. Even when she'd gone out during the week and walked around the village for exercise, she'd felt hemmed in.

But in the last day or two she had started to find some comfort in the enclosure. It was peaceful here. Folded away in these hills, she felt safe. No one knocked on her door and ran away. There was no jeering. And the two sisters entranced her. They were like characters in a book that she didn't want to put down.

Not that she was spying on them. Nor was her behaviour – to use the word that had been bandied around in court some months ago – voyeuristic. That hadn't been a particularly helpful description Dee, the therapist assigned to her afterwards, had said. It suggested a potential sexual motive, which didn't apply in her case. Well, of course it didn't. She hadn't felt anything like *that* for the Loftwoods.

No, the work to be done, Dee had informed her, was about appreciating the importance of other people's privacy. They'd discuss the meaning of personal space, she'd said. The difference between friendliness and imposition.

She was a nice enough woman, and eager to help, but she'd conducted those weekly sessions as if she was speaking to a child. There'd been no choice about attending them either. The magistrate had made it clear that – along with the restraining order – they were an alternative to a stretch inside. That had been an option open to him, he'd said. Trespass and harassment were serious offences.

'Mrs Loftwood terminated your employment and the next day found you in her house with a stolen key,' he'd said. 'That was a criminal act, Miss Fallon. Make no mistake.'

But she had no previous convictions, she'd never set foot in a courtroom before. She'd not denied what she'd done or made a fuss over her arrest. And with that in her favour, the magistrate had concluded – in a tone of munificence she was most certainly meant to detect and respect – that he believed she would be more likely to understand the effects of her conduct through a course of psychiatric treatment than a custodial sentence.

And so she'd been sent to Dee, gentle, patient Dee, whose endless questions were, in a way, worse than being judged and reprimanded. A far more duplicitous method of instilling the remorse they thought she ought to have.

'How did you feel, Joyce, when Mrs Loftwood told you to leave?' she'd asked.

'What thoughts were you having before you went back to her house?'

'Can you appreciate why your actions caused her and her son distress?'

'Was there something you specifically wanted from them?'

To learn, to *see*, Joyce had told her, and then explained – rather well, she thought – that life couldn't be lived entirely from one perspective, that one's own subjective understanding wasn't ever enough. You thought you knew what love was, say, but then you saw how it was between other people, like the Loftwoods, and you realised that your grasp of it had always been so narrow and shallow. And that was the point. Without close observation of other people, how could you ever hope to appreciate all the subtle nuances of emotion? And wasn't the purpose of being here, as a sentient being, to experience every intricacy of human feeling? To exist *at all* was such a miracle, such a fleeting opportunity to accrue knowledge. She couldn't waste it. She didn't want to get to the end and feel as though she'd only ever floated on the surface of life. That seemed a worse offence than the ones she'd been accused of in court. Squandering a gift like that, she'd hate herself.

Dee had jotted it all down and hadn't disagreed with the philosophy of living life to the full, only that there were less invasive ways of going about it. The type of intimacy Joyce wanted had to be consented to, she'd said. It couldn't be assumed. It had to be mutual too. Had she had any such relationships in the past? A long-term boyfriend or girlfriend?

No.

No, she'd need a better understanding of the things that closeness would demand of her first, she'd said. It seemed to her imprudent to go headlong into something as serious as a – she'd searched for the right word – a *coupling*, without being fully prepared.

'But it's fine to work things out with someone else as you go along,' Dee had assured her. 'Most people do. It's perfectly normal. No one's expecting you to know everything before-hand. Do you feel as though you ought to?'

A little confused by the question, the answer being so obvious, Joyce had said, 'Well, yes, of course,' and Dee seemed pleased, if not a little surprised, that she'd been given a straightforward reply.

Now she could say what was wrong. The diagnosis presented itself. Joyce was a perfectionist. It was, these days, a recognised psychological condition. One that might be alleviated by setting achievable life goals or developing strategies to cope with perceptions of failure. Those were the kinds of things they worked through in the eight one-hour meetings stipulated by the court.

It wasn't about perfectionism. Dee had missed the point completely. But Joyce hadn't put up any resistance. That would have only caused problems. It was better that she simply got through the sessions, presented herself as enlightened at the end, proved that she was no further threat to society, and slipped out of sight.

She'd treated the exercises Dee had given her just as she'd treated lessons at school on electromagnetism and Boyle's Law – as information that needed to be retained and regurgitated in order to pass a test, but nothing more, nothing to do with *life*.

So when Dee had asked her how it felt to have been caught in the Loftwoods' home, she'd given the required answer of 'ashamed, guilty', while thinking that 'careless' was actually more accurate.

It had all ended just as she felt as though she was coming into the presence of a kind of love she'd never seen before. It was the same here with the sisters. At the very point at which she was being forced to leave, she was on the verge of understanding something essential.

Beatrice came out to the yard rubbing her arms against the cold, and after exchanging some gentler words with Alice, she took her head and held it to her prow of a bosom. Yes, they had their differences, Alice drank and Beatrice was a scold, but it was only ever trivial stuff and it didn't come close to doing any serious damage to their affection for one another. They always reverted to kindness like this.

And that was all anyone could hope for, wasn't it? To be with someone who, no matter what you said to them or did to them, was never fundamentally changed by it. That they would be the same person at heart that they'd been yesterday and would be tomorrow.

It was devotion, thought Joyce. That was what Beatrice and Alice could teach her. Calling themselves sisters, dressing the same way, sticking it out in this house together year after year, that was dedication you didn't often see.

It was being here in Barrowbeck that made it possible. Context mattered. She'd come to learn that the depth to which feelings ran was entirely dependent on situation.

Would Melanie Loftwood have loved her little boy, Sean, if he'd been like any other child? Wasn't it his unfortunate situation that enabled him and his mother to know love so profoundly?

And wasn't it the fact that Barrowbeck was so remote and quiet, and the winters no doubt long and grim, that compelled Beatrice and Alice to pull together, regardless of how often they quarrelled? Well, naturally. In the end, the happiness of one was the happiness of the other. The sisters knew that, and Joyce had seen such sweet little acts of reciprocal attentiveness between them when she'd happened to pass their private lounge, the door of which was always open a touch to let the cats in and out.

She'd watched Beatrice administering Alice's eye drops, giving her a kiss on the nose after each one and dabbing away the dribbles from her cheeks. The next night, it had been Alice's turn to play nurse and she'd rubbed a bright pink cream into Beatrice's ham of a foreleg while they watched a documentary on dormice. The following evening, Joyce had glanced in to see Beatrice feeding Alice morsels of fruit cake – their treat for 'all that heavy lifting', she'd heard her say – and Alice brushing straw out of Beatrice's dry grey hair, which, unwrapped from its workaday bun, hung down past her shoulders.

And presumably there were more intimate pleasures they bestowed upon each other in the bedroom they shared. A room that Joyce had only glimpsed a few times when one or other of them had happened to come out. Matching mahogany wardrobes. Twin beds, both neatly made. Liver-coloured velvet curtains tied back. The nets at the windows ruched like items of elegant antique lingerie. A large wooden clock on the wall with *Tempus Fugit* imprinted in gold leaf around the circumference of the face.

That was Beatrice through and through. Must get on. Can't stop. What's next?

Below in the yard, she looked at her watch, a silver bangle sunk into the podge of her wrist, showed Alice the time, opened the door onto the back pathway, and then the two of them began to clap loudly.

Within a few seconds, the more audacious cats that went out hunting in the undergrowth appeared, slinking around Beatrice's ankles and padding into the house. Alice counted each one with a nod of the head as they passed, and knowing exactly how many more were still to come, the sisters kept on mustering until those that had been even further afield arrived. The last was a large Siamese, which Beatrice scooped up by the belly and held to her chest as she locked the gate – not only with a key but with an iron bolt.

They'd never called the cats back in before. Yes, it looked as if it was going to rain, but then it had been raining on and off for days and that hadn't bothered them. Perhaps since the sisters holed themselves up for the winter, they kept their cats indoors too and they had to be content with roaming the house rather than the village.

After helping Alice to her feet with her free hand, Beatrice led her inside, friends once more, leaving the dogs barking for the same attention that the cats had received, or to be fed, or just out of habit. They went on all day like this sometimes. And at night, if Alice went outside for a cigarette, she'd set them off again and Beatrice had to get up and shout them into submission.

It couldn't help that they had so many animals to look after as well as the house. And if the place was getting the better of them, as Beatrice had claimed, then what might they say to some hired help?

They wouldn't have to pay her anything, thought Joyce. It was clear enough that they didn't have the money to take on staff if they had to breed rabbits to make ends meet. She'd be happy with just bed and board.

If they wanted credentials, she could say that she'd spent her life in the service of others. She'd been a live-in carer, a cleaner, an enthusiastic Rotarian, a nurse.

She'd moved around more often than most people and so she was a dab hand at DIY too. It was often just a case of improving or repairing the little things. That made all the difference to a place sometimes. She could get to all the jobs that Beatrice and Alice had been putting off for years. Sand down and repaint the banisters. Put up some new wallpaper. Tighten the hinges on the wardrobes. Clean the black mould from corners that were too difficult for the sisters to reach.

She'd put the idea to them when she went downstairs to pay the bill, she thought. They'd no doubt decline at first. They had their pride. They had each other. And that had always been enough. Why would they think otherwise after so long? They would need a little time to weigh up the benefits of having a third party in the house.

So what if she were to accidentally miss the bus? she thought. The sisters would have to put her up for at least one more night. They wouldn't leave her out on the street.

Not when there wasn't anywhere else in the village she could stay.

That wouldn't make her a dishonest person, as the magistrate had so resolutely concluded. She hadn't any malice in her. She wouldn't be deceiving Alice and Beatrice for some selfish gain but giving them time to consider her proposition. There was nothing wrong with that.

She'd bided her time with the Loftwoods. She must have watched them from her living-room window for at least a month before she initiated any kind of conversation. She'd felt quite sorry for little Sean, always the last child to be collected at the end of the day, waiting in the empty playground with his teacher. But it wasn't out of any kind of neglect. His mother couldn't have been any more apologetic when she arrived. Joyce could tell from her gestures that she was mortified at being late, not only because she'd kept the teacher hanging on, but because it was time that she could have spent with Sean. The way she held him, the way he held her in reply, it was as though they'd been apart for months not hours. And walking back to the car, she would shower him with far more affection than other parents showed their children. She didn't just love the boy; she was *in* love with him. There was a difference. She had for him a kind of veneration.

In order to see the two of them at closer quarters, Joyce had started to walk past the school entrance at around four fifteen, four twenty, which was when Sean's mother usually turned up. She looked to be in her mid-thirties, Joyce had guessed, with blonde bobbed hair and the demeanour of someone trying hard to keep things together. She smiled for the boy's sake.

Under her open cagoule she wore a royal blue polyester skirt suit with a badge that said MELANIE LOFTWOOD: CASHIER. The outfit was, quite noticeably, a size too large for her, as if she'd thinned out quickly and recently. Sean, too, tended to look rather lost inside his uniform. His shorts hung below his knees and the cuffs of his jumper had been rolled back several times. He looked a dainty, easily breakable thing. And he was shy too. He wouldn't make eye contact with anyone other than his mother. When Joyce had exchanged a smile with Melanie, he'd stared down at the pavement. And once it had become customary for them to cross paths, and they'd started giving one another a mutual 'hello', he would at least glance up but with an anxious sort of expression and cling tighter to his mother's arm.

But then one afternoon, the wind plucked a painting out of his hand and Joyce rescued it from the gutter, giving her the perfect excuse to speak to them.

The boy held the returned picture to his chest with the possessiveness of a child half his age, still mistrustful of Joyce despite her kindness. Yet he began to thaw a little when she praised his skill. They all looked so happy, she said of the three people he'd painted. All were grinning in the slightly unhinged way common in children's artwork.

'Who's this then?' she said.

'Me and Mummy. And Daddy,' Sean replied.

Melanie gave him a smile and cupped his cheek.

'He works away,' she said to Joyce.

'Ah. I see. Here, let me.'

Joyce held the car open so that Melanie could strap Sean into his car seat. As she checked the belt was tight, she looked through the rear windscreen at the line of standing traffic and seemed anxious.

'Have you far to go?' Joyce asked.

'Tonight? Beech Park,' Melanie said.

The children's hospital.


Joyce hadn't brought it up in conversation when she saw them next. That *would* have been intrusive. And wasteful. It was far better that the disclosure about what was wrong with Sean came from Melanie herself, because then it would indicate that she trusted her. But trust had to be earned and so if she could cultivate a rapport with Sean, she'd thought, then perhaps Melanie would feel more comfortable about 'opening up' as the phrase went.

To that end, she made a point of speaking to the boy first whenever she met the Loftwoods on the street, squatting down to be on his level, asking him what he'd been doing at school, who his friends were, if he liked his teacher, the usual things. Gradually, he began to answer at length, and she'd pick up on certain details with great excitement.

In response, he began to bring her gifts. Things he'd made in class. A collage of autumn leaves. A model of a bear. A picture of her. All of which she praised as if it had been the work of a great master. Children liked that sort of thing.

Occasionally, there were more family portraits. Mummy, Daddy and Sean at the seaside. Mummy, Daddy and Sean at the zoo. But they had to have been drawn from memories or wishes, as there didn't appear to be a Mr Loftwood around at all. Still, Melanie was so adamant that he was 'stuck abroad' or 'coming home soon' that it seemed as though she wasn't only trying to comfort Sean but persuade herself that it was true. It was so delicate an illusion that Joyce hadn't attempted to tease out any of the details for fear of upsetting her. And so all she'd known of Mr Loftwood was a face in poster paint: big and bearded with a very red mouth.

'He looks kind,' she'd said.

'He is kind,' Sean replied.

'He looks like a bear.'

'He is a bear.'

'Is he strong?'

'Very strong.'

'Could he lift up a car?'

'A bus.'

'How about an aeroplane?'

'How about *two* aeroplanes.'

Children instinctively understood that there were no limits to what might be accomplished.

There developed such an easy-going relationship between her and Sean whenever they met that Melanie began to think her a professional.

'Are you a teacher?' she said one day.

'A childminder,' Joyce replied.

It hadn't been a lie as such. She had some experience. She'd looked after her nephew all the time, in the days when her sister had still been talking to her.

'But you had no official qualifications, Miss Fallon?' the magistrate had asked her, in one of his derisive rhetorical questions.

Nothing formal, no. But if that had been important then Melanie would have asked for a certificate. And, as Joyce had attested in court, she hadn't pushed anyone into anything. It had been Melanie's decision. The magistrate couldn't argue with that. When he'd suggested that Joyce had really been using the boy to insinuate herself into the family – for whatever reason – it was only speculation.

His suspicions had apparently arisen due to the absence of a proper contract. But there'd been no need for one, Joyce had pointed out. Her employment had been on a purely ad-hoc basis. She'd simply offered herself as a service for Melanie to call upon at short notice if she knew she was going to struggle to get away from work on time.

And so perhaps once a week, twice if she was lucky, she'd pick up Sean from school, walk him back to his house, make him his tea, help with his homework, sometimes put him to bed if Melanie was running very late. Though that didn't happen often. She wanted to spend every second she could with him.

The cancer in his blood had been flushed out a year before and although he was in remission there was a strong chance that it would return. There was some history in the family that apparently upped the percentages. The men on his father's side were riddled with weak immune systems. And whenever Sean was ill, Melanie understandably assumed the worst.

But, for Joyce, those had been the best times – when Sean was off school and she'd stayed with him at home, dosing him with painkillers, checking his temperature, feeding him soup, watching him sleep.

To see him unwell like that was upsetting, of course, but these coughs and colds only pulled him and Melanie closer. The way she sat on his bed and held him when she got home from work, it was beautiful, like a pietà. She adored Sean in the proper sense of the word. In the sense that everything he said and did, every word and gesture, was sacred. And all this when the boy had nothing more than a sore throat or a phlegmy chest. Imagine the love that would bloom when he became really ill, Joyce had thought; when he was diagnosed with leukaemia again. It was inevitable that he would be. Cancer was determined to get its claws into him. She wanted to be there when that happened.

But it had all turned sour long before then. It was her own fault, really. She ought to have been more discreet.

'There were some thirty or forty recordings on your dictaphone, Miss Fallon,' the magistrate had said. 'Each one an abuse of trust. It can't have come as any surprise that Mrs Loftwood sacked you on the spot when she discovered them. What cause you had to violate her privacy so egregiously, I can't imagine.'

It was only so that she'd have some record of Sean and Melanie's conversations, not for anything lurid or sinister as the magistrate had implied. It had been serious research for a scientific analysis of human interaction.

'But can you see how it might have looked to Mrs Loftwood?' Dee had put to her in one of their meetings after the hearing. 'From her reaction, you must have known that what you'd done was wrong.'

Melanie had been confused about her motivations, maybe. And Joyce had freely admitted that to be a failing on her part. She'd not been able to explain herself well enough to make Melanie see that she was paying her and Sean a huge compliment. That they were so valuable. They had so much to teach her.

'Still, she told you to go,' Dee said.

'Yes.'

'And then you went back the next day. You hid in the spare room?'

Well, yes. She had. Though 'hid' made her sound shifty.

'I waited for them,' she said.

'All right, you waited. But for what reason, Joyce?' Dee had asked, in that calm and unprejudiced manner of hers. 'All this scrutiny of other people, what are you actually looking for?'

'The purest expression,' she'd replied.

'Of what?'

Of everything.

Love, guilt, grief, anger, desire, dedication, whatever.

Just to witness a single moment in which such things were complete and unadulterated. That would be something, wouldn't it?

At that, Dee had put down her pen and closed her notebook. 'But does that actually feel possible to you, Joyce? Do these futures you imagine seem real?'

Yes, they did. Without a doubt. They had to be.

Dusk came, and it started to rain in a loud, heavy assault that set the brown ferns nodding on the fellside. The deluge seemed to spur the sisters into a redoubled industriousness downstairs. One of them went around closing doors. The other was at work in the kitchen putting away a great many saucepans. Perhaps she ought to go and offer to help, thought Joyce, and sow the seeds of her proposal now.

She packed her things – it didn't take long – and at a quarter to five went down the stairs, almost falling over the listless, preening cats, the population of which had tripled since they'd all been brought back indoors.

An envelope sat on the reception desk with *Miss Fallon* written on it. Inside was the bill. Next to nothing for a week's stay.

She left the money and called out 'Ladies?' and waited for one or other of the sisters to emerge. But it sounded as if they were too busy to hear her. Beatrice was backbiting at Alice again, snapping at her over the sound of brush-strokes and the grate of a shovel on a stone floor.

They'd be too distracted to listen to her at the moment, thought Joyce. They'd politely dismiss the offer of assistance and that would be that.

No, she'd leave as she'd been asked to do, and then come back with a tale about the bus setting off early and see if they might put her up for one more night, and so on. Perhaps later in the evening, when they'd done what they needed to do and were sitting in their lounge she might knock and ask if she could talk to them.

After putting on her coat and picking up her case she went out through the front door and stood for a moment under the lintel to unfurl her umbrella. The road was already awash. The streetlamps a dull orange. The reek of wet soil and wet soot in the wind. A dismal evening. Good. It meant that no one was likely to be about. No one to notice that she was taking a longer route to the bus stop than necessary. No one there to give her unhelpfully helpful directions or to go ahead on her behalf waving at the bus driver to hold on.

Stepping over the mulched leaves in the gutter, she crossed the street as the downpour intensified. She could barely see the tops of the fells now for the low cloud. It was no doubt like this here every day in the wintertime. No wonder that the sisters wanted to shut themselves inside.

She'd enjoy the contentment of that, she thought. The stuffy heat of those Victorian radiators. The permanent smell of something baking in the kitchen. The glow of the television in the evenings. Sitting on the settee with the sisters. A witness to their arguments, and the tender reconciliations that came afterwards.

Or she could go back to the flat in Longsight. And the looks. And the insults. And the late-night fists on the door.

She knew that if she was being serious about her studies, she couldn't discriminate between the emotional states she chose to examine. Resentment was as much a part of human experience as anything else and in itself was just as fascinating as love. But she was here now, and it was a poor scholar whose attention skipped from one thing to another. Only a focused enquiry produced results of any meaning. The varieties and gradations of hostility she'd come back to another time. It followed her around doggedly enough. It wasn't as if it was going to go away.

*

Passing the post office and the doctor's surgery, both closed up for the day, she came to the green in time to see the bus departing before it should have done. By the church clock it was still a few minutes to five. The driver wasn't after hanging about, just as the sisters had warned. But this was the proof that none of this was accidental, thought Joyce. Just as Alice had been blown into Barrowbeck to be with Beatrice, so she was meant to stay too.

The bus passed the war memorial and the church and then disappeared down the road that led out of the village. Now she could say quite truthfully that it hadn't been her fault that she'd missed it. The sisters would feel nothing but sorry that she'd gone out in such awful weather for no reason. Still, to make sure that they took sufficient pity on her, she folded down her umbrella and walked a circuit of the green in the rain, waiting for the bells to ring out the hour before going back to the guest house.

The front door was locked but she still had the key that Beatrice had given her when she'd first checked in. Inside, the hallway was in darkness. Presuming that their last guest had gone, the sisters must have retired to their private rooms.

Joyce turned on the lights and went to the foot of the stairs, wanting to get her apology in straight away so that it seemed as genuine as possible. 'It's just me, ladies,' she said. 'The bus went early. I'm sorry.'

She listened but got no reply. Was it odd that the cats had all disappeared? Perhaps not, the cats often did vanish like smoke. But then even the dogs out in the yard made no noise. There was a chilliness in the hallway too, and when she put her hand to one of the radiators it felt tepid. Beatrice surely didn't turn them off to save money. She didn't expect sickly, wraithlike Alice to see out the winter in a cold house.

Her hair dripping, Joyce went along the hallway past the door to the kitchen and the dining room and then came to the short flight of steps that led down to the scullery. Assuming the room would be wall to wall with rabbit hutches, apprehensive about startling the poor things when she pulled the cord for the strip-light, she found only stacks of boxes, cans and bottles. There was a scattering of straw, but the bales had all gone. What the sisters had done with them, what they'd needed so many *for*, she couldn't work out.

Back up in the hallway, she heard one of the dogs pining in the room at the very end, the door of which had a metal sign reading NO GUESTS.

'Ladies?' Joyce said, knocking lightly. 'Are you in there?'

Getting no response she turned the handle, bracing herself for the dogs to come out barking and snapping. But there was no movement at all. The only thing that met her was the smell that had come off the sisters whenever she'd been close up to them. It was strong in here, though not quite so unpleasant now, more a haybarn sweetness.

'I'm sorry, I don't mean to intrude, but the bus left before I could catch it, and I didn't know where else to go,' said Joyce, barely able to get inside as all the furniture had been pushed to the edges of the room. She had to twist and sidle in between the arm of a chintzy, cat-clawed sofa and the corner of a pinewood table.

There, she found the clothes the sisters had been wearing that day neatly folded into two piles, their shoes paired, the shoes of a giant and a doll.

'Beatrice? Alice?'

She tried to summon them by name, but got no answer, and worked her way in, cracking her shin on a rocking chair. She swore, groped in the shadows, found the stem of a floor lamp, bent down to locate the switch, fiddled with the button until the bulb came on, and then standing again and turning she saw it.

A huge mound of straw, tightly wound into a nest. In the cooling air, it steamed ever so slightly.

Pulling over a chair to stand on, Joyce looked down inside. Under a thin layer of thatch she saw the sisters in matching white nightgowns curled up with their cats and dogs. They were all asleep already, deaf to the rain on the windows, their bellies and chests rising and falling. The dog that she'd heard whine a few moments before had only been dreaming, and it settled its head on the neck of the mongrel-looking thing lying beside it.

The sisters too lay spooned into one another with their

legs drawn up, Beatrice curved around Alice's back with a hand on her thigh.

How wonderful it must be, thought Joyce, for them to bed down together like this and miss the winter. To wake up when it was over and have another year there waiting like a blank page had to be the most precious of gifts. But if she was meant to be here, then she was meant to experience this perfect intimacy for herself. The sisters had left room for her. She wouldn't wake them if she were to climb in too.

# A Celestial Event

## 2010

I got to Bill's early and let myself in, finding the house loud with music that, given the circumstances, seemed far too bright and joyful. After closing the front door, I called for him and looked in on the empty living room, where he had some jazz number going on the record player, and then called again and got no answer. And just for a moment I thought . . . Well, they say that when one goes, the other sometimes follows from a broken heart.

But when I went into the kitchen, I could see him through the window setting up his telescope in the backyard.

'I won't be a moment, Frank,' he said through the glass, when he noticed I was there. 'Help yourself to a drink.'

He seemed as breezy as ever, as if nothing had happened at all and Gracie was about to descend the stairs, genial and smiling, as if it was any other Society night. The pretence might have comforted him, but this striving for ordinariness only upset me all the more.

The kitchen wasn't spotless. If it had been, it might have indicated that he was skipping meals. Nor were there towers of dirty plates to suggest that he'd stopped caring about the little things that, he liked to say to Gracie, separated them from barbarism. Nothing was amiss. He wasn't just surviving. Quite the reverse. He'd obviously tried to make the place as welcoming as it always had been. As well as the music, he'd put up a small, artificial Christmas tree by the back door and set the lights so that they blinked in randomised patches of colour. On the table sat a decanter of sherry and five lead crystal glasses. And in a modest imitation of the spreads Gracie would lay on when it was her and Bill's turn to host a Society meeting, he'd turned out an ingot of duck pâté onto a plate and arranged some bread rolls in a basket along with the waxes of cheese that didn't get opened at the wake.

'All set,' he said, as he came into the kitchen rubbing some warmth back into his hands. 'I just need to give the lens a clean.'

I asked him how he'd been.

'Me? Oh, fine fine,' he said, as though he was only recovering from a cold.

'I'd have come and seen you,' I said. 'But I thought you'd want some time to yourself.'

We'd all thought that – me, Virginia and Duncan. It had been a genuine assumption genuinely made. But when Bill had telephoned earlier that day to ask me over, I felt terrible about having kept my distance since the funeral. It must have seemed as if I was ignoring him.

You can only go on what you know, I suppose, and quite wrongly I'd thought that Bill would be feeling just as I did when my Katherine went. The last thing I'd wanted to do then was socialise. In fact, I'd not been able to face seeing anyone for weeks. But everyone was different, of course, and Bill's reaction couldn't have been more opposite to mine.

It's after the funeral that bereavement truly begins. Prior to that, the numbness of the loss and the distraction of all the bureaucracy required to tie up a life acts as an anaesthetic. You go through the motions, as they say. It was like that for me with Katherine. Our Sadie and Amanda stayed on for a few days, but they had lives of their own, jobs to go back to, and once they'd left for Manchester and Leeds and I was in the house alone, the pain started to do its worst. I certainly hadn't been able to smile like Bill. I was hardly placid. In fact, I'm not sure I'd ever felt so much anger in me before. It was the kind of anger a child might feel at having something taken away from them for no reason. An indignation at the rank unfairness. Why *couldn't* I have her back? It wasn't much to ask. She was only one person out of billions. What difference would it make to undo her death?

Such thoughts plague you at a time like that. And other thoughts. Worse thoughts. But not for Bill, it seemed.

As he rooted about in the cupboards above the sink, he whistled along cheerily to the music from the other room. And when he found what he was looking for, a square of chamois leather, and noticed me staring at him, he said, all hale and hearty, 'Come on Frank, lad, pour the drinks. They'll be here soon.'

He patted my shoulder and went back out to see to his telescope. His bowtie was crooked, I noticed; its lopsidedness the only crack in this facade of normality he was trying so hard to sustain. It was a small detail but one which proved unequivocally that Gracie was gone.

Had she been there she'd have smartened him up straight away and attended to that yellow dicky bow as though she was putting the finishing touches to a ribbon on a present. Then she'd have thumbed something off his chin, held his face like a chalice and brought his head down from its great height to kiss his brow.

All that love. He'd been so unexpectedly blessed.

He'd come close to getting married a couple of times in his younger years, Bill, but for one reason or another – mostly the cold feet of the other party – it hadn't ever quite worked out for him and by the age of sixty-nine he'd long-since resigned himself to bachelorhood. But then, by chance, he'd met Gracie when she came with her choir to sing Nine Lessons and Carols at Saint Gabriel's.

She'd been given the responsibility of opening 'Once in Royal David's City', and on the very first note Bill had turned in his pew to look.

They hit it off, swapped phone numbers, he started driving over to see her, she came to the valley, and they were married a few months later before the end of March. Well, what was the point of hanging around at their age? Bill said, as if he thought we'd disapprove of him getting wed so quickly. But none of us had any reservations about that. He was quite right. On the threshold of our seventies, we couldn't pass up opportunities of any kind, especially in Barrowbeck, where life – or our equivalent of it – revolved in a very small circle.

No, I was pleased for Bill. The only sticking point was whether he might sell up and move away to live with Gracie and, selfishly, I didn't want him to leave. Or rather, it was more that I wanted Gracie to stay. By then, I was as hooked on her as Bill was.

She was one of those people lucky enough to have grown old elegantly, meaning that time had practised upon her gently and the changes it had wrought were inoffensive. No unsightly warts, boils, glaucoma, bristly chin, reptilian wattle, spider veins or tooth decay for her, but a liveliness in her eyes, and cheekbones that had kept their shape. And although her hair was cut short, it was still thick and more sandy than grey.

I wasn't only attracted to the way she looked. I give the description to make the point that she'd stayed youthful because of how she was in herself. She'd somehow managed to ward off the cynicism that hardens like a corn in old age and retained a passionate fascination for other people's lives that, I must admit, seemed like an affectation when I first met her. But then what a pleasant surprise it had been to realise it was entirely sincere.

When you were with her it felt as if you were in one continual embrace that, despite her seeming younger, was somehow maternal. The others in our circle of friends felt exactly the same way. Virginia would cry into her shoulder about her son, Terry, who was inside again, and Duncan confessed to being at the end of his tether with the demands of his bedridden mother. And Gracie got things out of me, about Katherine particularly, that I'd not shared with anyone before. But I never felt as though she was prying. She only ever asked anything in order to be able to offer some words of comfort or encouragement. And that was what made her company so addictive. I mean, how often do you find someone who's that concerned about your happiness?

Bill called to me from outside. 'The sherry, Frank,' he said, and I unstopped the decanter.

We always had a glass of sherry before our, what would you call them? Classes? Soirées?

They were Gracie's idea, these get-togethers. It was she who suggested we try and teach one another something new.

There was always something more to learn, she said. It didn't matter how old we were.

Why we'd never thought of it before, I don't know. It seemed such an obvious thing to do, when at our age we knew full well how easy it was to languish in habit and apathy. But Gracie was one of those perceptive types who could just *see* so clearly what other people needed. It was why Bill fell for her. Why we all fell for her. It's not an over-statement to say that when she moved here, she woke us up. Her interest in us roused a confidence that we didn't know we had, or we'd lost somewhere down the line.

We'd never taken our private hobbies all that seriously before. I think we'd probably been a touch self-conscious about how much they meant to us if I'm honest. We'd certainly never considered ourselves expert enough to impart what we knew to other people. But Gracie could dismiss any self-doubt with just a look or a touch or a wave of her hand. We ought not to hide our lights under bushels, she said.

She made us feel almost earnest. A word that I hadn't applied to myself for a long time, not since my thirties when I'd worn a red rosette and knocked on doors to get the vote out. We'd never have come up with anything as grandiose as the 'Barrowbeck Cultural Society' by ourselves, but when Gracie named us so it seemed just right.

Every Friday night at seven o'clock we'd meet at some-one's house. We'd eat together, have a glass or two of sherry and begin the lesson. Virginia would pick out something from her collection of classical records and talk us through the *Goldberg Variations* or one of Beethoven's late sonatas (listen to me, an aficionado now) or a Mahler symphony or something more challenging by Britten. We'd never realised before how knowledgeable she was about music. Nor, I suspect, had anyone known how much I revered Robert Frost until I began to hold those poetry readings in my front room. And who'd have thought that Duncan was so skilled with a pencil? Or that he'd get us drawing with only a little embarrassment at our efforts?

We'd take it in turns to play host and enjoyed the routine, but Bill's session was always something of a moveable feast, one that was dictated by the schedule of the heavens and the whim of the weather.

The two things being favourable that night, it was the reason he'd insisted on us coming over. The December sky was crisp and clear and, according to Bill, there was to be a wonderful celestial event.

The doorbell rang and he came in from the yard to answer it with a bemused look on his face. It was always open house on Society evenings. No one ever stood on ceremony. But things were not as they were. Everything had to be recalibrated now. As Bill's friends, it was our responsibility to help him do so. And I wondered if by just walking in as usual I'd clumsily endorsed his delusion that everything was fine.

They'd come over together, Duncan and Virginia, and followed Bill into the kitchen from the hallway making the same kind of small talk I'd made, no doubt thinking the same thoughts about the music and the Christmas tree and noticing, as I had, that there were one too many glasses on the table.

As they chatted about the weather – Duncan anxiously scratching at his beard, Virginia thumbing the wooden beads around her neck like a rosary – they sent furtive glances my way. What was Bill doing? Did he honestly want to give us an astronomy lesson *tonight*? It had only been a couple of days. Was he really well enough to be entertaining us?

Those were the questions we all wanted to ask him straight out, but we took the winding backroad of discretion instead.

'You really didn't need to go to so much effort, Bill,' said Virginia, appraising the display of cheeses.

I agreed and said, 'We'd have been all right with just a drink, you know.'

'Aye, we weren't expecting all this,' Duncan added.

'It was no bother,' said Bill. 'I couldn't let you go hungry. I'll get you a knife. Frank's being mother.'

I handed Virginia a sherry. Then gave one to Duncan and Bill before pouring my own.

'You missed one,' said Bill, nodding at the spare glass on the table.

I filled it halfway and expected him to drink to Gracie, but he put it to one side and raised a toast to something completely different.

'Here's to it staying clear,' he said. 'They say it might snow later.'

We sipped and looked at one another, and to fill the awkward moment Virginia said, 'You know, we're all intrigued, Bill, about what it is you're going to show us.'

'I've been watching it for the last two nights now,' he said.

Since the funeral then.

'And? Go on,' said Virginia, eyeing his dishevelled bowtie, itching to straighten it as much as I was.

He smiled at her. 'You don't want me to spoil the surprise, do you?'

'Well, I suppose not, no, but . . .'

'It's just the most beautiful thing,' he interrupted her. 'You wait. It won't be long now.'

He checked his watch, knocked back his sherry, and went out into the yard again, his hands on his hips as he gazed up into the sky.

With him gone, Virginia turned to me, and said, 'What the hell is all this, Frank?'

'I think he just wants some company,' I replied.

'I wouldn't have minded that,' she said. 'But he's acting as if nothing's wrong. Is he trying to prove something?'

Duncan helped himself to another drink. 'Would you rather he was in tears, Gin?'

'Of course not,' she said. 'But it's not healthy for him to be like this. Do you think we ought to get someone to come and see him?'

'What, a head doctor?' said Duncan. 'The poor bastard.'

'Look, there's no right way to be at a time like this,' I said. 'At least he seems happy.'

'It's not real, though, is it, Frank?' said Virginia. 'How can it be?'

It *was* an act. Of course it was. I knew that. It was just the effect of shock. It would pass. And the truth would eventually work its way in. He'd have to try and find some consolation somewhere, just as I'd had to do after Katherine. But all that would happen in its own time. There was nothing we could do to make him better any quicker. We couldn't hope to steer him into rationality. All we could do was accompany him through the stages of his grief, however strange they were.

Looking at the surplus glass of sherry, Virginia said, 'I still don't understand how she could have gone through with it. She must have known what it would do to him.'

She'd said the same thing over and over since it had happened, hoping perhaps that if she did so often enough someone at some point might be able to tell her why Gracie's desire to end her suffering (whatever that had been and wherever it had come from) could have outweighed her urge to protect Bill from harm as predictably brutal as this.

A note might have shed some light on it all, but she'd left nothing.

'She couldn't have thought much of us, could she?' said Virginia, sitting down at the table.

'What do you mean?' Duncan asked.

'Weren't we supposed to be her friends? Why didn't she say anything to us?'

'She hadn't known us a year,' Duncan replied. 'Perhaps she didn't feel as if she could.'

'But she didn't even say anything to her own husband,' said Virginia.

'Well, who knows what's going on in other people's heads,' Duncan said. 'And if someone's determined . . .'

'It was cruel of her,' said Virginia. 'That's all I can say.'

Duncan rubbed her shoulder. 'You don't mean that, Gin. Come on.'

She took another mouthful of sherry and said nothing more. She didn't really believe that Gracie had ever intended to mislead Bill, or us, in some malicious, calculated way. The poor thing clearly hadn't been thinking straight enough for that. And Duncan and Virginia were of the opinion that she must have been ill for a long time. Or that was what they wanted to believe was true, anyway.

'Perhaps she just pinned her hopes on Bill too much,' said Duncan.

'Meaning?' Virginia said.

'That she thought being with him would make her better.'

'Maybe.'

'And then when it turned out that it wasn't enough,' Duncan continued, 'she was too ashamed to say anything.'

Virginia wasn't swayed. 'Ashamed? Is that all?'

'Well, it's just a thought,' said Duncan.

And it didn't seem so implausible on the face of it. How *would* Gracie have ever told Bill that he was inadequate? But for her to have done such a dreadful thing to herself to avoid being honest with him didn't ring true to me. Had she been trying to cope alone with thoughts of that kind, it might have been a different story, but by marrying Bill she'd chosen to share her life and share it entirely. As a couple, they'd surely opened up the deepest parts of themselves to one another when they were alone. In which case, it seemed impossible that if Gracie really had been harbouring the sort of unhappiness that had the potential to make her do something so awful, she wouldn't have disclosed it to Bill, or that he wouldn't have been able to detect it in her. It made no sense for her to have picked him as a close companion only to then withhold the very anxieties that a soulmate might help reduce and relieve. And so, unlike Virginia and Duncan, I wasn't sure that Gracie had kept anything from Bill at all. I didn't think that there'd been anything *to* keep from him.

At the wake, none of Gracie's friends mentioned anything about her ever being unwell in *that* way. During those stilted conversations I'd had with her fellow choir members at the buffet table, when we'd run out of things to talk about, it would have been the perfect moment for them to say, 'Well she always struggled, you know,' or, 'Thank goodness she's finally found peace.' But there was none of that, and they'd furnished Bill with nothing other than fond memories of her.

Well, what else were they going to do? The point is, they seemed as baffled as we were, which I took to mean that what Gracie had done, even for much older acquaintances, had been completely out of character. Indeed, they'd all said how full of joy she was since she'd come to live in Barrowbeck, and while that observation in itself didn't mean much – anyone can *seem* to be anything – it felt true, nonetheless. Gracie was always smiling. She was the life and soul. So compassionate and generous and so driven to make people happy that it was, to her, like missionary work almost. And having been called, wouldn't she have felt a responsibility to keep going for the sake of others, regardless of whatever was disturbing her? Given that she'd been so devoted to helping us resolve whatever dilemmas we'd been having, it seemed odd to me that she wouldn't have wanted to see things through to the end and satisfy herself that we were on the mend. That would have given her great pleasure – and hope, surely?

It was impossible to say what had caused these passions to fizzle out. The reason being that she never once voiced any of her worries. And if it's by a person's troubles that you come to know them, then we didn't really know her well at all. Even what Bill could tell us seemed scant. He didn't appear to have much more information than we did about his wife.

She'd been a social worker, she'd moved around a fair bit, she'd never married, she didn't have any children, but he couldn't really tell us, when we asked, what choices or preferences had shaped her life in that way. It could have been that there was something about Gracie he didn't feel he could share with us, but it didn't seem as if that was the case. It crossed my mind that perhaps he and Gracie had agreed not to dwell on the past. Marrying one another had been the start of an unexpected chapter in their lives, wonderful for its newness, so why should they spend it talking about what had gone before? Still, it was hard to imagine that they *hadn't* had those conversations. Bill wasn't incurious. Not usually anyway. Except when it came to Gracie he was apparently content just to be captivated by her, as we all were; mesmerised by the way that, although she was such an enigma, she knew *us* so intimately, better than we knew ourselves. With anyone else, we might have been suspicious of that knowledge, paranoid about its occult accuracy, or felt a little too closely studied for comfort at least. But Gracie had no agenda other than to use her intuition in the cause of kindness. If she peered into us in some way, it was only so that she could better perform her ministry by ascertaining what tormented us most.

When I'd first met her, from the way she looked at me, I knew that she was able to see straight through the mask I was wearing. She'd been able to tell that I was still in pain about Katherine's passing, even though several years had gone by since then. She'd known, too, that I was afraid of the valley.

It was demanding at the best of times. Whatever life threw at you, it was all the more difficult to cope with it in Barrowbeck. It was a hard place to live. And a hard place to leave too. No one wanted our damp cottages. For Sale signs could rot away while folk waited for a buyer. Younger people, without anything to hold them back, went off to university or to find a job, like our Sadie and Amanda did, but my generation tended to stay, and we did our best to enjoy what we had and what we did.

When the girls moved away, Katherine and I buckled down to work. The years passed. We both ascended to the levels of responsibility at which we'd see out our careers. Head accountant at Hardwell's for her, sub-postmaster for me after Bob Stanley stepped down because of his emphysema.

But it was when I'd stopped working myself, and had time on my hands, that I'd started to see the village differently – or properly, I should say. I watched the same people doing the same things and saying the same things and thinking the same things and being outraged by the same things. However petty or inconsequential an incident might be, they milked it for as long as possible. Nothing odd about that. There wasn't much in the way of entertainment in Barrowbeck. But I began to see that living there was *all* about distraction, warding something off, evading something, and that I'd been doing it myself without realising it. Work had kept whatever 'it' was at bay, but now with no job to go to, I felt a profound discomfort at being suddenly unoccupied, and I'd wake up in the morning anxious about how I was going to fill so many hours.

That's not an uncommon feeling among the newly retired, of course, and Katherine in her magnificent and enviable pragmatism had made sure that she would be as busy at a pensionable age as she'd been all her life. She'd signed up to deliver Meals on Wheels, volunteered to be treasurer of the parish council, become a governor at the school, and so on. After a while, I'd thrown myself into similar things, tidying the church grounds, gathering donations for raffles, and helping to organise the village fairs that came and went throughout the year. But, unlike Katherine, I wasn't doing any of it because I particularly wanted to (who could possibly enjoy the savagery of parish politics?) but because staying active stopped me feeling quite so apprehensive. Or *anticipatory*. For I could be quite overwhelmed now and again by the feeling that something was about to fall on me. It was like the sensation someone might have standing by the wall of a high dam, acutely aware of the vast depths of water pressing at the other side.

When Katherine died, it broke. And what came out of it was fetid and toxic, as if all the fear and anger and bitterness that had ever occurred in the valley had been stored up and was now being let loose to flood into me. I drowned in other people's sorrows as well as my own. The grief I felt was too unbearable to be mine alone.

Bereavement seems like that, I know. And who's to say how vicious it can get and how deluded it can make you, but if that feeling of being swamped was some sort of mental hallucination then it was powerful enough to convince me that I really was being inundated from the outside by waves of accumulated suffering, old suffering. I could feel it emanating from the woods and the fields, flowing down the cloughs and along the river, swilling around the streets of the village. And all the places that I'd associated with Katherine became tainted.

Three years later, when Gracie came along, I still couldn't bring myself to spend much time out of the house. She saw that. She knew full well that I was avoiding something and that it wasn't doing me any good. So, when she moved to Barrowbeck, she started calling by in order to get me walking the old haunts again.

We'd go to Fitch Wood, where Katherine and I had courted as innocents. To the bridge between Pyre Meadow and Copelands Furlong, where she'd refused my first proposal of marriage, and to the top of Pilgrim's Fell where, a year later, she'd accepted. If it had been raining, Gracie would take me to look at the waterfall at Savick Clough that Katherine had loved so much, or up to Celts Cave, where Katherine and I would sometimes take Sadie and Amanda on Sunday afternoons so that we could throng the place with echoes.

Perhaps it was seeing the valley through Gracie's eyes, an outsider's eyes, that enabled me to think well of it again. When I was with her, there was nothing to be afraid of and I could recall Katherine more lucidly than I had in years.

'It's because she's not gone anywhere, Frank,' Gracie would say. 'She's still here.'

And we'd stand there in the wood and I'd listen to the trees and the rush of the river and I'd feel that Katherine was very close to me. I'd pretend that the hand in mine was her hand rather than Gracie's. I could see her subtle expressions, her eyes, the way she smiled, and smaller details that had faded since she'd passed on.

It wasn't only these vivid images that Gracie induced in me; I remembered, too, what it had felt like to be infatuated with Katherine, something which had been dulled along with the particulars of her face. I'd forgotten the intensity of love. Or I think I'd purposefully tried to dampen it down because it made me miss her too much. But after being nurtured by Gracie, I was ready to know it again.

I became too reliant on her, that's true. It's only natural to want to be with someone who can make you well when you've been sickening for so long. Virginia and Duncan were the same. Gracie was always guiding them through one thing or another.

She'd help Virginia write the letters that she hoped would start to thaw the ice with her Terry, who was in Strangeways then, I think. Or Durham. He'd been in and out all over the country.

When things were bad at Duncan's, Gracie would take his place at his mother's bedside, where her presence seemed to much reduce the old girl's distress.

And if I was feeling low, if I could sense the wall of that dam creaking again, I knew that an hour or two with Gracie would stop the cracks from forming.

I wasn't sure if any of us ever once thought about the strain we were putting on her. It must have taken a lot to carry us the way she did. But that couldn't have been it. That couldn't have been why she cut herself.

The only thing that made any sense to me (and yet really made no sense at all) was that whatever had worked its way into me after Katherine died had defiled Gracie too, very suddenly, and she'd tried to get it out – like those doctors of old might have bled a patient to balance the humours or eject a demon.

Was that what Gracie had been suffering from? Possession? Of a kind, maybe.

～

Outside in the yard, Bill was whistling again.

'God, listen to him,' said Virginia. 'He's not facing up to it, is he?'

Duncan watched him coming and going in the light from the kitchen window.

'I don't know,' he said. 'I think if I knew that I was going to spend the rest of my life asking "why" I'd put it off for as long as I could as well. It'd drive you to distraction having that question on your mind all the time, wouldn't it?'

'But what *does* he think's happened?' said Virginia.

It certainly wasn't the same as us. If we'd felt bold enough to share our theories with him, he'd have dismissed them out of hand, especially mine.

'He must see that Gracie's not here,' Virginia went on. 'How can he know that and smile?'

To that question at least, I could apply some logic. The only way that Bill could possibly be as happy as this was if he believed it was all meant to be.

I remembered him saying to me once after a sherry or two – it could have been on the day he married Gracie – that if astronomy had taught him anything at all, it was that everything was in the process of fulfilling a destiny. Every occurrence, however large or small, had been set into motion at the very start of the universe. And watching him through the window as he cleaned his telescope and whistled along to the music from the record player, it appeared as though he was still convinced that things were evolving as they were supposed to. If fate had brought him and Gracie together then what Gracie had done to herself had also been predetermined, and it pained me to think that he'd persuaded himself that this atrocity was in some way right and perfect.

He knocked on the window and Virginia wiped her eyes in order to give him an encouraging smile.

'Come on, it'll be here soon,' he said with the schoolboy excitement Gracie had always gently teased him about. 'Bring that glass with you.'

Duncan picked up the spare measure of sherry and went with Virginia out into the yard. I thumbed the wall switch and turned off the fairy lights on the tree so that they wouldn't interfere with our stargazing.

Being on the edge of the village, away from the other houses and any streetlamps, the night sky at Bill's place was pristine and the winter constellations so rich and lustrous that they showed up the ridgelines of the fells as silhouettes. It had dropped below zero, and we stood there as breath-smoking shadows while Bill studied the illuminated hands on his watch.

When the time became significant to him, he took the sherry off Duncan and, rather than swigging it as a medicinal shot against the cold, as I expected him to do, he set it down on the little cast-iron table by the wall with a peculiar precision, as though it was an offering. Duncan nudged my elbow, and I felt Virginia looking at me, even though I couldn't quite see her in the dark.

'Almost time,' said Bill. 'It shouldn't be long.' And then coming back to where we were standing, he glanced up, seemed to notice something, and quickened his last few paces.

'That's it. It's here,' he said, hurriedly positioning Virginia at the viewfinder of the telescope with his hands on her shoulders. 'Can you see it? It's very bright.'

'They're all bright, Bill,' she said.

'The brightest one.'

'Oh, I don't know. There are too many,' she said and made way for Duncan, who crouched and looked and then stepped aside equally mystified.

'You have a go, Frank,' he said.

It was a good-quality telescope, the lenses so sharp that it never felt as though you were looking *at* the stars but *into* them. Into the well-oiled clockwork of it all. The big cogs of time. And that's part of the appeal of watching the skies, when you think about it. The certainty of orbits and cycles. We can even say when something as startling as a comet will return to startle us again. That's why something unexpected in the universe is so troubling.

'It's shimmering,' said Bill. 'Have you got it?'

'What am I looking for?' I said. 'A satellite?'

'It's dancing, Frank.'

'Where?'

'Can't you see it? It's so bright.'

'A meteor?'

'No no,' said Bill. 'They burn up as soon as you spot them. Keep looking. It should be right there, coming closer.'

'I'm not sure which star you mean,' I said, and I let him take my place.

'A star?' he said. 'No, it's not a star at all. It's an angel.'

# Covenant

## 2029

At first, Evelyn thought that the man in the ditch was dead. But then he stirred and parted his lips, and murmured something she couldn't make out. He'd slipped, she thought, and hit his head on a rock under the bracken. Though there was no blood that she could see.

Climbing down into the muddy cleft, she touched his shoulder and recognised him as the one the people in the village called Benedict. She'd seen him every so often, muttering away to himself, and now and then he'd come shambling past the house on his way to the moor here. A small, thin chap who carried an old injury in his left ankle, one that made stout boots too uncomfortable to wear perhaps and so he'd opted for a pair of rubber wellingtons instead. They didn't match.

The yellow one lay a few yards off, half-submerged in the sludge, as bright and ridiculous as a duck's bill. It had evidently got stuck in the peat and in trying to pull himself free Benedict must have overbalanced and toppled into this gully.

'Are you awake? Can you open your eyes?' she said, taking one of his hands now and shaking it gently. His skin was deathly cold. 'Can you look at me?'

Slowly, he came round and sat up and stared at her as though she wasn't real.

'I'm Doctor Welland,' she said. 'The locum. Are you hurt?'

He was vacant in the eyes. Not fully conscious.

'Can you remember what happened to you?' she asked. 'Did you lose your footing or . . .?' but he ignored her questions and edged away. 'Wait. Don't get up,' she said, thinking he was about to try and stand. 'Take it easy. Give yourself a moment.'

He clamped his hands over his ears and made an agitated noise in his throat, meaning that she should stop talking, which she did and watched him fish out a little notebook from his inside pocket. It was half-soaked but he peeled it open at a new page and sat there poised with a chewed biro.

Once or twice, it seemed as if he was going to write something down but then shook his head.

'It's gone . . . gone,' he said. 'I can't remember it . . . not a thing.'

Whatever was wrong, it appeared that she was to blame, the look he gave her.

'Let me get your boot,' she said. 'Stay put.'

She went off to jemmy his wellington out of the mud and came back shaking crud off the sole.

'It's all right. Don't move. I'll do it. Give me your foot,' she said, kneeling down so that she could refit his boot but also get a look at his ankle. As she'd suspected, it had been broken at some point in the past and reset awkwardly. There was fresh damage too, and the tissue ballooned plum-like under his pale skin. He was going to struggle to walk without her help, but it was his head injury that bothered her more. Whenever she'd passed him in the village, he'd not been making much sense, and now that he was possibly concussed he seemed more confused than ever. His first thought had been to take out a notebook?

'I'd like to check for cuts,' she said. 'Can I take off your hat?'

He flinched away from her, wary, as people like him often were, of parting with their possessions, however filthy.

'Benedict, look at me for a moment,' she said, holding his stubbled cheeks as lightly as she could, trying not to startle him. Eventually, his gaze settled on hers. 'Do you have any pain?' she asked. 'How about dizziness? Blurred vision? Do you feel as if you're going to be sick?'

He shook his head tersely and she let go as he attempted to lever himself upright.

'Here, put your weight on me,' she said, and he gripped her shoulder with a hand gloved in muck.

She couldn't quite work out how old he was. Sixty? Seventy? Retirement age anyway, she thought. Gaunt and grey. Not much to him at all. She could have scooped him up in her arms, which might have been easier than trying to steady him as he limped through the heather.

'Did you fall?' she said.

'Fall? No no no . . . I was put to sleep,' he replied.

'You mean you fainted?' She considered the possibility that he'd had some sort of seizure.

'I'm given dreams,' he said.

'Dreams?'

'I never know when they'll happen . . . sometimes here . . . sometimes there . . . they catch me out . . .'

'Dreams about what?' she asked.

'Of what's coming . . . only I lost this one . . . you woke me too soon . . . I'll have to tell them . . . they depend on me . . . everyone does . . .'

Who 'they' were, she wasn't sure, and as he started shivering she thought that she might add exposure to the list of reasons for all this bizarre talk. It was hard to tell how long he'd been lying in that cold wet hole.

'Here, put this on,' she said, and took off her duffle coat to wrap around him.

The poor sod always looked threadbare at the best of times, but he'd never been as inadequately dressed as he was today. His blue anorak was as thin as a bin liner, his bobble hat more holes than wool.

He moved as quickly as he could on his swollen ankle, voicing his half of the dialogue going on inside his head.

'. . . I can't remember what I saw . . . I know . . . I *know* . . . but she woke me too early . . . yes yes . . .'

There was no point in trying to get him to explain what it all meant when he was so obviously flustered. Once she'd got him home and he was in familiar surroundings, he might calm down a little, she thought. And then perhaps she'd be able to draw out of him what had happened.

Eventually, they came to the brow of Pilgrim's Fell. The house she was renting, Prospect Farm, sat directly below on the fellside, and then further down, at the bottom of the switchback road and along the lane, was the village itself. It looked more than ever as though it had been constructed in anticipation of tempests. The glistening slate rooftops were all huddled in tight. If a place could look hunched, it was Barrowbeck. She had no doubt that Benedict had lived there all his life. The local eccentric. Laughed at.

As he lurched down through the mud and gravel on the path, yanking at her shoulder with each step, he kept on looking across to the limestone quarry on the south side of the valley, mumbling about the blight and the mutilation and 'the bastards . . . the bastards'.

It had opened the year before Evelyn had come to the village, and its presence had divided opinion, to say the very least. It still did. Those who'd taken jobs there were held up as traitors by those who'd protested and lobbied and petitioned to stop the mining company from getting its way.

Their efforts had come to nothing in the end, leaving them bitter and angry, and in the privacy of the surgery room they often vented their frustrations.

She'd be printing out a prescription for haemorrhoid cream or fitting the blood-pressure cuff when a patient would start on about the noise and the mess the trucks made and the way Celts Cave had been destroyed and – more to the point, Doctor – why was it that *their* valley had to be dug up to make other bloody people better off somewhere else?

Some of the stone was being used to build new starter homes in the suburbs of Halifax and Burnley, and some had gone off to be processed for its calcium oxide. Factories that churned out steel and plastics were ravenous for the stuff apparently.

Still, they needed the work here. She could see that. Anyone who was being honest with themselves could see it too. It was a poor place. The mill and the foundry had both closed down a long time ago. For some of her patients, a job at the quarry was the first steady work they'd had in years. They actually had some money now, they said. They could make plans. Live.

But at the expense of so much, *too* much, said the other side. What was that called? A pyrrhic victory?

Whenever anyone got onto this particular topic, she always listened and nodded and made sympathetic noises but never outwardly agreed with what they said, even though she could tell sometimes that they desperately wanted her to. She wasn't here to take sides. That way discord lay. Her time here would come to an end before it had even properly begun if she endorsed this and condemned that. Though, privately, she did think that the bite the quarry had taken out of the fell was immeasurably ugly, and she agreed about the racket.

During the day, there was an almost continuous thrum of heavy machinery and conveyor belts, and there were always trucks rumbling through the narrow streets of the village and along the lane to the outside world.

In the late summer, when she, Aidan, Ally and Sofia had moved to Barrowbeck, there'd been a haze of dust everywhere; now in the wintertime the rock waste that shuddered off the backs of the lorries turned to a grey sludge in the rain and the roads and the pavements were mired in the stuff.

That afternoon the site was mercifully silent. It being New Year's Eve, the shift had ended early. Still, 'bastards . . . bastards,' Benedict said as he chunnered his way down the footpath to the lane. 'It's all going to go . . . everything . . . everything . . . but when? . . . yes . . . I know . . . I know . . . the dream . . . I forgot the dream . . . but she woke me . . .'

After Evelyn had guided him through the gate by the house, he let go of her shoulder to head off in the direction of the village, still muttering to himself.

'Hey! Hold on,' she said, going after him. 'You can't walk back on your own.'

But he was too distracted to hear her concern and lolloped off slowly, scraping his instep down the road – which was steep and treacherous all the way down, a yellow salt bin on each corner. Even when it levelled out, it was a good mile into Barrowbeck proper. He'd not make it all that way without doing himself more damage.

'Look, let me drive you,' said Evelyn, holding him by the arm. 'If you want to get back, it'll be much quicker in the car. I promise.'

That seemed to persuade him, and he allowed her to lead him indoors.

As soon as she opened the front door, Sofia and Ally came down the stairs wanting to know where she'd been, and seeing her there with Benedict they stopped halfway, gaping at the poor old boy as if he was a mangy animal that had followed her home. Ally stared at his mismatched boots and the way his left foot was turned inwards. Sofia was instantly on the alert.

Perhaps she ought to have been more selective in what she'd read to them or the films she'd let them watch, thought Evelyn. Captain Hook, Long John Silver, all the warty wicked witches – she'd not quite realised until recently how gleefully the classics equated physical impairment with villainy.

'This is Benedict, from the village,' she said, as she closed the door. 'He's just taken a little tumble. Fetch Daddy, will you?'

The two children scooted back upstairs calling for their father and Evelyn ushered Benedict into the kitchen.

'Come and sit down,' she said.

'I can't stay . . . no no . . . I thought you were going to take me back . . . I need to tell them that I can't recall the dream . . . honesty is best . . . they always say so . . .'

'Just rest for a few moments', she said, 'while I get my keys.'

He was still reluctant but let her lower him into the rocking chair in front of the fire, where he jiggered his good leg nervously and went back to the conversation he was having with whoever else was in his mind.

She contemplated putting some ice on his sprain, but it wouldn't make much difference now and it was better that he got some heat into his body.

'You know you ought to take off your things,' she said. 'We can lend you some dry clothes. Would you like that? Benedict?'

Nothing. Not even Ally's excitable voice in the hallway caught his ear. Even when the boy burst into the kitchen, saying 'Daddy, this is him. Look,' he didn't react.

Aidan gave Benedict the once over with the same expression of antipathy as Sofia, who stood beside him, arms folded.

'What happened?' he said.

'I found him on the moor,' Evelyn replied.

'The moor? What were you doing up there?'

She gave him a face that said, *does it matter?* 'Fetch him a blanket or something, will you?' she said. 'Socks too.'

He sent the children off on the errand and stayed in the kitchen to roll himself a cigarette. He'd been outside chopping wood (presumably to let off steam) and his mass of curly hair was wild, his Aran sweater snagged with splinters.

'Was he lost or something?' he said. 'I thought if you were from the village you knew this place like the back of your hand. That's right, isn't it, mate?'

Benedict didn't look at him but creased his brow and tapped his fingertips on his cheeks. Evelyn tried a gentler tack.

'Is there someone you'd like me to call?' she said. 'Do you have a mobile? Will anyone be missing you?'

He didn't respond until the chimes of the kitchen clock roused him from his introspection.

'Can we go?' he said. 'You promised . . . you said it would be quicker . . . I can't sit here . . .'

'I know, I know,' she said. 'One minute.'

Taking her aside, Aidan said, 'Is he a bit . . . you know?'

'What does that mean?'

'Isn't he one of yours?'

242

'I don't think so.'

She wasn't sure he was registered with the practice, and she hadn't seen him in the surgery, which was strange, given the way he was. He was clearly beset by some significant psychological struggles. Not dementia. It didn't seem like that. Some personality disorder or other. Schizophrenia possibly. Perhaps he'd just forgotten to take his medication that morning. Or he'd run out.

'Let me call work and see if anyone can enlighten me about him,' said Evelyn. 'Make him a cup of tea or something, will you?'

Aidan lit his cigarette and went off to fill the kettle. Evelyn stepped out to phone the receptionist, Barbara, but there was no answer. She'd gone home to get ready for New Year's Eve. And Veronica, the nurse, didn't pick up either. She lived some distance from the village and was probably still in the car.

'No joy?' said Aidan when Evelyn went back into the kitchen.

'I'll call again later.'

'What are you going to do with him in the meantime?'

'I said I'd drive him to his house.'

'On your own? You don't know him. And if he's . . .'

'I think I'll be all right.'

The man was no more than six stone wet through.

'Can't he walk?' said Aidan. 'He managed to get himself up to the moor easily enough.'

243

'He's hurt his ankle,' said Evelyn. 'And anyway, I think he's concussed.'

'How would you know with someone like that?'

She looked at him and tried to work out if he was joking. It was hard to tell sometimes.

'I can't just send him on his way, can I?' she said. 'I have a duty.'

'He might not even be your patient.'

'And so I don't need to care about him?'

Aidan breathed out a mouthful of smoke. 'But I thought we were going to the village so the kids could do this New Year's Eve thing?' he said.

'We still can,' said Evelyn. 'I'll drop you at the green, take Benedict home and come and meet you, all right?'

'You say that,' Aidan laughed, without much humour. 'But I know you. You'll be on the phone for hours trying to sort his life out.'

'I can't just abandon him if he needs help, can I?'

'Hasn't he got a wife who can look after him?'

He meant it sarcastically.

'I've no idea,' said Evelyn, though she doubted it too.

Aidan nodded past her shoulder. 'Look out, he's on the move.'

Benedict was trying to stand, and Evelyn went over to resettle him in the chair.

'But I have to *go*,' he said, his voice rising. 'You promised you'd drive me . . . they wouldn't like me to waste time . . . there's not enough time . . . never enough . . .'

'All right, we'll go soon,' Evelyn said. 'But put something warm on first, for heaven's sake.'

Ally returned with a pair of hiking socks; Sofia had a blanket in her arms.

'Bring them over,' said Evelyn. She wanted them to see that, despite him rabbiting on, Benedict was entirely harmless. 'Say hello, then.'

Sofia manufactured one of the brief, fallacious smiles eleven-year-old girls seemed to have down to a fine art these days. But Ally stepped forward and gave Benedict a more genuine 'hi'. At seven, he still trusted his parents implicitly, and if Mummy said that it was all right to be near this nervous ratty man then that was fine.

'We're going to take him home,' said Evelyn. 'It's too far for him to get back by himself.'

'Does it hurt? Your ankle?' Ally asked Benedict, his face a picture of genuine concern. 'I broke a bone once too. It came through my skin.'

He pulled aside the collar of his sweater to show off the little scar over his clavicle.

Benedict stared at him and then at Sofia and looked up at Evelyn.

'They're so young,' he said, as though he'd only just noticed, and Sofia baulked at being thought of in the same way as her little brother.

'And getting older by the day,' said Evelyn, as she draped

the blanket around him. He refused the socks. As he did the mug of tea Aidan brought over.

'But they're just babies . . . they've hardly . . . and it'll soon be gone . . .' he said. 'The bastards.'

Aidan dabbed out his cigarette. 'That's a lovely mouth he's got on him, Eve,' he said and steered the children away. 'Come and get your coats on. You can sit in the back with me.'

He gave Evelyn a pointed look as he left. It was just like her to bring home a derelict.

Aidan brought out some old newspapers which he spread on the front passenger seat so that Benedict could sit down without ruining the upholstery.

'Where shall I take you?' asked Evelyn.

Still wrapped in the blanket, he was staring out of the window, looking up at the clouds.

'Benedict? Where do you live?' she tried again.

'Back Lane . . . Back Lane . . .' he said, a little irritably, as though she ought to have known. 'They'll be waiting . . . they'll want to know . . .'

'Who, Benedict?' said Evelyn, trying again to work out if these others he kept going on about were real or if he lived on his own. The latter, probably, she thought. She'd never seen him with anyone in the village. No one had come look-ing for him on the moor. There was no one to care where he went. No one to miss him. No one waiting at all.

'Go . . . go now . . .' He waved her impatiently out of the yard and onto the lane.

With the car doors closed, there was no escaping the smell of his sodden unwashed clothes, though Ally didn't seem to care or notice and only wanted to show Benedict the straw manikin he'd made.

Sofia on the other hand pulled her scarf tighter around her nose and looked just as morose as her father.

'Can't I open a window?' she said, as they turned the corner by Moorfoot Farm.

'Let's keep Benedict warm, eh?' replied Evelyn, eyeing her in the rear-view mirror. 'We don't want to make him feel any worse, do we?'

But before she'd finished speaking, Sofia had screwed in her earphones and was glowering at what passed by outside.

She'd found the transition to Barrowbeck much harder than Ally, who was so easy-going and generous that other children were smitten with him immediately and he collected loyal pals without any effort. He had no idea how blessed he was.

But for Sofia, trying to ingratiate herself with a coven of local girls who'd been friends with one another all their lives had been tough. Impossible actually. There'd been fights, name calling and then a sort of uneasy stalemate which had more or less lasted the rest of the autumn term. Now, she was counting down the months until she could go to secondary school away from Barrowbeck and start anew there.

Perhaps then, thought Evelyn, she might stop hating me quite so much.

It didn't matter how often she'd explained her reasons for wanting to move here – that the job was a rare opportunity, that they'd be in beautiful new surroundings – Sofia still seemed to believe that the decision might as well have been taken on the flip of a coin. In her mind, it had been nothing but selfish.

Of course it was going to seem like that to her but then she didn't know anything. And that was the point.

To call it an 'affair' made it sound like something short-lived. But it had been going on for at least two years – as far as Evelyn knew.

For the sake of Ally and Sofia, she'd never once challenged Aidan about it. She'd kept to herself every feeling of betrayal, shame, rejection, culpability and fury so that the children didn't ask what was wrong and wouldn't be hurt by finding out. She'd never considered it to be anything other than her duty to carry on and give nothing away. That was what the children needed and deserved. None of it was their fault.

Only, on the day she'd heard about the upcoming position at the surgery in Barrowbeck – to cover a sudden resignation on health grounds – she'd sent off an expression of interest the same afternoon. It was the thought of being able to show Aidan that she could puncture the little bubble he lived in and force him to make a choice between this Naomi and his family. He'd had it too easy. She'd been making it easy *for* him. Because she'd said nothing, she'd allowed him to believe that this other woman was somehow incidental, a detail.

The arrogance of that had become astonishing to her. That he could hold in such contempt the many contracts he'd put his name to, both official and implied, angered her in a way she'd never felt before. There were the vows that they'd taken as husband and wife – not just words to her – but he now had a covenant with his children too, which was deeper still, and demanded a more profound sort of devotion. To jeopardise that in any way was, to her, inconceivable, and yet it didn't seem to trouble him that what he was doing (night after night) had the potential to tear up their lives. It was hard to believe that he hadn't ever considered that. It was hard to believe that sex with *her*, his woman, however filthy or transcendental it might be, was worth more than Ally and Sofia's happiness.

He could seem so indifferent about the way they both adored him. Ally was his bounding puppy. And Sofia, like most girls edging into puberty, was both fascinated and frightened by her father. She complied with his requests immediately while resisting Evelyn's, however small, with a defiance that grew stronger by the day.

And that was what incensed her the most, thought Evelyn. That Aidan could make her so envious of him. After a night in London or a week away at some book fair in Europe, he'd been able to just stroll back into the house and enjoy the instant adoration of his little subjects, who knew nothing about what he'd been doing while they slept.

Had she wanted to punish him for that? Undoubtedly. Was that selfish, if it meant uprooting the children? Possibly so. But she'd thought that if coming to Barrowbeck changed things then it was worth it. If Aidan woke up and saw what he actually had, then it was for the good of them all.

He'd tried at first. Knowing that he'd been caught out, he'd attempted to make amends – or mitigate the consequences rather – by giving the venture his wholehearted support. He'd been the one to talk Sofia round when she was glum about leaving. He was the one who sold Barrowbeck to her. For the first few weeks he'd been as excitable as Ally about being somewhere different and Evelyn had felt her impulse to move here vindicated.

Only, it hadn't lasted. Over the autumn, Aidan had been editing a long and weighty book on English history, and since he'd completed his work he'd become restless again. She'd heard him getting up in the middle of the night and making murmured phone calls downstairs. She'd seen him sitting in the car sending text messages. She'd not asked him anything about it but had engaged him in proxy confrontations instead. They'd argued about anything and everything. Ridiculous things. But they'd both known what it was really about. She'd come close to unloading everything sometimes, she'd almost laid it all out, and it was getting harder to swallow it back. It was better to walk away. That was why she'd put on her coat earlier and gone up to the moor.

It was a good job she had, otherwise she'd never have found Benedict. He might well have been lying in that pit all night. Dead by the morning certainly.

Once they were down the hill and on the flat of the valley floor, they came to the larger houses at the edge of the village. Austere places, thought Evelyn. The one called Doonrigg, with a blighted past that no one seemed willing to disclose to her, was fenced off and boarded up and sat in thickets of wet weeds. Ally had never liked it and, as always, kept his eyes closed until they had gone by.

After passing Loud Clough and Savick Clough – she was slowly getting to know the names of all the ravines in the fellsides – they were onto Reed Lane, presumably named after what had once grown by the river. There was no vegetation there any more. Only the concrete yard of the old ironworks, flashing by behind the railings of the fence, the site long abandoned.

By the main gates, the road made a dog-leg and changed its name to Smith Street and then Old Butchery as it ran on towards the abattoir – as quiet that afternoon as the quarry. The bend around the high walls brought them to the lights by the chip shop, and then the short run of Jubilee

Terrace led to the village green, which was teeming with exuberant families all heading towards the river.

At the junction by the school, she turned right onto Waterside Road, by the Lion, and then stopped to let a line of people cross. From the grandparents to the tots in push-chairs, each clutched a little straw doll.

With a wave of thanks, they went into Pyre Meadow, between the road and the riverbank, where a brass band was playing, and everyone was starting to gather to 'throw in the year'.

Her patients had been talking about it for weeks, especially the children, who had been most concerned that whatever they'd been brought in for – chilblains, tonsillitis or a chest infection – wouldn't prevent them from taking part. Their parents, too, had been genuinely fretful at their little ones missing out.

It was one of many enduring traditions here. Every shop and business closed at lunchtime on New Year's Eve, even the surgery. It was sweet that it meant so much. Every other person she'd treated in the last month had taken out their phone to show her a photograph of their manikin, these foot-high effigies they made of themselves out of straw. Some were plain and simple, others more elaborate and dressed in little handmade clothes and hats.

As tradition dictated, they were constructed in some degree of secrecy. Ally and Sofia had insisted on it. As the stems of dried hay were wound together, one spoke aloud the sins and sorrows of the last twelve months so that they became entwined with the twists and braids. And then on New Year's Eve these figurines were tossed into the river to be carried away, cleansing the village.

She'd made one too. But Aidan hadn't bothered. He didn't feel as if they'd been here long enough to act like locals. That had been his excuse. What he really wanted to do was follow in the wake of these straw poppets and float out of the valley himself. She didn't think he had any real regrets anyway.

'It's no use now,' Benedict said as another family hurried over the road in front of them carrying their models. 'It'll make no difference . . . it's gone too far . . . there's nothing anyone can do . . . it's a matter of when . . . bastards . . . bastards.'

Aidan muttered something and then patted the back of Evelyn's seat. 'Drop us here,' he said. 'Then perhaps the children might hang onto their innocence a little longer.'

She pulled in by the war memorial and they got out, with Ally, sweet little Ally, giving Benedict a polite goodbye.

'I'll come and find you,' said Evelyn. 'I won't be long.'

Without looking at her, Aidan closed the door and went off across the green with the children. Ally held his hand. Sofia looped his arm.

'Please,' said Benedict, wanting her to set off again. 'Please take me to the house.'

Evelyn did as he asked and he directed her away from the green, past the church and through the twisting streets called

The Lots. Here, the old cottages were squeezed together. One front door was only a window away from the next. Various family businesses had somehow wedged themselves in. A wool shop, a place that sold gardening tools, a butcher's.

Out onto a straight road again, Benedict said, 'Here, here,' and motioned to the turning between the stone-mason's, Hardwell's, and a pub called the Jester, where those who worked in the quarry liked to drink. A few came out of the front door now, zipping up coats and pulling on gloves, their straw men under their arms.

'How can they smile?' said Benedict. 'After what they've done . . . they broke everything . . . further . . . further.' He flapped Evelyn onwards – then left and left again.

She'd been out to see a few patients in their homes since she'd come to the practice, but she didn't know Back Lane at all. It looked to be the poorest part of the village, and although most of the thin terraced houses were still dressed in Christmas lights, it didn't disguise the fact that they were in desperate need of repair. On every frontage, the grey rendering was either cracked or flaking off. Roof slates were missing. A few windows had been boarded up. There were lines of slimy green moss where broken gutter-ing had allowed rainwater to wash down the walls for years on end.

'Here,' said Benedict, and Evelyn pulled in by a strip of communal scrubland – the dumping ground for rusted radiators and broken furniture and cars covered with several autumns' worth of leaves. A small bonfire smouldered further along the street.

There were steps up to the front doors of these houses but not all of them had handrails. At Benedict's, the stone risers were steep and shallow and had been worn almost smooth. A bit of rain and it'd be like climbing up and down slippery blocks of ice. It was easy to see how he'd come to give himself that limp, thought Evelyn. He'd done well to only break his ankle and not his neck.

'Let me help you,' she said, and got out to make sure that she was there to take his arm before he tried to walk.

She held him tight all the way to the top. The door was unlocked and he detached himself, leaving her outside as he went in, calling for someone called Miriam and using the abundance of furniture to support his weight.

The steps might have been dangerous, but the house was just as hazardous inside. The hallway was cluttered with chairs, plants, a telephone table, a bureau desk, a grandfather clock. All of it looked dumped rather than placed, acquired rather than chosen. Things Benedict intended to sell, maybe.

At the foot of the stairs, which were stacked with yellowing paperbacks, Benedict held onto the newel post and called for this Miriam again. She must have heard him the first time, as she appeared immediately and came down with a look of concern.

'I couldn't remember it,' he said, when she joined him. 'I forgot the dream . . . she woke me . . . it wasn't my fault.'

Miriam looked to where he was pointing and saw Evelyn standing in the doorway.

'I found him up on the moor,' she explained, her act of altruism giving her licence to step in over the threshold, she thought. 'I'm Doctor Welland. The locum at the surgery.'

Miriam nodded. 'I know who you are.' Of course she did. In a place like Barrowbeck, a new doctor would hardly be anonymous. Still, Evelyn didn't particularly like the way she said it.

She was about the same age as Benedict with a cap of grey, close-cropped hair. Not his wife. No, that wasn't their relationship. A sister, then?

But then three other people emerged from one of the downstairs rooms, a mixture of ages, all of them curious and uneasy about Evelyn's presence, and she wondered if the house was used for Care in the Community with Miriam as the supervisor. She had an air of officialdom about her.

'I couldn't write down the dream,' Benedict said to these new faces. 'I tried to remember it . . . but it was gone . . . she should have let me sleep for longer . . .'

They all looked at Evelyn, and she found herself smiling back with something like an apology.

'I was worried he'd hurt himself,' she said. 'He's turned his ankle.'

256

They continued to stare: a thick-set middle-aged woman in a poncho embroidered with clouds, a young man in a lumberjack shirt, and a pretty girl in her twenties wearing burgundy corduroy dungarees.

'Go and sit Benedict down,' said Miriam. 'I'll be there in a moment.'

The young man took hold of Benedict's elbow and helped him into the room at the front of the house. The others followed, listening to the old boy's explanations, assuring him that none of it was his fault, and giving Evelyn accusatory looks.

Miriam ought to have been overjoyed that Benedict had been found – for the sake of her job if nothing else. She ought to have been mortified that she'd missed him going out in the first place. But she seemed oddly unmoved by the fact that he was wet and filthy or that he'd been up on the moor by himself.

If those who lived here were free to leave whenever they liked, then it clearly wasn't the right place for him, and this Miriam needed to be keeping a closer eye on him until she found somewhere more suitable. It was negligent of her to let someone as confused and accident prone as Benedict wander at will. What *was* her role here exactly if not to ensure that the people in the house were kept from doing themselves harm?

A few decades ago, Benedict would probably have been committed – in the old parlance – and yet he might have been better off. He might well have found some tranquillity in the routines of an institution. To say that they'd all been grim, punitive prisons was untrue. Some people had lived happy lives in those closed-off worlds.

There'd been a place for psychiatric patients here in the valley until the eighties, Evelyn seemed to recollect, at the old hall that had stood next to Fitch Wood. It was a ruin now, nothing more than a single crumbling wall and a chimney breast in a field, but there had once been a sort of working farm in the grounds, and it wasn't difficult to imagine that Benedict would have thrived there with so many things to occupy his time and his mind. Instead, he drifted about aimlessly and dangerously in the custody of a woman who seemed unconcerned about his welfare.

'I don't know how long he'd been unconscious for when I found him,' Evelyn said to Miriam, in a bid to try and convey the seriousness of the situation. 'I would like to examine him properly before I go. I want to satisfy myself that it's not concussion. Is this typical for him?'

'Typical?' said Miriam.

'The way he's behaving, I mean. Is it just his condition?'

'You've lost me.'

'Well, does he take any medication?'

'I'm afraid I've no idea,' Miriam said.

'But you do look after him here?'

'Of course we do. We all look after one another.'

'No, I mean, you're in charge. You, personally.'

'Me? No.'

'You don't work for the Trust?'

'The Trust?'

'The Mental Health Trust.'

'You must have me confused with someone else, dear.'

'Then you live together? Here?' said Evelyn.

'That's right.'

'You're all friends?'

'More than that.'

'And yet none of you went out looking for him?' said Evelyn, trying her best to keep her voice light.

'We do care about him,' said Miriam. 'I can't tell you how precious Benedict is to all of us.'

Evelyn inwardly scoffed. If that were true, then why would they have let him go out dressed as he was?

'Look, could I see him?' she said. 'Just for a minute or two.'

Miriam held the door to the front room open for her and she went in to find Benedict sitting on a shabby sofa, still in his wellingtons, still shrouded in the blanket, his notebook open on his lap. The others were gathered around waiting for him to write something.

A table in the middle of the room was covered in a large map of the valley with certain areas outlined in red. Placards in the corner of the room read NO QUARRY! and OUT! On the wall were dozens of little scribbled-on sheets of paper that had been torn out of Benedict's notebook.

'No . . . I can't see it,' he said, in distress. 'It won't come . . . it's gone for good . . .'

The young girl in the dungarees, with the bump of pregnancy just showing, clutched Benedict's hand as he broke down with frustration.

'It'll come back to you,' she said.

But he laced his fingers around the back of his head and bent forward and the woman wearing the poncho tried to comfort him instead. As she leant down to pat his knee, the necklace she had on dangled and turned, the heavy gold pendant fashioned into the name 'Celeste'. Her name, presumably.

'You just need to give it a minute, love,' she said.

What he needed was for them to leave him alone, thought Evelyn and said, 'Listen, Benedict. You must be exhausted. Why don't you have a hot bath and go to bed?'

'I have to fetch it back,' he said. 'It's on me . . . I'm the one given the dreams . . .'

'You don't have to do anything apart from rest,' said Evelyn, kneeling in front of him now. 'Why don't I help you to your room?'

She noticed the others watching Miriam, wanting her to intervene.

'He can go to his room later,' she said. 'It's important that we try and get what we can.'

'But look at him,' said Evelyn. 'His clothes are still damp.'

'It's in there somewhere,' said Benedict, prodding himself

hard in the forehead. 'I know it must be there . . . if I could just dig it out . . .'

'There's no need to get upset,' Evelyn said. 'It doesn't matter.'

For saying that, the others rounded on her crossly. Of course it mattered. It mattered a great deal. Didn't she understand?

Miriam touched her shoulder.

'Please,' she said. 'I have to try and help him remember.'

Evelyn got to her feet feeling powerless, but she couldn't force them to let her do her job.

Miriam drew up a chair and sat down opposite Benedict. Taking his hands, she said, 'Lie down. Close your eyes.'

He nodded and did as she asked. Miriam placed her hand on his brow and gradually slowed his breathing.

'Allow the pictures to come,' she said. 'Let your mind open.'

Benedict made no response for a minute but then said, 'I see us . . . we're in the church . . .'

'That's something new,' the young man said with a look of optimism. 'He's not been shown that before.'

'We're ringing the bells . . . like we planned,' Benedict went on.

'Can you say when?' asked Miriam. 'What day is it?'

He shook his head. 'I don't know . . . there's nothing that . . . I can't tell . . . I can't look hard enough . . .'

Miriam shushed him out of his agitation and continued to caress his forehead.

'Well, can you see us *getting* to the church?' she said. 'What's it like outside? Go back a little way if you can.'

'We're crossing the field.'

'Good.'

'It's cold . . . there are no leaves on the trees,' he continued. 'Paul's running . . . he's telling us to hurry . . .'

'I am?' said the young man. 'Why?'

'So we can warn everyone.'

'And before that?' Miriam said. 'Where are we? Can you see?'

He took his time to answer. 'Out on the street . . . Anika's crying.'

The pregnant girl looked at the young man, who tried to soothe her sudden unease with a pet of her hair and a kiss on her ear.

'But why do we leave the house in the first place?' said Miriam.

'Because we know that it's about to begin,' Benedict replied.

'How do we know?'

'We have proof.'

'What kind of proof?'

'Proof that these dreams are all true.'

'How?'

'A gold watch,' he said.

'I don't understand,' said Miriam.

'We're all looking at a gold watch on the day it happens,' Benedict went on. 'We're here in this room . . . I can see us . . . *it's ten past three*, we're saying . . . *ten past three.*'

The others looked as confused as Evelyn felt herself.

'Whose watch, Benedict?' asked Miriam.

He furrowed his brow, then said, 'The doctor's. Hers.'

They all turned to Evelyn. The young man grasped her sleeve and pulled it back.

'Look,' he said, brandishing her wrist, showing the others the flashy timepiece Aidan had bought her for their first anniversary. 'It *is* ten past three.'

'Ten past three, you're right,' Celeste in the poncho verified.

'What does that mean? Ten past three? What are you saying?' the young girl, Anika, said.

'It means it's today,' said Miriam. 'Now.'

'Now?' cried the girl, looking around. 'It's really going to happen?'

She held her belly and sat back against the table.

'What the hell are you talking about?' Evelyn said. 'What's going to happen?'

Miriam indicated the sheets of paper on the wall. 'Benedict's been seeing this day ever since the quarry opened,' she said.

'Something's been trying to show him what's coming,' said Celeste. 'It's been giving him dreams.'

'Premonitions,' Miriam said.

'And they've all been true,' the young girl cut in. 'It's all going to go. Everything. It's coming. Today. Oh, Jesus.'

She buried her face into the young man's chest and he rocked her slowly with his chin on the top of her head, scared and restive himself.

'What's *coming*?' said Evelyn.

'The beginning,' Miriam replied.

'Of what?'

'What do you think?'

The young man said, 'It's punishment, isn't it? For what these bastards have done to the valley. We just didn't know *when* it was going to happen.'

'Until now,' Miriam said, looking at Evelyn's watch again.

'Oh, for the love of God,' she said. 'This doesn't prove anything.'

Miriam frowned. 'It proves everything.'

'You think Benedict's been seeing signs and wonders?'

'How else did he know the kind of watch you were wearing?' the young man said.

'Lots of people have gold watches,' said Evelyn.

'And lots don't,' the girl replied.

'He probably saw it earlier,' said Evelyn. 'When I found him on the moor.'

'Did you?' Miriam asked Benedict. 'Did you notice the doctor's watch?'

He said not.

'He just doesn't remember,' Evelyn said. 'He wasn't exactly with it. He might well have a head injury. I've still not been allowed to check. Can I do that, Benedict? Please?'

'I think we'd know if he'd hurt himself,' said Miriam.

'I'm asking for his permission, not yours,' Evelyn replied.

'But we have to go,' said the young man. 'We have to warn everyone. It's what we said we'd do, when the day came.'

'Then go,' said Evelyn. 'But Benedict needs to stay here. If you really cared about him, you'd see that.'

'You're saying we don't?' the young man said. 'What the fuck do you know?'

'He could have died,' Evelyn retorted.

'Aye, well, he didn't, did he?'

Stressed by the impending argument, Benedict finally took off his hat. Underneath, his bald scalp had only the moles and marks of age. There were no cuts or bruises or lumps. No blood anywhere.

'There you are, doctor,' said Miriam. 'I hope that sets your mind at rest.'

'For Christ's sake, come on,' the young man said, taking Anika's hand. 'We're wasting time.'

Solemn and dazed, they left the room, Celeste too, and the three of them went to fetch their coats from the cupboard under the stairs. Miriam helped Benedict to his feet and leaning against her he stumbled towards the door as Evelyn tried making one last appeal.

'Benedict, you must stay off that ankle of yours,' she said, following him out into the hallway. 'Rest, at least until tomorrow. I'll come back then and see how it is.'

'Tomorrow?' the young man said, pausing to frown at her as he looped a scarf around his neck.

'You should leave,' said Benedict, looking at Evelyn with the most intense sadness. 'Get away from the valley . . . your children . . . so young . . . Just babies . . . this is only the start of it . . .'

Inching past the jumble of furniture, the young man opened the front door, letting in the cold air and the distant thumps and fanfares of the brass band by the river. He went out first, then Celeste, the pair of them carping at Anika to keep up. Miriam took Benedict's arm to guide him down the steps. And then all five of them made off along the street with as much urgency as they could manage.

Anika was crying, as Benedict had described, but only because she was so frightened by whatever had been planted in her head. Anyone *would* cry.

Celeste put her arm around her shoulder but out of exasperation rather than compassion and almost marched the girl along.

Evelyn went after them a short way and saw that the street came to a dead end at a mossy wooden gate. Beyond that was a small square of pastureland that stretched to the wall of the church grounds: a shortcut back to the heart of the village. Once through the gate, the younger man set off running, imploring the others to hurry, and they followed as quickly as they could, slopping their way through puddles and cattle muck. Benedict lumbered along with Miriam half-carrying him from time to time. Their frenzy seemed to increase as they crossed the field. The girl sounded as though she was having a breakdown. Celeste snapped at her. Miriam too. Benedict shouted at the sky.

Evelyn had no wish to follow them any further, but wondered if she ought to call the police. Could anyone just go into a church and start ringing the bells? The poor priest might not be able to stop them if they were determined.

He must have heard them shouting, as he came out of the rectory now, pulling on his coat.

Father Wilding, was it? She'd treated him for conjunctivitis not long ago. He'd seemed affable enough. Down to earth. She could just about hear his voice on the cold air as Miriam and the others entered the churchyard and gestured with urgency at the bell tower.

He led them there straight away and unlocked the door to allow them in. Was it just intended to pacify them? Perhaps they'd come calling on him before and he'd found that playing along was the best way to mollify their distress in the heat of the moment. Still, Evelyn thought she should make sure that he wasn't being harassed. He'd probably appreciate having another person there. Her name would crop up anyway if they relayed this dream or augury Benedict had supposedly had about her, and so she ought to go and try and explain what had happened.

Back in the car, she made her way to the village green and parked close to the church. Over in Pyre Meadow, the brass band was still playing, with the bass drum pounding away as everyone who'd gathered by the beck began slinging their manikins into the water. She picked out Aidan, Sofia and then little Ally, who seemed hesitant to join in. He was waiting for her, wanting her to be there when he threw in his straw boy.

He'd been so serious about it all week. Daft lad. Agonising over his sins while his father skulked in the work-shed talking to *her*, making plans. Even now Aidan was walking away from the children, smoking, checking his phone.

Evelyn got out of the car and thought that Ally had seen her. He was waving at someone anyway. She gestured to him that she wouldn't be long and locked the door before heading towards the church steps. She'd speak to the priest, make sure he was all right, and once that duty was done, she'd return to the more important one and carry on playing her part in the show of unity she and Aidan had been putting on for the children these last two years. They'd watch these wicker dollies floating away and listen to the music for a while longer. She'd drive back up to the house, he'd cook, she'd drink, they'd all eat too much. Then they'd set out a board game maybe, watch a film, try to stay awake until midnight, and see out the last few hours of 2029 as peacefully as possible, the four of them on the settee with the fire lit and the wind in the chimney. But she wouldn't let herself be fooled into thinking that *perhaps* . . . and *if only* . . .

No, it was all coming to an end. She was tired of pretending that they might be getting somewhere. So was Aidan. To carry on would be pointless. Coming here had achieved nothing. Had she ever really thought that it would?

She felt weightless for a moment. Unreal. One span of her life was coming to a close, the next was indistinct. It might be tomorrow or the day after, but Aidan would soon leave and then things would start to change – for Ally and Sofia the most. The pair of them caught in the middle of all this stupidity, the children of children.

She stopped for a moment to put on her hat and gloves. The cold was really biting now. It had been overcast all day, but it felt as though it was starting to go dark already. Even for Barrowbeck, it was too soon for dusk, not even half past three according to her watch. Yet the light in the valley was draining away so swiftly that the streetlamps were beginning to come on all around the green. Along Saint Gabriel's Lane and Lime Walk and East Edge. Then down the side roads, Victory Row and Underwood Place.

And as the bulb in the lamp above her bloomed into its

sickly orange glow, the church bells began. Not to sound the hour, not yet. Not in jubilation at the coming new year. But in a raucous, discordant pealing that echoed around the streets, around the whole valley.

The brass band stopped playing. Everyone on the river-bank turned and looked upwards. The sky grew darker still.

It was the children who started to run first, hurrying their parents across the grass as it began to rain harder than Evelyn had ever seen it rain here, or anywhere, before, as though the whole sky was falling in.

And perhaps it was an illusion, a fluke of light and moisture, but it seemed to her that from on high, the segments of a rainbow were tumbling down through the clouds like the pieces of a vast, broken bridge.

# A Valediction

## 2041

It was highly unusual for an intrusion alert to come up at Site 26. Normally, whatever passed through Barrowbeck, from a bluebottle to a gull, was immediately picked up by the cameras and ninety-nine times out of a hundred logged as benign. There hadn't been an issue of potential trespass for years. But an alarm had been activated, and for the last twenty-four hours 'Intervention Required' had been flashing on Kay's tablet screen.

The video recordings from the time the alert had been triggered showed nothing visible to the naked eye. The various analytic trawls had ruled out bugs in the system and the drone sent to perform an aerial inspection had reported a clean sweep. Still, the cameras had tracked the movement of *something*, which on the map of the site showed up as a red line travelling quickly east–west. And, as the Agency was duty-bound to investigate any possible incursion until criminal action could be ruled out, this was one of those rare

271

occasions when employees had to actually leave the office and undertake an inspection in person.

Kay had been to Barrowbeck before – once shortly after the Thirty-One Flood and once when they'd closed the place off for good a year or so later – and along the valley road which had once led to the village, the place could, at certain moments, look as it did on the old photographs she'd seen.

There were cloughs of tumbling water. Slopes of bracken rising up to limestone crags. And along the ridges, the shapes of solitary trees stood against the January-blue of the sky.

Except, they weren't silhouettes but had been burnt in the last moorland fire in the summer or the one before that maybe. And there were no sheep grazing on the hills any more. The shadows of clouds passed over empty pastures now.

'Another ten minutes or so,' Kay said, for the sake of talking, as much as anything else. Next to her in the passenger seat, the new girl, Natalie, had barely spoken in the hour it had taken them to get here, and her reticence made Kay feel as though she was being judged, which she probably was.

She'd have come on her own, but Agency staff were required to make any real-life visits to the sites in their district in pairs and the regional manager had been keen for her to take Natalie along.

To see an actual flood-zone first-hand was something that all new recruits were encouraged to do, so that they could grasp the scale of what they were dealing with. The Agency needed its trainees to recognise that the magnitude of the devastation across the country far exceeded the money available to undo it, and that 'controlled decline' really was the only viable policy. It was an exercise designed to neuter any sense of self-righteousness too. Apprentices, like Natalie, had to be purged of any delusions about *saving the planet* that they might have picked up on their Environmental Management courses from craggy, sentimental professors.

Though they needn't have been worried about her. She'd come to them devoid of any romanticism for the way things used to be. For her, damage was to be catalogued not cried over.


'Girl' wasn't an epithet Kay would have ever used in Natalie's hearing, but she was very young. Only – what? – twenty-one or twenty-two? A water baby, certainly. One of those kids born into a warm wet world who'd known nothing else. She'd have only ever seen snow on films and photographs. She wouldn't be able to imagine that England had ever been cold enough for ice and blizzards.

'You know,' said Kay, 'once over, the river would have been frozen at this time of year.'

'Oh yeah?' Natalie said with an affected interest, but she really meant *so what?* To her, it was perfectly normal for January to be as mild as April once was. Nothing unusual at all in seeing daffodils out three days into the new year.

Though they were smaller and fewer now. Not that she'd know.

'It's a long way away, isn't it?' she said. 'The site, I mean. It's remote.'

Kay thought about it and said, 'I suppose it is, yes.'

They were hardly going to the ends of the earth, but to Natalie it probably seemed so. People didn't travel far in England these days. They couldn't. Not without permits. No one went on holiday abroad any more either. Who would want to throw themselves into the infernos of Murcia or Crete anyway, even if they could get there? There were no airports now. Only military ones. Heathrow and Gatwick and the like had been decommissioned five years ago, as relics of what, to Natalie's lot, was a past of unconscionable and baffling lunacy.

Even though the graph that plotted emissions and temperature rises had been around for decades, and was so simple that even a child could understand it, people had still turned up in their droves, even in the 2020s, for cheap fortnights in the sun. Even when their own towns and villages were flooded, or alight with wildfires, up, up they flew to 'get away from it all'.

Put like that, it did seem mad.

There'd been some who refused to believe that there was a problem at all, let alone accept that they were contributing to it in any way. Some assuaged their guilt by persuading themselves that it was all right once a year. And a great many more were resigned to the fact that it was all too far down the line anyway and that they might as well enjoy themselves. All attitudes that Natalie's generation simply couldn't understand.

She looked up at the hills on her side, then the river flowing past as a foaming muddy torrent.

'What if something happens while we're here?' she said.

'Like what?' replied Kay.

'Well, who knows what we're going to find.'

Now that she was actually in the valley, she was getting jittery. She would have spent almost her entire time at university learning about and researching the Thirty-One Flood. She would have taken hundreds of VR tours of the worst hit places in the Northern Belt, like Hebden Bridge and Mytholmroyd – maybe even Barrowbeck – and might have even felt as if she knew them, but out in the field it was very different.

'I mean, if we need help, then what?' she said.

'We're being tracked, don't worry,' Kay replied. 'Anyway, there'll be nothing there.'

Natalie frowned at her. 'But the cameras saw *something*.'

'They're only like human eyes,' said Kay. 'They only pass information on. It'll be a glitch in the processing. There'll be ingress into one of the motherboards at the Hub or something. I guarantee it.'

Natalie shook her head. 'It would have come up in diagnostics.'

'Those programs aren't always right. They can be fallible.'

'Maybe in your day,' Natalie said, and then added a half-smile to mitigate any insolence. But as far as she and everyone her age was concerned, computers didn't make mistakes any more. They couldn't. They thought too quickly and too deeply for error.

'Look, we wouldn't be here at all', said Kay, 'if the tech was working properly.'

'It is,' Natalie replied.

'A hundred and fifteen cameras and not one of them could work out what it was looking at?'

'The system's still learning,' Natalie said. 'It'll come up with an answer soon enough.'

'It's had since yesterday,' said Kay, which was an eon when the processors sorted through a million pieces of data per second.

Natalie shrugged, her faith unshaken.


A little further on, by what little remained of the old Squire's hall, they stopped at the gates that now blocked the road, and Barrowbeck itself finally came into sight at the end of the valley; tiny-looking under the fells, an island in a wide brown tarn.

The sun lit the east side of the village and cast the shadows of the buildings winter-long across the surface of the water. It was oddly pretty. Or there was a rugged sort of attractiveness about the place at least. The church, the mill, the school, the houses and cottages were all built from the same tough Pennine stone, and from this distance it looked as if everything would stand for another thousand years. But the mortar was dissolving around each and every brick. The old wooden lintels were softening. Beams and rafters were gradually mouldering away.

The slow corrosion was monitored by pole-mounted cameras, as tall as the old streetlamps, which scanned the site 24/7. And from here it was possible to make out a few of what had been dubbed 'the jellyfish', the plastic half-domed devices that floated about the village, constantly measuring the levels of giardia, cryptosporidium, E. coli, lead, red diesel, kerosene and a thousand other contaminants in the outflowing water.

Should a rise in toxicity pose a threat to the bigger rivers the beck joined when it left the valley, preventative action would be initiated, but currently the village was considered a low-risk site. The pollution its deterioration caused came within the legal limits. 'Acceptable Discharge' it was called. The topic of Natalie's university thesis, apparently.

~

Beyond the high metal gates with their rusting KEEP OUT signs, the lane quickly disappeared into the lake that now filled the valley, and the rest of the journey had to be made by boat.

Kay checked her tablet again. There was no point in going through the process of suiting-up if the anomaly with the cameras had been resolved while they'd been driving here. But she would have received a notification if that had been the case, and 'Intervention Required' was still there blinking away next to an exclamation mark in a yellow triangle.

'We'll go straight over to the Hub,' said Kay. 'I'm sure that's where we'll find the fault.'

'And if there's nothing wrong?' asked Natalie. 'What then?'

'Then there'll be a fault somewhere else.'

'Or there's no fault at all.'

'I told you, don't worry.' Kay directed her attention down to the village. 'It's deserted,' she said, and got out.

The sunlight had only just started to lean into the valley, but it was warm already. Bright, standing water steamed lightly with evaporation. Insects clouded. She should make the most of it being so temperate, thought Kay. Spring would be hot. Summer unbearable, even here in the north. The previous year, it had been forty, forty-one for days on end. In the south-east, forty-five, forty-six. Forty-eight, on August the twenty-first. And on that day alone there'd been hundreds of deaths across London. And hospitals had started seeing cases of dysentery and cholera in patients from the Thames estuary.

The sites the Agency managed were often steeped in a fetid soup of algae and bacteria and chemical froth, and on any visit every precaution had to be taken so as to minimise contact. While the winch lifted the dinghy off the trailer, Kay and Natalie put on waders and yellow hazmat suits, but even a face mask couldn't fully cut out the stench of the water, rank as it was with sewage, effluent and putrefied vegetation from the meadows rotting under the surface.

What sat here now was more a swamp than a lake, and when they set off the boat's wake quickly closed up again behind them.

They passed clumps of dead beech and hazel that had once been part of Fitch Wood, then the Wesleyan chapel and its manse, both half-submerged. On the peripheries of the village were a few solitary farmhouses, as empty as skulls, windowless and graffitied. Natalie shifted in her seat to take them in, then turned the other way as they puttered towards a stonemason's with the name HARDWELL'S painted high up across the frontage.

Beyond that was a pub called the Jester with the sign still hanging from an iron bracket showing a fool dressed in motley and a coxcomb. The building itself was a shell. What had been the barroom swelled with filthy water and debris as the wash from the boat swept in through the glassless windows.

A while back, there'd been a spate of videos showing people breaching security fences and exploring flood-zones by rubber dinghy, in the way that folk used to break into abandoned asylums and derelict schools for fun. But, like every viral fad, it had quickly passed, and if Natalie was afraid of finding people here bent on vandalism or theft, then she was worrying about nothing. The looting had come to an end long ago. There was nothing left to take. Nothing that was worth the effort of getting here or being slapped with one of the hefty fines they handed out for trespassing. All that remained were the odds and ends of the lives that had once been lived in the knot of narrow terraces the boat took them into: Arthur's Lot, Richard's Lot, Henry's Lot. Probably built around feudal partitions of land, each street shaped to boundaries that had persisted since Domesday.

In one house there was a cuckoo clock above a fireplace. In another, a fancy mirror still hung on a wall papered in green paisley. In the next street, a large silver Christmas star revolved from a light fitting in what had been the butcher's – Lampland & Sons, established 1890.

Being above the waterline, the bedrooms of the cottages were better preserved. Even though the windows were grimy with moss or half-obscured by the weeds that hung from the gutters, it was still possible to make out chintzy lampshades and forgotten ornaments. But it was all slowly spoiling, nonetheless.

Once out of that fusty warren, the boat continued towards Saint Gabriel's, passing close to what had been the graveyard. The tops of granite crosses were thick with weed. Stone angels, in poses lachrymal and pensive, contemplated the water lapping around their waists. The other memorials were either under the surface or had been taken away to be replanted in the municipal cemeteries of the towns and cities nearby.

The diocese had thankfully emptied all the plots before the Flood, but it had been a protracted battle to get them to do so. Even after the long, wet winters of 2029 and 2030 (the so-called Precursory Weather Events) when the village had been overwhelmed and the graveyard had sat under water for weeks on end, they still wouldn't accept that unless they moved the bodies the river would, and soon. They'd accused the Agency of overreacting and scaremongering, and taken them to court in the end.

They'd lost, of course. The science had trampled over any spiritual objections they'd put forward about the dear departed being denied eternal rest. But even after the verdict, the local clergy and the parishioners had manned a makeshift blockade to hold back the diggers and the black vans.

It was more denial than demonstration. No one here had wanted to believe that the big flood, the flood of floods, would ever materialise. When it *had* come to pass, a decade ago now in 2031, and Barrowbeck had been inundated to the point of being uninhabitable – like so many other places that year – there'd still been those who refused to be evacuated, even under the threat of arrest. They'd tried to live on in the upper rooms of their houses without gas or electricity, cooking on camping stoves, convinced that the water levels would eventually drop as they'd always done in the past, and then it would just be a case of sweeping out and carrying on. Only, the rain hadn't stopped, and the river had risen higher by the day.

Supplies of food had inevitably run out, and when it became impossible to get anything into the village, those still left here had finally conceded defeat and gone to live miles away in one of the encampments alongside the M6 or one of the sprawling conurbations of pre-fabs the government had slung up on the outskirts of Sheffield. Though not without protest. Barrowbeck was where they *belonged*. They had a right to be in the homes they'd paid for. That was understandable, and Kay had never had anything but sympathy for the displaced, even if they were deluded.

'It's hard to believe, isn't it?' said Natalie, her voice fuzzy in Kay's earpiece. 'Why anyone ever thought places like this would be rebuilt.'

Kay looked at the church, the water almost up to its boarded-over windows, and then at the half-drowned houses that marked the edges of the old village green.

'Well, if you'd lived here all your life . . .' she replied, to which Natalie made a dismissive gesture.

'That's not reason enough.'

'No?'

'To spend so much money for the sake of, what, a few hundred people?' Natalie continued. 'Did they really expect that to happen?'

Yes, plenty had. Most people had. In the weeks following the Flood, when the rain had finally stopped and the country had come up blinking from the shock, thoughts had naturally turned to salvage and restoration, and there had been a general assumption that everything ruined would be replaced. Those who'd been relocated believed that they'd be able to return at some point to wherever they'd come from. The water would be pumped away, the streets cleared of mud, the buildings somehow made usable again. The money would come from *somewhere*. No one had ever considered that certain places would have to be abandoned.

But it had been impossible to repair everything. And for a year afterwards, as the Agency had conducted its assessments of the devastation, they'd had to choose what to save and what to let go. There had been vocal and sometimes violent protests as every so often a place like Barrowbeck was declared permanently irretrievable.

There had been all kinds of wild theories about the selection process, mostly that it was riddled with various agendas that had nothing to do with the place in question. Towns and villages were added to the Reject Pile, as it became known, as acts of political retribution. Poor areas of the north were being disproportionately marked down as not worth saving. Meanwhile, the companies that manufactured the materials for makeshift housing were raking it in.

MPs had resigned. The Agency had been lambasted. But then an algorithm had been developed to take over all the decision-making.

Unsurprisingly, a significant number had believed it to be just as biased; some still did. But they were truly unfounded anxieties. The algorithm was (like Natalie) unimpeded by nostalgia, loyalty, affection or desperation, and made its conclusions on the basis of facts alone. Its efficiency had eliminated financial wastage, and both the speed and precision of its executive orders had averted significant human casualties, most recently in Hull when the system had initiated the closure of a road next to a huge Victorian warehouse, the foundations of which had effectively turned to sand because of floodwater and corrosives. And had the collapse of the place (which occurred as predicted) come as a surprise, the death toll would have made for grim reading.

But for the algorithm to work, it needed input and, aside from detecting incursions, the prime function of the cameras was to consume real-time information in a constant stream. Barrowbeck might have been deserted, like fifty-nine other sites around the country, but the data its decomposition generated about the way in which buildings of a particular construction or of a certain age fell to pieces could be used to safeguard other places deemed to be more important.

The Hub, which housed the server for the cameras, had been sited on the flat roof of the school so that it was well above the water. The boat crossed what had presumably been the playground and past the windows of the assembly hall. Inside, the plaster was coming off the walls in scabs, and green slurry lapped against the stage where a piano sat covered in a thick fur of mould. But, miraculously, there were a few paintings still stuck up here and there. Scribbled suns and aeroplanes. A picture of the river winding through the village like a blue snake. And stick figures on the bank throwing little versions of themselves into the water.

The boat auto-moored to the zig-zag metal steps around the back of the building, and Kay assisted Natalie off the deck to help her find her footing. Being so unused to wearing these cumbersome suits, and it being so hot and claustrophobic in masks, climbing was strenuous and Kay heard Natalie breathing just as hard as she was by the time they got to the top.

The strips of tarry waterproofing felt were peeling at the edges but the structure itself was still sound enough to walk on and Kay led Natalie to the Hub which sat at the far end. It was as shat upon as the church tower. But apart from the guano there was no obvious impairment to the outer casing and so Kay opened the doors to get at the racks inside. These units weren't completely impervious, and she expected to find evidence of rain damage.

'Let's have two sets of eyes on it,' she said to Natalie, who took the torch from her belt and probed the beam into gaps between the switches and patch panels.

It all looked as it should. The diodes flickered from the heavy traffic of data.

'Show me the tracking map again,' Natalie said, and bringing out her tablet, Kay swiped onto the screen that highlighted the movement of whatever it was that had caught the attention of the cameras. The line ran directly across the map of the village.

'That's why it has to be a glitch,' said Kay. 'Look at the speed it was going.' It had only taken a matter of seconds.

'It has to have been some kind of bird, then,' said Natalie.

'One the system hadn't seen before or couldn't fathom out? It's doubtful.'

'So what now?'

'We mark it as resolved and go home,' said Kay. 'The Hub's fine. And there's obviously nothing here, is there?'

Natalie's goggles steamed and cleared as she looked around uncertainly.

'Listen,' said Kay. 'Even if the cameras did see something, it's gone now. It came and it went.'

She pointed out the trace of this brief visitation on the screen again and Natalie conceded the point.

'We can't wait around forever to see if anything comes back. We've done our job,' said Kay and ran through the checkboxes on the tablet.

The form completed, she authorised her conclusions by scanning her retina, and passed it to Natalie to countersign by doing the same.

The pulsation of 'Intervention Required' finally stopped and Kay closed up the doors to the Hub.

\*

As they'd been working, the sky had become overcast, and it began to drizzle. The fells seemed even closer and steeper. The quarry on the north side of the valley loomed over the village, the bottom of its grey mouth collapsed into a long scree of rock and earth that ran all the way down to the water.

Even before the Flood, it must have been a difficult place to live, thought Kay. They must have always felt at the mercy of something here: the remoteness, the quiet, the dark, the cold, rain, rumours, each other. But somehow, they'd endured it. And for so long.

'Don't you think it seems unfair?' she said as they made their way back to the stairs.

'What's unfair?' said Natalie.

'That it's all gone. That they couldn't save a single thing.'

'Such as?' Natalie said.

'I don't know.'

'A brick? A building?'

'Something, at least. The war memorial?'

'What would be the point?' said Natalie. 'What would you do with it?'

'Just keep it, I suppose.'

'As a souvenir?'

'More than that,' said Kay.

'For posterity?' Natalie looked at her and began her descent to the boat.

She said it with such derision that Kay didn't reply. She didn't really know what they ought to have conserved of

Barrowbeck or why it felt so important to do so. She hadn't quite formulated her thoughts about it well enough. Only that it seemed such a waste to let everything disappear. To think of all those who'd been and gone. To think of all they'd ever done and said, all that they'd overcome or failed to achieve, everything they'd laughed at or cried about. If it was only ever going to come to this dissolution, then what had it all been for?

There had been people here for two thousand years before the Flood. They'd found a Celtic axe-head when they'd churned up the graveyard, and before that a potholer had come across some amber beads and prompted some archaeological interest in the valley. But nothing had come of it. And it was too late now. No one would come here again. Certainly, no one would ever *live* here again. The water would carry on rising, and the buildings would eventually fall down and be submerged for good and there would be no trace of anything.

But it was happening all over the country. It'd be death by drowning for England. No one was really prepared for it. No one high up knew what to do either. There was only a certain amount they *could* do. Rivers kept becoming lakes and the sea kept on gnawing away, especially in the east. Over the next twenty or thirty years or so, the coast of Norfolk would start to look like the coast of Norway. And most of East Anglia would be swallowed up, mile by mile, until Peterborough and Cambridge were next to the sea. Hundreds of places would be overrun.

An age of mass migration was coming. With millions of people to rehouse, there wouldn't be time to argue about what had been lost. The next generation would need to be pragmatic, ruthless administrators, willing to enforce the directives of the algorithm.

Natalie would do well, thought Kay, as she joined her in the boat. She was exactly what the country was going to need. To her, History was entirely dispensable. History was a joke. A time of tyrants and idiots. History was when people behaved like children, demanding what they knew they shouldn't have – two cars and new roads and flights to the sun – and now they sobbed over what they'd ruined because of it.

The boat swung slowly to take them back the way they'd come, and they crossed the open space of the former village green. The drizzle thickened to rain which beat loudly on their waterproof hoods and battered the skin of the water around them into countless ripples. Natalie sat there dripping and looking dejected.

'It'll pass over soon,' said Kay, though she wasn't sure it would. It might rain for hours. And she thought how dismal it would be getting back to the office. If the weather turned heavier still, if there was a storm, then the water-ploughs would be out on every route into the centre and slowing up the traffic. There'd be sirens going off along the Irwell and the Medlock, which were already brimming. There'd be roads closed. Diversions.

A memory surprised her of once either meeting or leaving a lover on a wet afternoon somewhere. She saw the stained toes of her suede shoes, a yellow umbrella, a steamed-up bus.

The name of this boy had gone, along with whatever feelings she'd had for him. The rain gave the recollection a seasoning of melancholy and romance that perhaps hadn't been there at the time. Or maybe it had. She'd been susceptible to both once. How old, or rather how young she'd been that day, she couldn't be certain. Young enough to think of herself as a girl seeing a boy. Euphoric at being desired. Heady with the first enthralments of sex.

The images came and went, and it seemed now like an event from a completely different epoch of human life. She'd never realised how great a luxury self-absorption had been back then or what a privilege it was to have such petty neuroses. There had once been nothing more important than knowing one was loved.

And now that seemed so small. Or perhaps it mattered more than ever.

'The boat's starting to fill,' said Natalie, her voice crackling in Kay's ear.

'It bails itself out. Don't worry,' she told her.

'Shouldn't we take shelter?'

'Where?'

'At the school maybe?'

'All the way back there?'

'One of the houses then.'

'We'd have to get out and wade,' said Kay. 'Do you want to be up to your hips in this?'

'It'd only be until the rain stops.'

'It doesn't look as if it will.'

'You said it would,' Natalie replied. 'I thought you must have looked at the forecast.'

'I did,' said Kay. 'But places like this have their own weather. You'll learn that.'

Natalie was about to argue back when, as they were entering The Lots again, something hit the underside of the hull and surfaced next to them, smooth, dark and glistening. Not one of the plastic jellyfish but a section of tree trunk, perhaps, or the flank of a large dead fish, it was hard to tell.

But as it drifted away, it rolled over and a face – of sorts – stared up at the sky. The head was only attached to the rest of the rotten body by a few leathery strings of skin and sinew.

Natalie cleared her throat but didn't seem fazed. Her concern was more about protocol.

'We report it and leave it,' said Kay. 'Let Reclamation decide whether to follow up.'

Though she didn't think they would. Not for a floating body. Once it slipped under the water again, a thousand divers could search for a thousand years and never find it. They wouldn't use up resources for just one corpse.

It was hard to say how old it was. It might have been a trespasser who'd drowned or a body that they'd missed when they'd emptied the graveyard. Or it was something even older that had been preserved by Barrowbeck's mud.

'Well, that must be what set the cameras off,' said Natalie, watching the remains bobbing in their wake. 'It would have confused the system if it couldn't see the face properly. It might not have known it was human.'

But Kay wasn't convinced.

How could a body have moved as quickly as the cameras had reported, even if it had been borne along in a fast-flowing current? No, it was something else. For a few seconds, in a freakish, inexplicable way, the cameras must have caught something that was both imperceptible to the human eye and incomprehensible to the computer system.

That line of trajectory on the map, thought Kay, it wasn't transit but an upward departure. Something had escaped and flown away. Something that had been living inside that corpse perhaps.

And she thought of those Victorian paintings of deathbed scenes: the soul rising vaporously out of a spent and supine body and into a starry beam of light; all tears wiped away, all the frailty and grossness of a human life transfigured and forgiven at last.

# Acknowledgements

Thanks first of all to Justine Willett of BBC Radio 4, who originally commissioned 'Voices in the Valley', the series from which many of the stories in *Barrowbeck* are derived. I am indebted also to the wonderful Jocasta Hamilton and Lucy Luck for their unwavering support and incisive advice throughout the writing process. And to the editorial team at John Murray – Katharine Morris, Dave Watkins and Howard Davies. Sara Marafini has created another superb book cover. Anna-Marie Fitzgerald and Alice Graham continue to champion my work and keep me connected with readers. Lastly, thanks to Jo for always being there. This is for you.